CU00928278

~bookstrings~

Twice Sold Tales

CHAUTONA HAVIG

PUBLICATIONS

Fonts: Adorn Condensed, Albino Lovebird, Berton
Cover Illustration: Joshua Markey
Cover Design: Chautona Havig
Edited by: Haug Editing and TWE Editing

The events and people in this book, aside from any caveats that may appear on the next page, are purely fictional, and any resemblance to actual people is purely coincidental. I'd love to meet them!

FICTION / CHRISTIAN

Dedication

To Cathe… thanks for making the research trip with me. Sorry for zonking out on you for most of the evening! You've been a dear friend for over two decades now, and I'm grateful to have you in my life.

Here's to three or four more decades!

One

Books: because reality is overrated.

Today's T-shirt said it all. Although, Harper Brevig really would have preferred one that said, *Fictional characters: because people are overrated.* She just hadn't found one yet.

Late June mornings in Red Wing, Minnesota were temperate enough that while she didn't *need* her super-thin jacket, she also didn't swelter with it on and wouldn't before she reached her store. She'd been told that not offending potential customers with her snark shirts was the secret to keeping her bookstore from going under. Who knew?

Turning off East Avenue onto 3rd Street, she made her daily stop at Hanisch's Bakery. As usual, Jamie the barista tried to talk her into oatmeal or a breakfast wrap. Once, she'd even suggested the quiche. Harper's, "Real women don't eat quiche," had stunned Jamie enough to keep that suggestion from ever being made again. Or so she hoped. If she could only find something to say about the oatmeal. Point out that her hair wasn't blonde, so Goldilocks food wouldn't work? No… Jamie would say the food was for the bears, and she, Harper Brevig, was most definitely a bear in the morning.

Better not.

"Just the breakfast sandwich. It's veggie day." Her

reminder to herself about not making a face came a second too late, most likely. Jamie had also tried to convince her either to not eat the veggie sandwich or to save it for better days. Harper thought it made sense to get the worst day of the week out of the way at once. Done.

And besides, if she didn't eat a veggie sandwich, when else would she get those nasty green things into her body? At least this came with bread and egg to disguise it.

Bag in hand, she crossed the street at a diagonal, eying the public works crew as they watered the flower baskets that hung from the downtown lampposts. Stretching out their long watering poles, they gave each hanging basket a good soaking before moving to the next.

Hers looked healthy enough, but what did she know about plants? Harper's experience thus far had been to become an expert in burying their remains under the cover of darkness while her landlady slept in blissful ignorance.

Well, except for that time that the plant had only been faking death and had started growing next to the lilac bush in the backyard, exposing her for the fraud she was. Apparently, not only could God make a tree, but He could also resurrect plants she thought she'd killed.

She'd applied for the job as plant waterer her first summer home from college, but she hadn't gotten it, and considering her track record, maybe the woman who interviewed her had known something. *Too bad she didn't tell me so I could have saved all those plants a slow, miserable death.*

The day promised to be a scorcher as evidenced by the realization that she wanted out of that thin jacket… *now.* So much for it not being *too* hot for a lightweight hoodie. Harper pulled keys from her canvas bag and unlocked the store doors, taking a moment to flick a boxelder beetle from the vinyl S of "Twice Sold Tales" on the glass.

The biblichor of her new (a few) and used (a lot) books struck Harper as it did every morning. She stood there after locking the door behind her, eyes closed, inhaling the wonder of her favorite place in the world. *If only I didn't have to share it with the rest of Red Wing.*

When Harper had first inherited the bookstore from a great aunt she hadn't actually liked, she'd loved the idea of staying after the doors closed, sorting books, dusting shelves, and— oh, who was she trying to kid? She'd known she'd get lost in some book every night, but wasn't that the perk of owning a store full of them?

Only her increasingly later and later arrival at home and the way she barely made it to the store to open in time had eventually forced her to arrive a couple of hours early and go home within an hour of closing. Harper always took a book home with her, of course. She wasn't stupid.

In the small office on the top floor of the building, Harper spread out her breakfast. Her electric kettle clicked on with the press of the lever, and she pulled out her little basket of bagged teas. Maybe the vanilla Earl Grey... No. The blackberry merlot. Maybe even over ice. Yes...

Her water bottle would do until it heated, steeped, and cooled. With a quick prayer of thanks, she pulled up her Bible app and let it read the next chapter to her as she ate the detested veggie sandwich.

"'First Corinthians chapter two. 'Are we beginning to commend ourselves again? Or do we need, like some people, letters of recommendation to you or from you? You yourselves are our letter, inscribed on our hearts, known and read by everyone. It is clear that you are a letter from Christ, the result of our ministry, written not with ink but with the Spirit of the living God, not on tablets of stone but on tablets of human hearts...'"

Living letters... that was almost as good as a book, and considering all that a lifetime entailed, perhaps life was a book and events were those living letters. So that would make peoples' lives epistolary "novels." What an amazing thought! Harper missed whatever else Paul had to share with the Corinthians, captivated as she was by the idea that maybe... just maybe... God could write a story worth reading—in her life.

A curled-up piece of bell pepper lay on the wrapper

as Harper licked her fingers at the end of her breakfast. Eat the disgusting stuff or consider it the pepper's fault for being stupid enough to fall out of the sandwich? She wadded it up and dumped it in the bag from Hanisch's. "You snooze, you lose." Besides, as it was, there was probably a piece of the nasty stuff stuck in her teeth to mortify her later.

Just as she'd settled into her comfy chair by the windows, Dumas' *The Black Tulip* in hand and wondering why Dumas was so obsessed with throwing his characters in prison, she remembered the previous Saturday afternoon's "visit" from Darcy Tolonen and her twin book dementors—two terrorists masquerading as three-year-old boys. Harper had been so irritated at the devastation left in their wake that she hadn't bothered to clean it up, thinking Mondays were the perfect days for such cruelties.

"Their fingers are the soul-sucking kiss of death for poor, defenseless books. I should ban them from the store."

She wouldn't, though. You couldn't do that these days, or so she'd been told. Parents talked, and if you didn't love every person's progeny and sing their praises, they'd gang up on you and the next thing you knew—out of business. Every business owner insisted it was so. If it weren't for that whole eating thing and paying taxes on the building thing, and insurance thing, and... *life* thing, she'd close the store and just hole up in there all by herself. Wouldn't that be a dream?

No people to complain that they can buy a book cheaper on Amazon or that a used book had a fuzzy corner on the back of an otherwise pristine copy at half the cover price. No one asking her to spend time finding out the cost of a book only to say, "Well, I can get it cheaper online and faster too. I'll just order it from home. Thanks." As if "Thanks" negated the waste of her time and the jab against her not being able to compete with companies with warehouses the size of her town—or nearly.

Aunt Lorene had given her a chance to avoid a

withering job in an office somewhere (since librarian positions had been harder to find than computers with floppy drives), and here she sat pouting because she still had to work. Shameful. At that thought, she shoved herself out of the chair and locked her office on the way back downstairs. It was a risk, but she went ahead and unlocked the shop door, flipping the sign to "open" so she wouldn't forget.

The tumbled books, two with torn covers, which lay sprawled across the floor nearly made her revisit the idea of a Tolonen ban. Those mothers... they were probably buying online anyway. At least her stock would be saved from the ravages of the destructive duo.

"Oh, well. If there's no use crying over spilled milk, there's no use stewing over strewn tomes. Or something."

Harper repeated that to herself, over and over as she stacked books here, sorted others over there, and took a mental inventory of losses. That visit had likely cost her thirty dollars. With customers like that, not being in business was cheaper.

One by one, the books found their homes on the shelves—all but the ones that needed removal from "circulation" and the ones that would have to be discounted—until the door chime alerted her to her first customer of the day. A glance at her phone prompted a groan. A quarter till opening. So much for hoping no one would come in early. "Be right with you!"

"Take your time, Harper. I've just come to return that book and choose another. Maybe read a while before my hair appointment."

Mrs. Klair. The highlight of every day. If every customer were like Emme Klair, her job would be anything *but* work, and the world would be a better place. "I'm just back here cleaning up after the Tolonen terrors. Holler if you need me."

"I'll do that." When Harper jerked her head up to see the dear old thing smiling down at her, Mrs. Klair added, "Unless you need help?"

"Only with my attitude." And to prove it, she added a heavy sigh.

When she finished, Harper had just enough time to change out of her shorts and snark shirt and into "professional" attire. She had a uniform. Black slacks and a white button-down shirt. Sweater in winter. Short sleeves in summer. Boring.

That should be my name. Harper Boring instead of Brevig.

At a quarter to eleven, Mrs. Klair brought a battered copy of *Return of the Native* by Thomas Hardy to the front. "I've never noticed this one. Haven't read it in years. I'll take it."

Harper struck out *Childhood's End* on the notepad by the register and scribbled, *Return of the Native* below it. "All set. Oh, and I just read a Christian fiction novel I think you'd like." She reached under the counter and pulled out *The Road to Happenstance.* "I read it night before last and loved it enough that I ordered the next two books in the series. They'll be here tomorrow. Think Mitford meets Mayberry with just the faintest question of whether there's a bit of magical realism going on or not."

The rest of the day went relatively well—steady sales, pleasant customers who didn't hang around to bug her, and no Tolonen terrors or their minions to mar the perfection. For that, she'd walk home and grab her car for supper at Culver's. With fried cheese curds. She could still taste that pepper from breakfast, despite her soup cup and sandwich for lunch. Cheese curds would solve it. Yep. And only fifteen minutes to go.

She dug into her mail while she waited for "close o'clock" and changed her mind about Culver's when she saw it. Another insurance bill.

Great.

Two

Parenting Tip #13: When all else fails, make 'em laugh.

The little cream house on Wilkinson Street might not seem like much to some, but for Noah Lampe, it signaled the beginning of an amazing, terrifying, unbelievable adventure. Unshaven, which wasn't that uncommon, he sat in a lawn chair in his "all-weather" porch with a mug of coffee in hand and stared out at the rock wall and trees. The chair wobbled as he shifted, and Noah made an asterisk on his mental to-do list next to "find affordable furniture for the porch." That put furniture right beneath "buy a pool for the back corner."

Bennie would like that—some place to swim and play while he was at work. And since Megan Hansen couldn't drive yet, taking Bennie to the Y or the water park was out of the question. Besides, it would save a lot of money over the course of the summer. And since he didn't know what having a son would cost, well, it seemed prudent to be careful.

Prudent. When had he become his father, using words like prudent, anyway? A smile formed at the mental picture of Bennie offering him a shy smile. When he'd become a dad like his father. That's when. He only hoped he'd be half as good as Dad had been.

And the terrifying wonder returned. He, Noah Lyndon Lampe, was a father to an almost seven-year-old he hadn't known about until four short months earlier. Four months of awkward visits with a little boy who just wanted his mother back *and* to have a father for the first time in his life. Four months of house searching, bank account draining, toy selling (he still missed the jet ski, if he were honest), home inspections, and parenting classes. The list still felt endless, despite finally taking full custody on Friday.

Noah's mother insisted on calling it their "gotcha" day, but he refused to do that until the name-change paperwork had been completed. That day, Benedict John Pedersen would become Benedict John Lampe. *That* would be the closest thing to a "gotcha day" as he could have with his own son.

Meanwhile... prudence. He'd have to learn a thing or two about that one.

A shuffling behind him sent his heart racing, but Noah made himself turn slowly and smile at the little guy. "Hey... you're up early."

Again with the shy smile, but at least Bennie stepped closer. "Can I come in?"

The poor kid. He asked before stepping into any occupied room. Good training or something Noah didn't want to think about? The kid's lip quivered, and Noah got out of his own head. "Sure. Come here." Despite the light tone he'd used, Bennie winced. "I want to show you something."

That seemed to relax the little guy. He seemed small for his age, but what did Noah know about the size of kids? He'd been an only child, so no nieces and nephews for him, and he wasn't close to his cousins—not *that* close.

Bennie's feet pattered across the concrete floor and stopped just out of arm's reach. *Note to self: buy area rug ASAP.* The kid's toes would freeze in winter. *Second note: find a way to convince the kid you won't hurt him.*

That thought broke his heart. Noah dropped his head, staring at the floor. When he'd composed himself, he looked up again to find his son in a perfect imitation of

14

himself. "Hey, Bennie?"

Without raising his head, the boy looked up at him. "Yeah?"

"You have no reason to believe me, but I'm going to tell you anyway. I won't hurt you. I'll make mistakes, and I might even get frustrated with you—more like frustrated with me because I don't know how to be a dad yet—but I won't *hurt* you."

"Thank you."

He had to get out of there before he lost it. Fighting back tears he didn't understand and anger he didn't know where to direct, Noah rose and started toward the kitchen to hide his emotions. "Know what you want for breakfast?"

It was the wrong question. His caseworker had told him to allow some choices but that Bennie needed the security of someone else leading the way. Apparently, he'd been made to decide too much for himself.

Noah's heart squeezed. The poor kid had obviously been hurt enough that hearing he wouldn't be hurt required a thank you. If fists through a wall would help and not terrify his son, Noah would have gladly sacrificed both of his right then.

"Whatever." The word shot through his thoughts so fast, he almost missed it. "I can make peanut butter sandwiches. I know how, and I'm not 'lergic."

Time to do that take-charge thing he'd been assigned. "How about some scrambled eggs and toast? I think I have orange juice, too."

"Yeah."

Beating eggs didn't offer quite the same satisfaction as punching walls or pounding nails, but he did his best to pulverize them within an inch of… whatever eggs had to be pulverized into. Just as he poured them into a sizzling pan, he heard a quiet, "What?"

Steady… he needed to keep steady. While reaching for the spatula, he looked over at Bennie. "Hmm? Did you need something?"

15

"You said…" The boy faltered and turned away. "I'll go get dressed."

He'd gone two steps before Noah's brain kicked in. "No. Wait."

The kid stood stock still—whatever that was—and even without seeing his face, Noah knew he flinched. "I said what? You can ask me things, Bennie. I know you don't know me well, but we can't get to know each other if we don't talk. So what did I say that you didn't understand?" *And please don't let it be that I won't hurt you. I can't take it.*

"Show me." The words came out in a whisper.

Show him what? The eggs? *What does that have to do with what I said?* Then the scene returned to him. He'd planned to tell Bennie about the pool. "Oh, right! Sorry, bud. I got sidetracked." He rubbed his belly. "Can't think straight when it's growling for breakfast. It just eats up all the brain cells while it waits."

The boy's lips twitched as if he really wanted to smile.

That's all Noah needed. He dropped his voice to the deepest rumble he could make and said, "I'm gonna eat every one of those brain cells if you don't feed me." He grabbed a banana from the bowl on the counter and ripped it open, taking a giant bite almost before he'd peeled all the sides down. "There," he mumbled around a mouthful. "Don't eat all my brain cells! I need them or Bennie will have to have *all* the brains in this family."

This time a giggle erupted. "You're silly."

"You betcha, kid."

"The eggs are burning."

The words sounded innocuous enough, but the wide-eyed plea the kid sent with them ripped up his heart. "Oops!" He shuffled the spatula in the pan. "There. Not too bad. Just a little brown in one spot. I'll eat that part."

Bennie stepped a bit closer. "I can do it."

Without thinking, Noah reached out to ruffle Bennie's shaggy hair and deflated as the kid shrunk back from him. "Sorry, bud. Just trying to push your hair out of your eyes. I'll—" Bennie smoothed his hair and stepped a bit closer. At any other time, Noah might have told him not to get too close to the stove, but he couldn't bring himself to do it. Not now. "I'll eat the overdone spot. Happy to."

Another giggle escaped. "They're burning again."

Noah grabbed the banana, ate what was left, and stirred like crazy. "Not as dark this time." To his belly he said, "I gave you food! You were supposed to leave those brain cells alone."

This time the giggle became an actual laugh. After watching for a moment, the kid added, "I could put the bread in the toaster."

Without a word—Noah couldn't have spoken if he'd tried—he pulled out the loaf of bread and dangled it between his thumb and forefinger before finding his voice. "Have at it."

Dragging a chair across the floor—Noah tried to hide his dismay at what it would do to the finish—Bennie turned the back to the counter and climbed up. A sign he'd been taught by someone how to do it safely. Once the slices had been dropped into their respective slots, Bennie knelt down on the chair, arms folded on the counter and his chin resting on those arms. Watching.

If it wouldn't have ruined the moment, Noah would have snagged a picture of it. Instead, he scooped eggs onto plates and asked if Bennie wanted cheese. The boy turned his head and watched as Noah sprinkled shredded cheese on the largest pile of eggs. "Yeah."

Probably should correct that. Make him say "Yes, please" and all. But not yet. The kid can barely stand to speak to me right now.

He passed the butter dish and a butter knife. "Can you spread 'em?"

"Yeah."

Anyone listening would have thought the kid was as bored or surly as could be, but the look he gave Noah— tentative but eager, too. Best Valentine's week gift ever. Terrifying… but amazing. He looked so cute there in his Spider-Man—wait.

"Did you change pajamas?"

Bennie leaned back so far that he nearly fell off the chair. "No."

Noah started to convince himself he'd been wrong about that, but then he remembered the crazy story he'd told Bennie about Spider-Man swinging through the town, searching for the perfect place for them to live and finding this house. Right here. Pointing out that bedroom window... no. It had *not* been green dinosaur pajamas.

He must have taken too long to think, because Bennie scrambled down from the chair and bolted just as the toast popped up. Great. Now what should he do? Address the lying? Who cared which PJ's a kid wore? Let it go for now?

With one last look at the steaming eggs—eggs that would be a cold, gross mess by the time this problem was solved, Noah climbed the stairs and hesitated at Bennie's door. Knock or...? It hadn't been pushed all the way shut, so Noah opted for middle ground. He knocked as he inched it open. "Bennie?"

The room—empty. So was the kid's bed—the mattress bare and the bright red sheets gone. Maybe it wasn't right, or maybe it was his job. Noah couldn't decide which, but he went into the closet and rummaged through the duffel bag the boy had brought. Underneath a photo album were four mini-Depends-looking things. They had a name for them, but while Noah couldn't remember what they were called, he knew what they meant. Poor kid.

He clambered down the stairs and into the living room, rounded the kitchen wall, and took the basement stairs two at a time. Bennie stood before the washing machine, stuffing the bedding in as fast as he could, tears streaming down his face. "I'll clean it. I'll clean it. I'm sorry. I'll—"

Maybe it was pushing things, but Noah couldn't help himself. He scooped up the boy and held on tight. "It's okay, Bennie. It's okay. You don't have to worry about it. Things happen."

"It's all my fault. I forgot my Pull-Up."

You forgot? You fell asleep during the movie, and I put you to bed. You were out for the count. It might be true, but the kid was too freaked out to hear it yet. "Hey… it's no…" He stopped. Mortification could take a hike. This kid—*his son*—was more important. "If it's anyone's fault, it's probably mine."

"No. I—"

"Do you know what heredity is?"

A sniffle preceded what Noah took for a no. With the kid's head buried in his neck, it could have been a nod, but Noah went for obvious. "Well, it's like… okay. Do you remember the first day I got to meet you?"

The boy gave a decided nod. "Yeah."

"I walked into that office and there were all those people. Lots of kids with lots of adults, but the second I saw you, I knew you were *my* son. Do you know how?"

Again with the shake—he'd read the signals right anyway. Bennie lifted his head a bit and looked at him. "How?"

Man, the kid was getting heavy already! It'd kill his back, but Noah abandoned the half-filled washer and carried Bennie up the stairs to the kitchen. He set the boy down at the table, handed over the eggs and spread butter on the cooled toast. When he seated himself, he leaned back in the chair and pointed to his head. "That spot by your forehead? I bet when you get your hair cut, the lady always complains about it. Says it's impossible to make it lay right."

Bennie nodded and the tension that had reformed began to dissolve again. "Mommy called it a cowlick. She said it drove her crazy."

The wince that followed left more questions. Crazy because it reminded her of Noah? Not possible, was it? They'd only gone out a few times before she took off for the cities. She probably hated how hard it was to manage. Their crazy curly hair and that cowlick.

"Well, that's heredity—when you look like your mom

19

or have six toes like your grandpa."

"I don't have six toes!"

Noah grinned. "I don't either, but my mom does."

The kid giggled. "She does not."

As Noah took a bite of his cooled but at least somewhat warm eggs, he nodded. "Sure does. You'll have to ask her to show you. It's cool."

"Her-re-dit-ty." Bennie drew each word out as he dragged his fork through the eggs. "So my hair is that?"

"Or *hair-ed-i-ty*." Bennie looked confused, so Noah just nodded and tried to ignore that his first dad joke had flopped. Badly. "Know what else is hereditary?"

The kid shook his head and scooped up eggs on his fork, clearly done with the conversation now.

"Bed wetting. I wet mine until I was eight."

Those big brown eyes stared at him. He blinked and then blinked back tears. "You did?"

"Yep."

"I tried to clean up…"

Hide it, you mean. But again, that was something to address later. The kid needed to feel safe, right? No need to make him feel ashamed for something he couldn't help. Silly as it was, Noah had chosen his parenting strategy from a toilet paper commercial. That mom sitting with her potty-training daughter and not getting frustrated when she had to "go again…" That's who he wanted to be. And he'd do it.

After a few more bites, Noah stretched out as relaxed as he could make himself. "Hey, Bennie?"

The kid froze.

"You don't have to take the sheets off the bed. We'll get pads to put down, so we only have to wash those. It'll be easier." In a stroke of genius, if he did say so himself, he added, "It'll be your job to take it down to the washer if it gets wet and put a new one on, okay?"

The next scoop of eggs filled the kid's mouth, but still, Bennie grinned and said, "Okay." Half the eggs landed on his shirt, and to Noah's delighted disgust, it looked adorable.

I've lost my mind.

They'd finished eating and loaded the dishwasher before Bennie spoke again. "What were you going to show me?"

It was the first question he'd asked since arriving that sounded natural and relaxed. Noah nearly cheered and cried at the same time. What was the boy talking about? Show— "Oh! I know. C'mere." He led Bennie through the sun porch and pointed through the window. "See that spot right there?"

"Uh-huh…"

"I'm thinking we should put a pool up there today. What do you think?"

No one could accuse his son of making rash decisions. Bennie stared at the spot for a good minute before turning to him and nodding. "That looks like a good spot. Will you swim?"

"Do you want me to?"

Bennie's head rose and lowered. Once. A single nod. For Noah, it might as well have been "I love you" or "you're my best friend."

"Next up… There's this list my mom and I put together—all the fun stuff we can do this week and next. And then maybe some fun stuff before school starts. There's a hockey camp…"

Bennie shook his head. "I don't like hockey. People get hurt."

That was a first. In all the times he'd ever spent with his son, not once had Bennie said anything so decided. "Well, there's also soccer, I think." From the look on Bennie's face, that wasn't much better. "Is there anything you've ever wanted to learn? Basketball? Swim team?"

The way his son stared at the floor made him wonder if there'd been too much HGTV in the kid's life. But then it came. A whispered, "Yeah."

He'd never have been able to explain it to anyone, but standing in the sunroom, the early morning sunlight doing

21

its best to work its way inside, Noah felt the first crack in the wall separating him from his son's heart. "What is it? If I can afford it, we'll make it happen." It might be a crazy thing to promise, but anyone looking at his son's face in that moment would have done the same. He just knew it.

"Dancing."

Dancing? Noah ordered his face not to show the alarms going off on all his senses. "Um... what kind of dancing? I think there are classes here for... oh, tap?"

Bennie shook his head.

Well, that was a relief. "Um... hip-hop?" It wasn't his cup of joe, but he'd manage.

"No... like at Christmas with the tree that gets bigger and the girls on their toes."

Noah swallowed hard. It didn't help so he did it again and finally his voice decided to cooperate. "Ballet?"

A grin the size of Minnesota stretched across the little guy's face. "Yeah! Can I do that?"

Even as his heart screamed, *No, no, no! Not my son! Hockey! Even* tap *would be better than twinkle toes!* Noah pulled out his phone and said, "Let's see what they have for kids your age. I don't know if I can afford it, but I'll try." *And meanwhile, should we see some kind of therapist?*

Three

It's read o'clock.

With the last book wrapped in brown paper, Harper placed them all in the wooden tray that made up the top of a giant puzzle table and squished them together. Next up: draw a picture across them all as if they were one single canvas. The journal Aunt Lorene had left for her for when she needed to know how to do things said to put "yardsticks on two sides to keep the books from sliding while you draw."

Very helpful information… if Harper had a clue where Aunt Lorene kept said yardsticks. The storage cupboard proved empty. Under the counter—likewise. She tried on top of shelves, behind shelves, and even down in the unused basement portion of the shop. No yardsticks anywhere! She had to do this. Last summer she'd gotten away with hiding away in her shop since Aunt Lorene had just died that January, but now…

Just as she was ready to wield her trusty Sharpie without benefit of stabilizing yardsticks, the memory of canopy poles being taped to the lid of the box prompted her to look *under* the table. Yep. There they were. Duct tape to the rescue. Only Aunt Lorene…

And they worked too. With a glance at the giant train clock at the back of the store, she grabbed that Sharpie. Thirty minutes. Surely, she could draw an outline of the

23

giant books and shelves onto the covered books in twenty minutes. Surely…

Aunt Lorene had probably freehanded *her* pictures. One woman had commented on the Alice down the rabbit hole puzzle she'd created one year. A man had described the giant whale bearing down on a whaling boat. Someone else had told her about a tree where all the leaves were books. "That one was so hard," she'd said.

Red Wing would get a bookshelf with books on it and be grateful she participated in their stupid River Days. *Wish I could wear my* "I closed my book to be here" *T-shirt. Then people would really know what I think of them.*

Even with the templates she'd created, the shelves alone took fifteen minutes. After that, she plopped down templates of spine after spine, sometimes stacking them, other times keeping them standing, and occasionally making one or two lean toward an end or a stack. Having the templates made remembering to make different sizes easier, but she still only managed to get one row done before the shop bell jingled.

Another day, another dollar… another bill, most likely. I wonder if I should contact that guy that Anders tried to get to help last year. Maybe I should have let him stay. Bet he's expensive, though…

A nudge—she'd give the Lord credit since it was a good one—reminded her to greet the customers. "I'm back here if you need anything!" Maybe not exactly warm, but she didn't ignore them. Definite improvement over her first customer.

Even Harper groaned at the memory. It had been Mrs. Klair. She'd opened the door, smiled at Harper, and before she could say (her now customary), "Good morning," Harper had said, "What do you want?"

In my defense, I meant "What are you looking for?" but I got nervous.

Still… someday she'd have to learn to say "hello" first. Or maybe "good afternoon." "Welcome" might be too much of a lie. She didn't welcome anyone into Twice

At two hours after breakfast, Noah decided a donut from Hanisch's wouldn't be a bad idea. They turned right off Bush and onto 3rd Street. Noah pointed up at the sign. "Can you see that one up there? Can you read?"

Bennie shook his head. "I was supposed to learn last year." He refused to look anywhere but at the ground as if determined not to stumble and fall. "I didn't."

"Well, you'll learn when you're ready. Do you know your letters?"

Though Bennie only gave a single nod, he saw the boy looked pleased that he could say so. "I know *some* words. My name. Cat. Mom." He flushed. "I don't know Dad. Does it start with a D?"

Noah's heart constricted. "Sure does. Ends with one too. Just D-a-d."

"Got it."

If the fierce concentration that had assumed control of his son's features meant anything, Bennie had determined never to forget that letter combination. Noah started to squeeze the boy's shoulder and stopped himself just in time. Contact made the kid jumpy. Better to save those attempts for home. For now. Instead he said, "I knew you were smart."

"What letter do I look for?"

He nearly asked what Bennie meant and then got it. "Oh, right. Well, I was thinking donuts, and you don't get better donuts in Red Wing than at Hanisch's, so… you're looking for an H."

They were nearly upon it already, but Bennie's gaze was across the street. Noah tried again. "This side."

That determination grew almost fierce until the Bennie stood stock still. "That one? H-a-n-i-s-c-h-s? What's the curly thing?"

"A…" *Not comma… um…* "An apostrophe. It tells

25

you that something belongs to Hanisch—in this case, the bakery. Let's go in."

Even at nearly nine o'clock on a Tuesday, the bakery bustled with customers coming and going, some getting just a single treat, others with boxes. Eyes as big as the donuts themselves, Bennie stood before the case, mesmerized. Noah hunkered down on his heels next to his son. "Know what you want?"

"Which ones can I have?"

Something told him that giving a kid the choice of anything in the place was probably a really *bad* idea, but he couldn't have said no if he'd tried. "You can have just one, but you can have any *one* you want."

If the kid's eyes could get bigger, they did. However, Noah suspected it was an optical illusion. That boy's eyes couldn't get any bigger. Not possible.

Eventually, and after they let several people go ahead of them, Bennie chose the "Fruity Pebbles" donut. Noah chose the maple bacon like any sane man would and led his son—would he ever get used to that word?—to the tables in the coffee shop. Bennie sat with his head propped in one hand and picking bites off one by one.

"My mom does that."

"What?"

He pointed as Bennie pinched off another bite. "Eats her donuts like that—muffins and cookies, too."

"She's nice."

Was it wrong when it cut deep knowing that Bennie seemed more interested in his mother than in him? Probably. The boy's forehead wrinkled more than Noah's grandfather's. "Um…"

"Hmm?" His attempt at nonchalance failed. Too eager. He'd have to stop that.

"The head-ity thing."

Noah smiled. "Her-ed-i-ty."

"Yeah. Um… If I get…" He looked around to make sure no one was listening before whispering, "wetting the bed…" His voice raised. "—from you."

"And that cowlick," Noah added in a quick bid to make something more positive than the need for diapers at six, although cowlicks weren't much better.

"Yeah. But I get..." He pinched off another bite. "*This* from my grandma... then how come you didn't?"

"Because..." Noah took the last bite of his donut and licked his fingers as he did. "I get that from *my* dad. He was the best. I wish you could know him."

Bennie's lip twisted to the left like it always did when he fought emotions. "Maybe..." Now the lip trembled. "Maybe he's showing Mommy how to eat them—in heaven, I mean."

Though Noah doubted the theological accuracy of donuts in heaven, despite what locals had to say about them being "heavenly," he wasn't going to pop the kid's bubble. Not now. "Could be. Or he could be teaching her how to spit watermelon seeds. He taught me when I was your age."

The moment he spoke, Noah regretted it. Bennie would want watermelon—with seeds. And you couldn't get those at Family Fare. Then again, wasn't there a farmer's market outside city hall? They could walk over and see if someone there had one.

"Can you teach me?"

Noah grinned and nodded. "We'll go get a watermelon as soon as we get done here."

After thinking for a moment, Bennie picked up the rest of his donut and shoved it in his mouth. He mumbled something around it, and instinctively, Noah knew what it was. "I ate it like you."

Reaching over to ruffle the boy's hair nearly undid him. Bennie didn't flinch or pull away—not even a little. "Love you, kid." The words sprang from his thoughts to his lips before he could consider them. To cover his embarrassment, Noah jumped up and said, "Ready to go find a spittin' melon?"

Bennie nodded.

The day promised to be warm—really warm. Possibly

in the nineties. But Bennie didn't complain as they walked back up to Bush Street and down to 4th. White, red, and green canopies lined up and a few people milled about. Bennie inched a bit closer as a man walking a lab so big that he looked like a Newfoundland toward them.

"You're safe, Bennie. I won't even let him *lick* you."

A giggle reached him half a second before the dog strained against the leash. Bennie squeaked and jumped three feet sideways. The owner laughed and pulled the dog back. "He likes kids. Won't hurt you. I promise."

Bennie just stared, and Noah finally remembered to thank the guy before hurrying off toward the tents. But when they got there, he noticed Bennie watching the dog until it rounded a corner and disappeared. *I don't have to get him a dog, do I?*

A moment later, his son tugged at his shirt. "There."

Sure enough, there were watermelons lined up in the back of a pickup. The farmer had zucchini of course, but Noah didn't know how to cook it. His mom had always made zucchini and tomatoes, zucchini bread, zucchini casserole—none of which he had a clue how to make. "Can you pick us out a melon? Preferably one with lots of seeds."

Bennie beamed, and the woman manning the stall nodded. "I know just the one." She reached over by the wheel well and hefted a short one with wide stripes. While carrying it back, she seemed to be weighing it. "Eight dollars." Noah's sticker shock must have registered because she shrugged and said, "Non-GMO, heirloom seeds aren't cheap. Organic food is only possible because we take the losses that pesti—"

The ten-dollar bill he thrust at her stopped the sermon. "Not to insult you, but I've never bought a watermelon—ever. So… I wouldn't know if they were usually two dollars or twenty. But we're going to have a spittin' contest, and we need a good, seeded watermelon for that."

"This one will do you well." She turned to Bennie.

"Save all the seeds you can find. Dry them out. And plant them next year. You might get another watermelon out of it!"

It only took one glance at Bennie to know he'd be researching how to dry seeds before nightfall. They carried it back to his car and began the trek back down 3rd Street. They still had half an hour before registration for "Ballet Camp" (wasn't that an oxymoron?) began.

At nearly every store, Bennie peered through windows, but he made no comments. They passed the jeweler's, law offices, insurance office, the bookstore, Mandy's Café, and the little outdoor seating area that separated buildings. Bennie stopped and walked back to the bookstore, over to Mandy's, and then spun in a slow circle.

"What's wrong?"

"It's the only one painted white. All the other ones are…" he pointed to the brick buildings. "Like that. Why is this one white?"

Noah couldn't answer that. But he had an idea. "Let's go around back. I bet someone just liked the idea of a white building with that cool red door. I bet the back is red brick—or maybe bleached brick even." They wove through the tables and into the parking lot behind the stores along 3rd. Interesting… even back there all the buildings were unpainted except for those three—except back here, two were green.

"Well spotted."

"But why?"

He couldn't answer that, but maybe someone in the stores could. A glance at his phone told him they had plenty of time. "Let's go ask someone and see."

The coffee shop looked busy, and the bookstore had a sign directing them around front, so they trekked back around to the street, and he asked Bennie which one. "Books," the boy said. "Because you can find anything in books."

I doubt this is one of those things, but okay.

They pushed open the door and a bell jingled. From

somewhere near the back, a voice called out, "I'm back here if you need anything!"

Bennie strode forward, on a mission, leaving Noah to follow and *not* get a good look at a store he'd never visited. Where had his shy, almost shaking kid gone? They both came to a stop at the sight of a woman writing on… were those books? She looked up and he caught sight of her shirt. *It's read o'clock.*

Someone really *likes her books.*

All the boldness left Bennie. He nudged Noah, and by that miracle he now knew as parental intuition, he actually translated it properly. "Bennie was wondering why this is the only painted building."

The woman stood and dusted her knees. "It's not. Two buildings—or is it three? Not sure, up toward the Sheldon there's another painted building—two, actually."

"This one—these three here—" Noah insisted, "Are the only painted *brick* buildings. Front or back."

After wrinkling her nose in thought, the woman contradicted him. "No, there's a painted back a few doors down. Not painted in front, though. I wonder why I've never noticed we're the only painted brick…"

He couldn't let it go—not if he wanted to see that wrinkle again. And he did. Well, as long as he didn't laugh. But it really was the funniest thing he'd seen in a long time. It made her nose look part Shar-Pei with all the little wrinkles. "Nope. Just this one. Two greens and a white."

With a huff, she beckoned them to follow. She unlocked the door, propped it open, and pointed down at the corner. Sure enough, one more white back.

"Huh… I just looked and I did not notice."

"Not very observant, are you?" She turned on her heel and went back inside. When he didn't follow, she stuck her head back out the door. "Are you coming in, or should I lock it again?"

By the look on Bennie's face… they were going in. Great. Books. Yay.

Four

Bedtime. Book time.

H ead pounding, stomach growling, nerves worn to a frazzle, Harper dragged herself up the path and over to her side of the large, Victorian house she called home. Well, she called one small "wing" of it home, anyway. The porch sent a welcoming beam in the growing darkness. Set in the center of the "O" in her "Go Away" doormat was a tiny potted plant—another sacrifice from her landlady. Myrna Underwood had it in her mind that if a bookworm like Harper didn't have a cat, she needed "plant pets" to keep her company.

"So much easier than pets too—you only feed them once a quarter and water them once a week or so..."

Harper had barely kept her shock in check. *You have to feed plants?* That tidbit still freaked her out a bit. Balancing the plant and tote bag handle in one hand and fumbling for her keys with the other, she managed to get through the door before Myrna came out to chat. A flick of the light switch with her elbow turned on her favorite lamp. It was tiny, but perched atop a set of Thornton Burgess books she'd bought because they were pretty... and cheap, it worked well enough. If she ever got the urge to *read* those books, she could just reach over and pull one off the stack.

Of stacks, she had many. Some were like the Burgess books—all one author or subject. Stacks of Christies,

Dickens, Nancy Drew—yes, she still liked the Titian-haired detective—and for reasons she still didn't understand, a stack of Winston Churchill's books on the second world war. Other stacks sometimes indicated genre—suspense, YA, romance. Others were just piled on as she brought home one or two at a time

And only a small portion of the books had come to live with her since inheriting the store.

Her minuscule entryway had room for wet boots and winter coats and that was it—not many at that. The living room blended into a dining room which blended into a small kitchen flanked by the smallest powder room known to man. The mirror had been attached to the slanted wall shared with the stairs, making looking into it… interesting.

With robotic movements, Harper washed her hands in the bathroom, angling her head to see that the gash she'd given herself from the counter hadn't started bleeding again, before moving into the kitchen. Frozen pizza into the oven. Timer set, drag herself upstairs.

Today's clothes filled the hamper, so she changed into sleep shorts and another snarky T-shirt and carried the hamper down to the tiny laundry-ish room out the back door of her kitchen. Her T-shirt had it right. Definitely, *Bedtime. Book time.* Just as soon as those clothes were chugging their way to clean. After four people had requested copies of *The Extraordinary Deaths of Mrs. Kip,* all in the span of a couple of weeks, she'd ordered herself a copy.

Her annual reread of a Jane Austen novel in July— this year's was *Northanger Abbey* (such a delightful satire on the Gothic novel)—had ended happily while she brushed her teeth before work that morning, so Harper could start the latest Christian fiction craze. At least it had to be better than the one about Jephthah's daughter. Right? She still didn't know why the Christian fiction market had swooned over that one.

Once back in her living room, she gazed about for a place for her plant—something that would give it a ghost of a chance before it became a ghost of a plant. Harper felt a slow smile form at that one. *If I could write stuff like that, maybe I could* write *books instead of hawk them to unsuspecting people who probably prefer Netflix.*

She'd learned her lesson about plants needing light when she'd put one on her underwear shelf in the closet. In hindsight, she'd been pretty stupid about that one. Keeping it watered in one side of her sink? Root rot. Why that could be a thing when you could just stick the roots in water without dirt, she still didn't understand. Plants were weird.

And when interred in her place, they had less chance of survival than prisoners of war in a Japanese death camp.

The timer went off the second she turned the first page of the Kip book. Finish the chapter and burn the pizza or… With an exaggerated sigh for her own catharsis, she set the book down and dashed to grab physical food to consume while her brain ate its daily rations. Did that make brains zombies that devour books? Now *that* was a T-shirt she'd like to have.

Harper stacked the whole pizza in slices on a salad plate. *It's like a salad too. Tomatoes, onions, grain, and cheese. Oh, and pepperoni. It's an* Italian *chef's salad.*

After promising only to read two chapters and then go to bed, she made it through twelve. Improvement— usually she'd have gone ten *times* the planned number instead of ten over. And this one… this lived up to the hype. She'd stick a few in the store window the minute the order she hadn't made yet came in.

The day's bill taunted her, hinting that maybe ordering more books that she didn't know she could sell wasn't a good idea. Harper stuck her tongue out at that thought. Or maybe it was just at the mirror as she brushed her teeth.

Taking time off work to spend with Bennie had been a good idea. He'd have to thank his mom again. They'd gone to the park, walked along the shore of Lake Pepin, and he'd even driven over the bridge into Wisconsin just so Bennie could say he had been to *two* states. They'd go south past Rochester and into Iowa sometime this week—after Bennie's morning ballet class.

The week-long "camp" would supposedly tell them if Bennie liked it enough to continue. Despite the expense of black ballet shoes—Noah's mom had to help him sew on the elastic strap—bicycle shorts, and t-shirt, Noah still prayed that Bennie would decide it wasn't for him. Otherwise, once a week…

Unless he was deemed not ready for strict ballet instruction. The education he'd received about what kinds of classes were available to kids Bennie's age… Most classes for kids under seven were "combo classes" and Bennie didn't want anything to do with tap. Just ballet. *"Like in the Nutcracker at Christmas."*

It was a good thing he hadn't known about stuff like this when he'd first learned about Bennie, or he might have run.

Noah stared at his bed before flopping onto it and snapping off the light. In the darkness, he pulled his hands behind his head and stared up at the ceiling. Was that true? He didn't think so. Just trying to form the words in his mind made him sick to his stomach. *No way. If my kid wants to jump around on a stage in tights, then he'll do it. Doesn't matter. He's* my kid. *I can do this.*

That thought might have turned into a prayer if the mental and physical exhaustion of trying to do this parenting thing hadn't caught up with him. All Noah knew was that one minute he'd started to ask the Lord something and the next, whimpers and sobs broke through slumber and jerked him into consciousness.

It took a moment to realize that it wasn't the neighbor's unspayed cat in heat again. Wait. He didn't have that neighbor anymore. He'd moved into the house on Wilkinson to give Bennie—

That's all it took. He jumped from bed, stumbled,

nearly face-planted as his feet tried to dislodge him from the tangle of sheets, and bolted for Bennie's room. If he could get the kid to the bathroom before it was too late…

Flinging open the door, he wasn't hit by the scent of urine. They had a chance. But when he sat on the bed, the little guy scrambled up into his lap, sobbing. "Hey…" He rubbed Bennie's back and held him tight. Who knew you could do that? "What's wrong?"

"Mommy's gone."

He'd been warned about this—prepared in the classes they'd insisted he'd need. They'd called them *parenting* classes, but much of it was layman's grief counseling 101. Which thing did you do in the middle of the night? He couldn't just drag the kid down to the kitchen table and insist he draw a picture to express his feelings. Also kind of late for a "Tell me a story about her" moment.

Instead, Noah just held his son and squeezed as tight as he could without crushing. He hoped. "Your mom loved you."

"Yeah."

That Bennie didn't sound convinced only hurt more.

Between sniffles and sobs, Bennie said, "Someone said that there's no heaven, so Mommy isn't there."

How did he answer that one? He had no idea what Tara Pedersen had believed about God. He wouldn't lie to his son about something so important, but he didn't want to hurt the kid, either. "God says there's a heaven, so I believe that all of His children go there. If your mommy was one of His children, she's with Him." It was weak on encouragement, but it was the best he could do.

"But is there a God?" The sobs began. "'Cause a God should keep mommies safe."

His own tears fell. He'd have liked to be able to say they were for Tara, too, but he barely remembered her and what he remembered wasn't flattering. They flowed for Bennie, soaking the kid's head. Noah tried again. "Some people think that bad things happening means that God doesn't care about us." Pleading with the Lord for wisdom, he continued when Bennie leaned a bit closer as if hungry to hear more. "But all I can think of is how terrible *everything* would be if He didn't care."

A quiet, "Yeah…" preceded a new bout of sobs.

Noah focused on comforting. It was too late—the clock glowed two-thirty-two—make that *early* for deep discussions. Instead, he held, stroked, and rocked the boy until Bennie finally grew heavy. After tucking him back in bed, Noah crept toward the door, but a whimper stopped him. Seconds passed and another followed. Without anything else to do, he slid under the sheets next to Bennie, pulled the boy close, wrapped an arm around him, and relaxed.

An hour later, with the clock still glowing, he started to drop off, one last thought clinging to consciousness. *If God works all things for the good of those who love Him, then God took this horrible thing and gave me something good out of it— Bennie. But what about him?* He'd have to *make* this change in the kid's life a very good thing—somehow.

Five

Parenting Tip #33: Never underestimate the cruelty of children

A cluster of cotton candy exploded down the steps of Cornerstone Community Church. Then the cotton candy clusters dispersed into blonde ponytails, brown buns, nearly black mini braids with colorful beads, and more. Pink tutus came off and shorts came on. Converse and Keds replaced ballet shoes. Giggles and whispers gave way to cries of "Mommy!" and "See you tomorrow." And amid the estrogenic gaggle of girls and women, Noah stood pressed against the wall with Bennie at his side.

Bennie was clad in biker shorts, a snug t-shirt, and black ballet shoes. He clutched a Walmart shopping bag that included his regular shoes and socks, a pair of cargo shorts, and a T-shirt. A Minnesota Vikings T-shirt, although Noah was a Packers fan himself. He figured Bennie needed all the odds that could be thrown in his favor, and in Red Wing, that meant Vikings.

A few little girls stood around, each whispering and pointing. One mother put a stop to her daughter's rudeness, but most moms were either talking or glued to phones. The woman next to him finally spoke. "Is that your…" She swallowed hard before forcing the word out. "Ssssooon?"

"Yes. Bennie. He's six."

37

Her brow furrowed. "This is the seven to nine class. I think you got the time wrong."

"Miss Courtney said he could try this class. He's not interested in tap, and the other one is a combo." By way of conversation, he added, "I was surprised to find a ballet studio above a church. I go to Red Wing Community myself." After he'd spoken, Noah realized he should have said "we."

"It works out well for both. Cornerstone doesn't need the upstairs during the week and the studio isn't open on Sundays, so Miss Courtney lets them use the studio for Sunday school rooms."

"Nice."

The woman started to say something, shot a look at Bennie, and shifted. "Has Bennie always..." Her face flushed red. "—been interested in ballet?"

He ruffled his son's hair and tried to act nonchalant, but he wanted to tell the woman what she could do with her questions, and none of his mental suggestions were even in the periphery of Christlikeness. "Since Christmas, didn't you say?"

Bennie nodded. "I saw the dance with the Christmas tree getting bigger and bigger."

A little girl—one Noah hadn't noticed—popped out from behind the woman. "*The Nutcracker*. But the tree really doesn't get bigger. Everyone else is actually getting smaller." She smiled at Bennie's nod. "I'm Abby. I've never seen a boy in class."

When Bennie shrank back into the small space between his leg and the wall, Noah wanted to say a lot of ungodly things. The mother hissed, "*Abby!*" To Noah, she added, "It *is* unusual. I wondered if maybe Bennie hasn't always... *identified—*"

Noah broke in before she could go further. "Biologically exactly as appears."

"I see."

"Well, there were men on the stage in the cities, and they had to start somewhere," Abby pointed out.

Maybe one person here was a decent human being. So far all they'd endured were stares, whispers, and insinuations. Maybe he'd made a mistake, but his rebellious side hated to let narrow-minded people win. Dancing was as much a sport as it was an art. Google said so.

The girl saw a friend and dashed off. The mother gave him a weak smile, muttered, "No offense…" and hurried after her daughter.

People didn't even add "intended" anymore. They just threw out the words like that wiped out the hurt and confusion left in their wake. He stepped away from Bennie so he could make eye contact and smiled. "Abby seems nice."

Though Bennie nodded, he also whispered, "Her mommy is scared."

"Scared?" That made no sense. "Of what?"

The kid's lip quivered just a bit. "Me."

There wasn't time to react to that. Miss Courtney came down the stairs and greeted the waiting girls—and Bennie. "All right ladies…" She shot Bennie a smile, "and our little gentleman," it's time to dance. Come this way, and I'll show you how you're expected to come into class…" Over her shoulder, she called to the parents. "Please be sure to be here in exactly one hour. We can't have unattended children. A second offense will mean termination from camp with no refund."

She'd been kind to Bennie, but those final words appeared to be directed at Noah. He offered to sit in the corner of the classroom. A few mothers gasped, and Miss Courtney shook her head, citing some kind of distraction. "Just everyone be here on time."

She may have *said* everyone, but again, her gaze was riveted on him. A couple of the little girls giggled and pointed. One turned away from Bennie and said, "Well I'm not dancing by *him*."

The sight of Bennie's face as he disappeared upstairs stabbed Noah's heart and twisted for good measure. What if they were mean to him? He'd never know unless he ever got the boy to open up. The memory of the previous night's cries ripped at him anew.

He'd intended to go sit at Mandy's Cafe until a couple minutes before eleven and then dash back across the street, but now he just wanted to hang out right out front—just in case. Classical music began upstairs, the signal for him to leave. Long past, really. He stepped out in the July sun and surveyed 3rd Street while propped against the brick next to the large, double glass doors.

Tourists wandered up and down the street. Most of them were retirees, out for a stroll in the "quaint town." He'd heard it all his life. Red Wing was "quaint," and now looking at it with an objective eye, he couldn't argue that— at least not downtown. The turn-of-the-20th-century brick buildings with their upstairs apartments did have that all-American "Mayberry" vibe. The old-fashioned streetlamps offered an extra welcome with their hanging flower baskets. A Kiwanis project, someone had said. Probably true too.

The white brick of the bookstore and Mandy's caught his attention again. Odd how Bennie had picked up on that—white all the way to the masonry cornices along the top. The upper windows glinted in the morning sun. Noah stared. He moved left a bit… and a bit more. Hadn't there been stairs? Not blocked off, either. Maybe there were more books up there, and if he could get up there…

Ignoring the crosswalk just a few feet to his right, he dashed between cars and pulled open the door. An older woman smiled at him from a chair to his right. "Good morning."

"Morning." This must be the owner. She should get someone with better customer service to man the store in her absence. Then again, people always said you couldn't get good help these days. But she'd had a cute nose wrinkle. And a fun T-shirt.

"Harper's upstairs, but I'm in here every day, so if you need something, I might know where it is"

Not the owner, then. "Thanks."

The first time he'd come in, Noah hadn't paid much

attention to the place. Bookstores weren't exactly his forte. Now he gave the store a good once-over. Despite himself, he liked what he saw. Instead of the dark, gloomy place he'd remembered his grandfather dragging him into, or the crisp, modern look of chain bookstores, this store oozed charm. White walls with those boards that were so popular? His friend's wife wanted their living room with it because some TV show recommended it. Something about boats, but he doubted "boat board" was it.

Most of the shelves were plain white shelves with a facing around their fronts, but here and there a low shelf of darker wood showcased books that must be more important. Back where he'd first found her with that table and the drawings, children's books of every size and color filled much of the space, and vinyl beanbag chairs seemed to fill the rest. He'd missed that before.

A tiny placard by the French doors leading into the space read. BEANBAG CHAIRS SANITIZED SEVERAL TIMES A DAY.

Though most of the books seemed new enough, some were clearly antiques—probably collectible. Simple signs pinned to each bookshelf told what you'd find there. Things like, THIS YEAR'S BESTSELLERS, BRITISH CLASSICS, AMERICAN CLASSICS, CHILDREN'S CLASSICS, GOLDEN ERA MYSTERIES, GARDENING, COOKING, LANGUAGES, PHILOSOPHY, RELIGION, CHRISTIAN NONFICTION...

That stopped him. Noah looked first at the religion shelf and then at the Christian shelf. He couldn't decide *why* he liked the differentiation. It was more than just that there were so many more Christian books than all the other religious books combined. He'd made his way to the stairs before he realized what it was.

Christian nonfiction. *It's like a statement of faith. If it's about Christ, it's true.*

The staircase was just as crisp and white as the rest of the store except that the steps were carpeted in the same warm brown as the hardwood flooring in the rest of the store. And the risers were painted to look like book spines.

Some had titles. Others didn't. He saw *Great Expectations, One Hundred Years of Solitude, And Then There Were None.* Was she waiting to find books good enough to write on them?

At the top of the stairs, Noah noticed the room had developed an odor—kind of musty, but different. He tried to remember what the library had smelled like when he was a kid and had to go once a week every summer. This wasn't it, but it was similar.

The room was chock full of bookcases packed with small paperbacks. A million spines begged him to take them home with a similar intensity to puppy eyes at an animal shelter. It was sad, really. All those old books that people had tossed aside. Had they not liked the books? Read too many? What made someone buy a book and then get rid of it?

He'd probably never know the answer because he'd never take the time to ask. Besides, he had more important things to do. Noah moved toward the front of the building. *Like get a look out those windows.*

Movement in the windows across the street and cattycornered to him answered his curiosity. He pulled out his phone, opened his photo app, stretched out the screen, and after a bit of adjusting, found what he wanted to see.

A little tow-headed boy holding onto a railing and trying to bend his knees into an awkward squat. Down… back. Up on his toes, and back again. Down… back up…

The whole thing looked boring as anything to him, but Noah could see the kid was having the time of his life. Miss Courtney stopped by his side and stretched his feet out a bit. Bennie went down, and then beamed up at the teacher when he came back up.

Okay, Lord. He likes it so far. Now what do I do?

Something about the guy in the "junk room" (as she silently called the upstairs used mass market paperback repository) felt familiar, so Harper stayed hidden in her office, trying to figure out how to sneak downstairs without him seeing her. He didn't move—just stood there looking out. She thought, anyway. It was kind of hard to see from the crack in the office door.

When she couldn't justify being gone for another minute, Harper pulled against the door's hinges as she opened it (to prevent creaks, of course) and dashed to the first wall of paperbacks—thriller/horror books that all had the same ominous typography and dark, brooding covers in various shades of doom. Peering around the end, she could only see the guy's back, so she skedaddled downstairs before he caught her.

And just in time. Mrs. Klair stood at the counter. As Harper approached, she held up a book of Dickinson's poetry and said, "I'll take this one today." Pulling *I Capture the Castle* from her purse, the woman slid it across the counter.

Harper grinned as she crossed it off her list and added the poetry book. "Did you like it better this time?"

"No... I feel there must be something lacking in me, but I always want to shake Mr. Mortmain and tell him to get on with the new book or to become a fishmonger, but *do* something—even if it's just be a decent parent to your girls so they don't end up the insipid idiots they're destined to be."

"But Cassandra isn't like Rose," Harper complained. "She has potential."

"Potential that will be wasted without cultivation by someone mature and sensible."

Harper stuck a bookmark in the book and pushed it over. "You've made my point for me, Mrs. Klair. Her father is neither mature nor sensible, which means she has more hope without his influence than with."

The door jingled before Mrs. Klair could come up with her own retort, and the Stadtlers marched in. Tammy waved as she ushered the kids back to the kids' room. Harper heard something about "one book that takes place before Grandma was born."

Mrs. Klair laughed. "My mind wants to go back to before the forties, but I'd bet she means before seventy or something." She waved the book of poetry on her way to the door. "I'll love this one for sure—a palate cleanser after that saccharine mess. See you in the morning."

Tammy paused in her perusing and stared. The moment the door jingled behind the older woman, she turned to Harper. "I've seen that before—you letting her take a book home. Does she do that *every* day?"

Harper nodded.

"But..." Tammy's gaze shifted out the window. "Doesn't she know the library is literally across the street?"

"She's lived here all her life, so I'd guess so."

Even someone as unobservant as Harper Brevig could tell Tammy had another "but" in there somewhere. When it didn't come, she relaxed. Good. The Stadtlers liked to talk—a lot. Both of them. The kids were sweet enough, and Harper liked children for the most part. But the *parents...*

Though she should have been rearranging the "new books" shelf—the ones she considered "on probation" until they'd proven to be worth a read—Harper pulled out her book about Mrs. Kip and flipped to her current page. Not all books lived up to the hype around them. Take that one about Jephthah's daughter. She hadn't *expected* that a book about someone who was sacrificed because her father was an idiot would be any good, no matter how "beautiful and heroic" that daughter was in her submission to her father's idiocy.

But other books had sounded *amazing,* and everyone who read them sang praises to skies full of hearts and rainbows. However, when Harper read them, the rainbows turned gray, the hearts fell, and the skies turned dark and gloomy—like her mood at being tricked into reading drivel. So a book about an old woman dying and moving into a nursing home for hospice? *That* hadn't been promising. Which made its goodness all the better.

With her finger stuck in her place, she hugged the

book to herself and gave a little hop. Good books were just so... *invigorating!*

Hands appeared in her peripheral vision—Tammy's. Harper would recognize the ridiculous diamond ring Tammy wore anywhere. Rare optimism prompted her to stick her finger back in the book and pull it close again. "Need help finding something?"

She did not add, *Like the door?* Which should count for lunch at Bev's Cafe. She'd even throw in some creamy cucumbers to justify it. If all vegetables came swimming in Bev's creamy sauce, Harper just might eat some a bit more often.

"A couple of things. First... *Middlemarch* or *The Brothers Karamazov?*"

"Brothers. Definitely. I think *Middlemarch* was named that because everyone wants to march away from it by the middle—if not before."

"Excellent." Tammy leaned forward. "Why don't you tell Mrs. Klair that she needs to check out books from the library? This is a store. You should be paid for your merchandise."

"At least she reads them. And she's nice." Harper sighed. "I like the routine, too. The UPS driver doesn't come every day, the mail guy isn't always the same, and... she is."

"You like routine."

Harper nodded. *Isn't that what I just said?* At least she'd finally learned to *think* thoughts like that rather than say them.

Dalton appeared with *White Bird.* "It's World War II."

Tammy picked it up and the boy's face dropped as she fanned the book. "Nope. Not doing a graphic novel."

"But it looks so good!"

Without a word, Harper scooted out from behind the counter and made for her favorite shelf in the children's section. No one looked at it—not really. It's just where she kept copies of all the books she loved and recommended. By genre or time period rather than author name. Between

45

herself and no one else, Harper wasn't always great with names. Down came the book she'd remembered, and she carried it back to the counter where Tammy, used to Harper's oddities by now, waited.

Harper pointed to *White Bird*. "That one's cool because it shows a Jewish girl being hidden from the Nazis in France. She's also not perfect, so you get to see character growth." She slid her selection across the counter. "*A Place to Hang the Moon* is more traditional fare—English kids being sent to the countryside to be safe during the Blitz—but with a twist so it's not the same old/same old. It's my favorite right now."

"So you agree that the graphic novel isn't as good?"

That she didn't scream her objections proved that growing up had its advantages. Harper just shook her head. "It's possibly better because of the character growth and showing kids that the war affected children in places other than Germany and England. You just didn't want a graphic novel, so I gave you what you wanted."

Emily giggled. Dalton grinned. Harper couldn't imagine what she'd said that was so funny, but even Tammy smiled. "All right. We'll take both and a solid copy of Karamazov. It's a reading challenge. We're supposed to read a 'daunting book' from our book bucket lists, and those were mine since I tortured myself with *Mill on the Floss* and *Atlas Shrugged* last year."

By the time they *finally* left the store, Harper had included a vanilla milkshake to her Bev's Western Burger dinner. She'd earned every single calorie that everyone told her would someday start sticking to her body and creating curves—likely in all the wrong places.

Six

A book a day keeps reality away.

If only life could be as simple as a T-shirt slogan. Harper stood in front of the mirror in the upstairs restroom and stared at the words written across her chest. Score one for voluptuous-less. Not even Aunt Tracey could say there was anything immodest about a guy reading *her* chest—so to speak.

A tiny, rebellious part of her— Not hardly. Every bit of her and more wanted to walk right back out of that restroom wearing the shirt. It wasn't rude or anything—not like her *"The book is open so your mouth should be shut"* shirt.

Still, Anders had insisted that she needed to be professional. Black slacks—today's were cropped almost to capri length—and a white shirt with no writing and did not look like it could *have* writing on it. Most of the time she stuck to button-downs, but she'd found a pullover with a pretty hem and neckline on final clearance at the resale shop on the corner last week. It was more ivory than stark white, but she considered it to be in the white family.

Right around that thought is when Harper realized she was procrastinating. Today was tax day. Just a couple of days before, her tax guy had to send the government her quarterly payment. And it was huge. So if she'd made that much, *why* did she have nothing?

The healthy account that had come with the store had

dwindled to a ghost of its former self, and with another insurance bill looming too. At least she'd listened to Tom the Tax Tallier and kept her quarterly payments in another account. Maybe she should have him tally up all the taxes and insurances and figure out how much she should add to that account every month. Then she couldn't order more books than she could afford.

What a depressing thought. All those poor books jailed in warehouses until someone comes along and gives them a nice home on a shelf somewhere. Forget "crazy cat lady" bringing home a new cat from the pound every week, gimme the books. Preferably daily.

That could be a T-shirt, too. *Crazy book lady.* Harper grinned as a postscript to that thought penned itself across the page of her mind. *(Cats optional).*

Well, if she failed as a bookseller, she could always try for a life of selling bookish merch—T-shirts, mugs (readers needed lots of those for tea and coffee), tote bags (to carry the books), even journals (to write about the books they read).

That settled everything. If she ran Aunt Lorene's business into the ground, she'd never hear the end of it from her still-bitter family. In brighter news, she might still be able to eat; although, she might need a second job to buy books.

The moment she unlocked the front door and wheeled out the reject cart—that is, the "so cheap it's nearly free" cart—Harper dashed back in to confirm her scrawled numbers were the right ones to write on the check to the IRS.

Tom assured her that yes, they were. Yes, they were a bit higher than last year, but so were her sales, and no… he didn't think the property taxes and insurance were unusual. Almost exactly what they'd been for the past few years. "If you are having cash flow problems, look to your expenses." That's when he brought up things like labor (she had none but herself), utilities (she had to have lights and heat or AC), losses (again, only the dementoddlers), advertising (was she supposed to do that?), and of course, merchandise—i.e. books (those she had… by the boxful).

Her heart sagged as dramatically as her shoulders as she wrote out the check, ripped it from the book, and slipped it into the envelope. She then printed the form he sent over and realized that he'd probably seen through her subterfuge regarding not being able to read her writing. Sure it was true, but they both knew she had the forms in her inbox. If only she'd remembered before she called.

At the same time as every other day that week, the same guy stepped into the shop, smiled at her, and dashed for the stairs. Harper would question his taste in books if he ever looked at them, but he didn't. As far as she could tell, he just went upstairs and stared out that stupid window—recording half the time—and then dashed off again.

The problem was, as far as she could see, there wasn't anything *to* see. The street? Who cared? A store? Was he a reporter trying to get the goods on the glasses place or Hanisch's? The church? Did he need prayer? Praying with others wasn't really her thing, but she could pull off a few words if she had to. But if that were the case, he could also just go over and ask someone to pray with him. People were in and out of there all day—especially this week with Courtney Madsen's ballet camp going on.

Harper turned to stare out the front window. Courtney. Upstairs teaching classes in a leotard and tights…. Probably short shorts. That pervert!

Never had Harper made it up the stairs two at a time. She did now. At the top, she darted around horror and came to a stop where creepy dad stood with his phone up. He flushed at the sight of her. "Um, hi."

"What do you think you're doing?"

"Watching that class." He said it like it was no big deal, but his eyes darted everywhere, and his hand shook a bit as it held the phone up but pointing in the wrong direction.

"Thought so." Harper backed away and pulled out her phone. "I'm calling the police. You disgust me."

That got his attention.

Thought it might, you...oh, I wish there were better words to describe people like you!

"Why? What'd I do?"

"In the old days, they called guys like you peeping Toms. Well, not on my watch."

The twist of his lips hinted he wasn't as embarrassed anymore. "Not peeping. Watching. Look." He turned the phone back to the window and moved it around. "There. Look."

You said that already, bossy. But Harper looked. He had a seriously good phone. At the slightest move, it went off somewhere else and got the wrong thing, but you could see *everything* in that classroom. She took the phone from him and stared at the screen as she panned the building and back again. Courtney Madsen—at least she wore a little skirt—one little girl... two little girls... all in pink tights and skirts, pink shoes, black leotards... still a lot of pink. And a boy. In bicycle shorts, T-shirt, and those same ballet shoes.

"Wait... is that?"

"My son, yes." He started to shove his hands in his pocket, noticed her holding his phone, and held out his hands for it. "He's in that class—the only boy and the youngest kid. And some of those girls and their mothers have been..."

That's all she needed to hear. She passed over the phone. "So you come up here every day to..."

"Make sure he's all right. He doesn't—I mean, I—" After a shaken head, he sighed. "It's a long story, but I can't let him feel insecure. He has to know that I'll be there in just a minute if he needs me." The phone went up and he started watching again.

Harper just stared. What was she supposed to do with *that?*

50

With ballet out of the way, hopefully forever, Noah packed Bennie up in his car and headed out to the "Family Fun" ice cream social at the historical society. It sounded boring as anything, but his mom had insisted it would be great fun. *"There's going to be a reenactment, old fashioned games, ice cream..."* At his raised eyebrows, she'd added, *"You need to do things with him that don't require a screen, or he'll be jaded before he's ten."*

That magic word, "screen," had done the trick. In his nightly self-taught crash course on parenting, he'd been finding lots of conflicting arguments on screens vs. no screens, but one thing that no one seemed to argue with was the need for kids to spend lots of time outdoors and lots of time interacting with *real* people, not just virtual ones in games.

"So... ready for ice cream?" Noah watched Bennie from the rearview mirror. The kid was still on cloud nine from their seed-spitting contest the night before. Bennie had made a funny comment just as Noah went to spit, and the "spit take" hadn't been focused enough to make a difference.

The way Bennie's face lit up as he smiled back... Could anything be more wonderful? How had he ever thought no responsibilities was a *good* thing. Easier, sure. Less terrifying? Definitely. But good? A second glance at the boy watching as the houses slipped past confirmed it. Nope. Not good at all. *This* was good.

Despite having lived in Red Wing all his life, Noah barely knew where the Historical Society *was*. Sure, he knew the street, but what kind of building was it? Had he ever gone there? School trip? If he had, he didn't remember.

Truth be told, he hadn't expected many people to be there, but the place teemed with people—old and young alike. Finding parking? Not so easy, and when he climbed out to help Bennie, he saw the first reenactor.

"Why's the army here?"

Was it weird that a six-year-old could tell that a guy dressed up in an old blue coat and pants with a gun over one shoulder was wearing an army uniform? Seemed weird to him. "They're going to show what an old battle in the Civil War would have looked like."

"Was that in Affffgaaan… something? Mommy's boyfriend was there."

Throat constricting and prayers firing off one after another, pleading for the kid not to get upset now, Noah shook his head and led Bennie across the street. "No, this was over a hundred—maybe a hundred fifty…" he tried to remember the end of the Civil War. 1864? 5? Something like that? "Yeah, like a hundred fifty years ago. Long time. It's when some of our states like Virginia and Georgia were fighting other states like Pennsylvania and New York."

With his luck, he'd just put one of those states in the wrong ballpark, but whatever. They asked when the reenactment would begin, did a gunny sack race (both of them fell flat on their faces), tried running with a plastic egg on a spoon (Bennie dropped his every two feet, and Noah stepped on his—twice), and yes, ate ice cream. At least the day wasn't too hot or muggy. Puffy white clouds floated high overhead and far apart.

But of all the oddest things, the reenactment held Bennie spellbound. They sat on the grass, watching as soldiers pretended to advance, fire, called out orders. Sitting cross-legged, elbows on his knees, head in his hands, Bennie never shifted his gaze. Every teacher's dream student. Unlike Noah who would rather have counted toothpicks—to keep his eyes open.

From behind him, a woman's voice pierced through the commands, the sounds of blanks firing, the chatter and squeals of children and murmurs of the crowd. "—have to go soon. We finished our read aloud last night, and it's Emily's turn to pick out a book. She's kept one eye on my phone all day. She's convinced that Harper will close the store early because of the social and we'll be forced to read one of the dozens of unread books we already own."

If you could hear eyes roll, Noah did.

Another woman took up the conversation. "I don't

know how you get your kids to sit around and listen to you read. Emily's what? Eleven? Twelve?"

"Almost thirteen."

"And she just lets you *read* to her?"

That caught his interest. What tween wanted someone to read to her? Wasn't it a bit... juvenile? Noah's mind conjured pictures of the woman sitting on the couch, book turned toward her kids who sat in a semi-circle on the floor, reading sideways or over the top of a picture book. You read picture books to kids. Didn't you?

"Well, we've always read to them—first just nursery rhymes or board books. Then picture books and chapter books. The younger kids have it easier because they're used to a couple or three chapters a night now. Anything less and Emily sneaks the book away during the day."

Sneaking a book. That was *not* something he would have ever done. The conversation continued—all the benefits of being read to and the bonding experience it was. That thought right there sealed the deal. As soon as they left, they'd go over to Twice Sold Tales and get Harper—whatever her name was—to recommend something for them to read. He swallowed hard. Aloud.

I missed diapers, Lord. And potty training. So I can suck it up and do this. Right?

Seven

Parenting Tip #41: Teach your kid that you'll stand up for him by standing up for other people. Or something.

The store buzzed with shoppers. One man wanted books about Red Wing—historical things or memoirs. Harper, in the same clothes he'd seen her wear every single day, led the man to a tiny display atop a crate that held other books. "These are all I have on the whole county. There's not a big demand for Goodhue County works. I'd try the Historical Society. They're having an ice cream social today, so if you get over there quickly enough, you might find something there."

She probably didn't mean to sound like she said, "Go away," but she did.

The guy gave her a strange look and shrugged before walking out the door. Another woman asked for Red Wing T-shirts. Harper—that was her name, wasn't it?—said something about the visitor's center or the Uffda Shop. Had something gone wrong? That was the second— Noah winced at the next.

"No, I don't carry *Goosebumps* in my store. You can find trash like that on eBay."

Maybe it had been a hard day. So far, he hadn't seen any other employees. Burned out? Hungry? *Hangry!* With all the customers, she probably hadn't had time to go get food. Maybe she'd forgotten a lunch? He could do something about that.

"Hey, Bennie. What do you say we run down to McDonald's and get Miss Harper (*that better be her name*) a burger?"

"Can I stay and look at books?"

As much as he wanted to say yes, every instinct demanded a definite no. "Sorry, bud (*where'd that come from?*). Can't. But we'll come right back. I think she's *really* hungry."

"Can I have fries?"

They tried to sneak out the back door, but it was locked. Three women chattered about the great books they'd found, but if the expression on Harper's face could be believed, she disagreed. And probably needed that food before she ran off every customer.

Noah paused by the register. "Coke? Root beer? Lemonade?"

"Huh?"

"Favorite drink with lunch?"

She wrinkled her nose. "Rooibos."

Try again. Stay patient. Pretend she's Bennie. "Fountain drink."

She shrugged and turned back to the guy waiting at the counter. "Dr. Pepper."

You would. Aloud he said, "Be right back."

"Whatever."

I should let you starve.

Only three people browsed the shelves by the time he returned. Bennie entered with palms up as if in surrender and made for the restroom at the back of the kids room to wash his hands. A woman asked for the latest Nora Roberts novel. Harper huffed and pointed at a shelf announcing, "New Releases."

"Third shelf from the top. Second or third from the right." Under her breath she muttered, "With all the other garbage wrapped in satin."

Noah set the McDonald's bag and cup on the counter. "Happy Saturday." At the suspicious look she gave him, he added. "Thanks for letting me hang out all morning this week."

That seemed to placate her but only just. He tried again. "I also hoped you'd give me your opinion on reading aloud to kids." *Please say it's overrated—that kids need to read themselves so they can develop some kind of brain muscles.*

"Essential." Harper—he had to ask about her name—peered into the bag. "You got me a Quarter Pounder?"

Noah nodded. "With cheese."

The woman appeared with Nora Roberts, three thrillers from upstairs, and a children's book with a picture of a bed piled high with people sleeping in and on it. "I'll take these. I just love your store."

"So do I—most of the time." She rang up the sale, took the woman's money, shoved books in a bag, and then gave an actual smile. "*The Napping House* is a great choice. Happy reading."

After giving her a queer look, the woman shook her head. "Well, it's for my sister's granddaughter. I didn't plan to read it myself. It just looked cute."

She'd just popped the hamburger box open when a man asked if she carried anything by Upton Sinclair—particularly *Mammonart*. Noah watched and tried not to laugh at the way she *didn't* repress her wrinkled nose as she said, "Um… try the top shelf over there above that row of outdated and worthless encyclopedias. If it's not with the other self-important works, I don't."

At least that guy found her funny. "I have to ask. My wife's brother collects just that sort of junk."

"He'd be better off collecting toilet paper rolls. They're softer."

That earned her a chuckle. "I'll have to suggest that. Oh… there is one. Great."

A woman rushed in and slowed as she took in the store. Though she slowed around each bookshelf, her eyes roamed. Harper (he really needed to ask about that name) sighed. "Restroom's in the back and to the right."

Face flushed, the woman thanked her and darted for the back as if fleeing the restroom cops. "Good one."

"You learn to read people."

This time the box made it open, and the top of the bun dropped into the lid before the next question came from Sinclair dude. "Got a recommendation for a good mystery? Something newish? I've been plowing through my Dad's collection, but he doesn't have anything from the past five years."

Without looking up, Harper ticked off several authors with each flick of an onion or pickle. "Jacqueline Winspear, Patricia Raybon, Richard Osman, Ashley Weaver, or... hmmm. Maybe James Hannibal or T. E. Kinsey."

Only then did Noah realize the man stood in front of the mystery shelves, pulling one author off after another. He dropped them on the counter just as the hamburger had been reassembled sans unwanted additions. Harper reached into the bag and came up empty. "Oh, seriously? What is with these places?"

He had to do something and fast. "Um... you sit and tell me what to do between bites." Noah inched around to the edge of the counter. "Can I come back?"

"Um—"

Taking that for a yes, Noah flipped books over and read the stickers on the back. The tablet mocked him. "Um..."

Step by step, and around mouthfuls, Harper walked him through the process. After typing in each one, he stuffed it in a bag and went to the next. "Add a bookmark from the jar..." The bookmark said Twice Sold Tales, Red Wing and in tiny print on the bottom Harper Brevig, proprietor.

Yes! At least I accomplished one—no, she's eating... make that two—*things today.*

"Come back anytime."

"I live in Idaho. It'll be a while." And with that, the guy waved and left.

Noah needed a nap. Or at least a caffeinated drink.

"Why'd you do that?"

If he was not mistaken, and he wasn't, Harper glared at him. "Just thought you might want to eat before it got cold."

"And why'd you do this?"

The door jingled and a family came in—three small children and two parents who couldn't have looked more impassive. One kid dove for a display with a matched set of something—probably classics. Another grabbed a random book that Noah couldn't identify, and the third threw his sippy cup at his father's backside. A glance at Harper showed her waffling between fury and tears—or tears of fury. "Keep eating. I've got this."

And why is this any of your business? You just came in for a stupid book.

Noah's heart plummeted to the floor where the kid's juice washed over it and his shoes. Book. Bennie! He'd forgotten all about his son! What kind of father *does* that? A glance at the back showed Bennie sitting cross-legged again, but this time his eyes bored into an open page.

A yelp from behind him shot his gaze over to Harper and back to the kids. The classics set was half a second away from becoming a garbage set. "Hey, there. Let me get that." The kid sent up a shriek loud enough to ensure everyone in town thought she'd been whacked with the books or maybe they'd all been dropped on her head. The father turned around and a flash of something appeared and disappeared in a matter of seconds.

"What is wrong, Allegra?"

"Books! He took my books!"

The man gave Noah a look that was likely meant to be reproachful, but again—completely inexpressive. "I believe my daughter was looking at those."

"Destroying them is more like it," Noah muttered as he scooped the last one up off the floor before "Allegra" could get it. Who named their daughter after an allergy medication, anyway? Or was it prophetic…?

"Children can be rough, but it's how they learn." The

man said it, but it sounded like a child's robotic answer to a teacher who called him out for bad behavior.

"Not in my store and not with my merchandise," Harper said.

Noah looked over and nearly butted heads with her.

"I'm going to have to ask you to leave." She dove for the book half a second after the little guy ripped the dust jacket off and into two pieces, all in one swift movement. "Just as soon as you pay for this book your son decided you would purchase."

"We're not interested in…" the man pieced together the dust jacket. "*Where the Crawdads Sing*, but thank you. And we haven't finished looking—"

"*Destroying*, you mean," Harper insisted. "If you don't leave now and with twenty dollars on my counter, I'm calling the police. I'm done with parents letting their kids destroy my shop."

The woman finally turned around, that same bland look on her face. "You're distressing the children," she said. "And we don't want to buy that book. We're going to see the movie."

"Do everyone in the theater a favor and get a babysitter," Harper snapped back. "But get your brats—" She dove for another bookshelf and planted herself between it and the child ready to empty it of its contents. "—*out* of my store!"

The kid wailed, screamed, sobbed. Now that reproachful look really did appear. "How could you make a child cry over a silly book?"

"Call the police."

She must have been speaking to him. Noah called.

With the same expressionless expression plastered back on her face, the woman picked up her shrieking child and tried to soothe him. But even her "Shhs" and "It's okays" sounded like it came from artificial intelligence. "We're going to go look in another store."

"Books!"

"We'll find some in another store."

59

Harper began to shake. "Twenty dollars and don't forget your destroyed book."

"The words are still there," the android—she just couldn't be a real woman—said. "It's still legible."

When a dispatcher asked the trouble, Noah spoke louder than necessary. "Yes, I'm a customer at Twice Sold Tales, and a family has come into the store. The children are tearing up the place and the parents refuse to stop them or to pay for damages. They also refuse to leave the store. The owner would like them escorted off the premises."

Even as the bizarre family left, the only hint of expression came when the man set the twenty-dollar bill on the counter. It may have been Noah's imagination, but he could've sworn the guy slammed it down—just a bit. For him, anyway. Harper called after them, "And stay out of the Uffda Shop! You can't afford the bill!"

The moment they left, Harper dashed to lock the door behind them. "That's it. I quit. I'm done for the day. I can't deal with these crazies!"

"Don't blame you. That was the single most bizarre thing I've ever seen."

Bennie appeared at his side, staring up at Harper. After watching her struggle to gain control of herself, he stepped forward and wrapped his arms around her. "I'm sorry."

The woman met his gaze and sent a thousand questions at him. Noah just shrugged. If only his son would hug *him* like that—with that same genuine spontaneity. After a moment, Harper wrapped her arms around Bennie for half a second and said, "Thank you."

Bennie stepped back and smiled up at her. "We're here to buy a book." He shot a look at Noah. "He's going to read it to me." His gaze dropped to the floor. "I can't read yet."

"But you will." She hunkered down on her heels and gazed at him. "I think… you… you like adventure. You want to see kids do things that matter."

Head bobbing with the speed and efficiency of a

bobblehead, Bennie became the poster child for hero worship. "Yes!"

"I've got just the book for you. Stay right there. I want to surprise you."

If he hadn't seen it himself, Noah wouldn't have believed it. Grumpy, snappish Harper Brevig had been... sweet. Charming, even. A look at Bennie sent his stomach plummeting to the floor again (and reminded him there was juice to clean up). He'd root for the Vikings if Bennie hadn't just developed a teacher-like crush on their bookseller. *Oh, brother. Not what I needed.*

Eight

If it involves books and pajamas, count me in.

And cramps weren't invited. Stupid gate crashers.

Closing the store early on a weekend, much less a day that drew in even more people with things like the ice cream social—not a good way to pay taxes and insurance bills. But curled up in bed with a stack of books that toppled every time she (stupidly) shifted, and a heating pad strapped (or it would be if she had a way to do it) to her middle, Harper sobbed her way through the final pages of Mrs. Kip. She'd order five of them and foist them onto every customer who walked in the door.

"Authentic love is the greatest joy there is, Miss Kelley, but it requires a thousand little deaths to self."

Those words had trickled into her heart through a crack she hadn't managed to plug up in time. The crack was now a gap, and the faster each letter of each syllable of each word flooded in, the wider it grew. Harper would've scrambled to shove anything possible in that gap—anything to stop even one "little death," but cramps, a pounding head, and mortification couldn't hope to battle Mrs. Kip's truth. Sara Brunsvold was a genius.

Why'd he do that? No answer came, despite her repeated question every twenty minutes. Noah was his name. His son, Bennie. Well, Bennie had whispered, "It's really Benedict—Benedict John Pedersen—but it's going to be Lampe like him soon."

Noah had been cleaning up the book-mentor—no, that sounded like a good thing. Well, the sippy cup kid *had* been a toddler, so demen-toddler worked. *More like demon toddler.* As if she actually needed the reminder, Harper added as an afterthought, *No kids for* me!

Regardless, Noah had been cleaning up the juice mess for her and hadn't heard their conversation. Why didn't Bennie have his father's name? It *was* his son. Anyone looking at them could see it, despite a difference in hair color. The kid's cowlick alone…

Thinking about Bennie wouldn't answer the burning question of the night. What had made Noah step in and help like that? Bring food? She knew when guys were hitting on her. This wasn't that. If anything, he hadn't even wanted to be in there. Bennie liked it, though. Little kids "always" "got" the magic of books. And they didn't play games. They were outspoken too—no trying to hide their real thoughts behind socially acceptable opinions.

Older people were like that too. Mrs. Klair had once said that at a certain age, you just don't care what people think anymore. *"It happens earlier for some and only near the very end for others, but it happens."*

People her age—except the neuro-divergent ones (thank goodness for them)—were too concerned with offending one group to realize that their sanitized and rehearsed opinions offended other groups. *"We've lost the art of allowing other people the courtesy of being wrong in our eyes."*

Who had said that? Harper couldn't remember. She did remember several references to "correct opinions" in Jane Austen's *Persuasion* and noted that the idea of "correctness," whether cultural, political, or societal fell under Solomon's "nothing new under the sun" banner.

Another cramp seized her, and a glance at her phone told her she could take another couple of ibuprofens. Reaching for her little bowl of cheese curds and the medicine bottle, however, made that cramp throw a tantrum of epic proportions. Her stomach roiled, but she chewed up three curds, downed her pills, and chewed three more before washing it down with lukewarm raspberry-mint tea.

Curled up hugging her pillow again, Harper waited for the painkillers to accept their assignment and assassinate the cramps once and for all. Another peek at her phone promised only eight more hours until relief. Her gaze slid toward the sleep pills. Just a couple more hours and she could sleep away the rest of her misery.

A slim volume in the middle of her precarious stack beckoned her. *The Haunted Bookshop* was just what she needed right now. Four books slid like Harper's shoes on ice and hit the floor, two made a dive for the edge before she stopped their trajectory, and the final one stayed rooted in place. She couldn't help but snicker. *Root Out of Dry Ground* by Argye Briggs.

For just a moment she was tempted to try it. The dust jacket had caught her eye a few weeks back, so she'd brought it home, but Morley…

No. Definitely Morley. After a day like today, she needed the funny old guy's philosophies on bookselling.

The dust jacket had a few more tiny tears along the edges since her last reading, so Harper removed it and slid it into the empty nightstand drawer, saved for just this purpose. The illustration above CHAPTER I brought a smile to her lips. This copy really was a treasure, even if it wasn't a first edition.

"If you are ever in Brooklyn, that borough of superb sunsets and magnificent vistas of husband-propelled baby-carriages, it is to be hoped you may chance upon a quiet by-street where there is a very remarkable bookshop."

The opening of *A Tree Grows in Brooklyn* had a similar feel and fit the day better, really. Being summer and all. Just for justice's sake, Harper pulled out her phone and looked up the opening lines.

"Serene was a word you could put to Brooklyn, New York. Especially in the summer of 1912. Somber, as a word, was better.

But it did not apply to Williamsburg, Brooklyn. Prairie was lovely and Shenandoah had a beautiful sound, but you couldn't fit those words into Brooklyn. Serene was the only word for it; especially on a Saturday afternoon in summer."

Harper hadn't liked *A Tree Grows in Brooklyn* the first time she'd read it. Grumpy Aunt Lorene had commented to another aunt—probably Aunt Robin—that Harper was a twenty-first-century Francie Nolan, and of course, she'd had to read it. At twelve, maybe she should've felt a kinship with Francie, being the lesser-loved daughter to the golden-boy son (or as good as), being a lover of books and stories, even her struggles with the truth when it never looked like *she* thought it should.

But unlike Francie, Harper had never wanted to write. No, she'd been incensed at the horrible librarian who hadn't nurtured a young girl's love of reading and had decided, even as she tossed the book aside unfinished, that she'd grow up and be a librarian. *Not* a bookseller like Aunt Lorene, because *no one* wanted to be anything like Aunt Lorene.

"And here I am. Becoming more like her every day. Is it irony or fate? I say *bitter* irony." With that pronouncement, she went back to her book.

People didn't write books like *Parnassus on Wheels* and *The Haunted Bookshop* anymore. Books where the author spoke directly to the readers were out of fashion. Did it count as "breaking the fourth wall" or whatever that was in movies? Probably. Or close enough.

The young man always brought a smile to her lips—had since the first time she read the book. Then again, she'd read it when she was nineteen instead of when she was twelve. That's when she'd given *A Tree Grows in Brooklyn* a second chance too.

All right, so it had been assigned reading in her twentieth-century American lit class along with *The Great Gatsby* (abominable) and too many of Hemingway's books to want to think about with a stomach full of cheese curds, tea, and drugs of the legal variety. Hemingway had written exactly one story she liked—assuming he really had written it. *"For sale: baby shoes. Never worn."* The rest had never lived up to that one in her opinion. For a guy known to be succinct, Harper Brevig considered him verbose.

The "This Shop Is Haunted" poem on page thirteen finally got its way. Harper snapped a picture of it and clicked on the Etsy app. She didn't buy hand-knitted cardigans or leather pouches. No vintage doilies or prints for her walls. But once a month or so—right around this time, actually—she'd find a new T-shirt she couldn't live without.

Tonight, she'd order that sign for her shop. She'd considered it at least twice a year since the first time she'd read it, and *now,* she had the shop to hang it in and the perfect place for it too. This is how thirty minutes after she opened the book, she'd only made it three pages—two of which were partially covered with illustration and that poem. But a beautifully typeset print of it would be on its way to her in no time. *Gotta love Etsy.*

Advertising—the whole of chapter one had to do with bookselling and advertising. Harper didn't do any of that. She didn't know how and held a firm (and understandable, given her history) belief that her doing what she didn't know how to do was a surefire way to ensure she botched it. Twice Sold Tales had become proof in that pudding for sure.

Some of Harper's favorite lines rushed at her next. *"A book is 'good' only when it meets some human hunger or refutes some human error."* Maybe that's why some books she hated at first reading and loved later… Harper's gaze strayed to the shelf of favorites where her battered copy of *A Tree Grows in Brooklyn* stood next to *The Count of Monte Cristo*, *The Secret at Lilac Inn*, and a completely falling apart copy of *The Mysterious Howling.*

"Maybe I wasn't hungry for Brooklyn when I was twelve."

"No advertisement on earth is as potent as a grateful customer." The line pulled her back into the book, and as

always, the illustration of Roger Mifflin brought to mind ideas of an old sea captain rather than a bookseller. Less than five minutes later, she'd ordered the book Rx on page twenty. It would match the other one, and if there were more, she'd sprinkle them all over the store. At least when she went bankrupt, she'd have nice art for walls she couldn't pay for in a house she didn't have.

By the time she got to Mifflin's insistence that booksellers were tolerant, she'd decided that Aubrey Gilbert was right and Roger Mifflin wrong—totally wrong. Advertising was her problem. She'd just have to go about it in a more... *unconventional* manner. i.e. one that cost her nothing—or very little.

Google insisted that she "optimize her online presence with branded social media." No, thank you. Harper had not and would never become a part of the self-absorbed social media craze. She much preferred her own self-absorbed *book* craze. Next up: become involved in her local community. She *was*. She paid taxes. Great, heaping gobs of property taxes! And she stayed open late when they had community events—usually...

Start a newsletter. Because people *wanted* their inboxes stuffed with *more* coupons, *more* stuff to read, *more*... whatever she'd have to send in those things.

Undaunted, Harper dug deeper. Unique things different bookstores offered. She couldn't take up a whole city block like Powell's. She hadn't been around since forever like The Strand. She did have enough junk books that she could create sculptures and doorways with them, but since people knew that The Last Bookstore in Los Angeles had done this, maybe it wasn't a good idea.

Then she found it—a book about a store in Ann Arbor, Michigan where the owner had plunked an old typewriter down on a desk and had rolled a piece of paper in it. Now he had a whole book of the things people had been moved to type on it over the years. Some broke her heart. Others made it soar. The guy who walked into the store with a friend and walked out in love. Wow...

But of course, someone had already done the typewriter. Harper refused to be a bookstore plagiarist, but she'd allow inspiration…

Except she found nothing. Not. One. Single idea. She broadened her search to other markets. Music. Crafts. Art. That one sparked the beginning of an idea. She wouldn't set up a canvas for people to add to all day. First, it broke the plagiarism rule, and second… paint and books didn't mix, no matter how much the profits from the sale of those paintings might help the homeless. Did Red Wing have homeless people? She didn't know. And she didn't want to know if she were truthful.

Another link took her to YouTube where some guy droned on about how important it was to have an email list. At the end of that one, she saw a reading journal flip through. And from there…

"A journal! It's like a typewriter, but maybe if I made a page or quarter page about my latest read, people would get the idea. It'd be like reviews but right there in person."

Harper's heart sank at the thought of little kids filling pages with scribbles, but seeing the woman glue two pages together when she made a mistake changed that idea. "Spiral. I'll get spiral. And bigger—like sketchbook sized. I can rip out pages that are ruined on both sides and glue the others. And maybe it'll bring people in."

Inside ten minutes, she'd filled an Amazon cart with markers, pens, "washi tape" (which she really couldn't see the point of), stencils, and stickers. (Washi tape stickers, too). A hundred twenty bucks later, she hit purchase and closed her phone.

She closed her book too, stacked it and the remaining pile on the floor on the side of the bed she *never* got out of (childhood superstitions die hard), and took her sleeping pill. After a quick trip to the bathroom and some scrubbed teeth later, she sank into the covers with her heating pad (not) strapped to her, the little AC unit chugging its heart out, and too excited to fall asleep.

Good thing she'd taken that pill.

Nine

Parenting Tip #47: You can fake it until you make it, but you won't fool 'em.

If Noah Lampe had been warned that there were *rules* about how to read books aloud, he'd have bought an audiobook and called it good. Actually, if he'd thought of audiobooks at all, he'd have done it anyway. Instead, he'd settled into his favorite chair and adjusted the floor lamp behind him before reading the opening line.

"'Once there were four children whose names were Peter, Susan, Edmund, and Lucy…'"

"Wait." Bennie stood still in the middle of the room, his face contorted with an expression Noah couldn't decipher.

"What's wrong?"

"You have to read on the couch."

That made no sense, but the kid was so earnest and certain, that Noah couldn't say no. He dragged his tired backside out of the chair and plopped onto the couch, stretching one leg out across the cushions. Bennie scrambled up into his lap as if it happened every day. *Whoa…*

Pulling Noah's arms over himself, he leaned back and got comfortable. "Okay. I'm ready."

Throat closing in on his vocal cords, Noah fought to get the next sentence out. "'This story…'" He made it to when Susan spoke before Bennie spoke again.

"But what does Susan *sound* like?"

Sound like? How should I know? A vague memory of his mother reading to him pushed itself forward and he heard her voice drop when Captain Hook spoke. "Right." He raised his voice to a reasonable falsetto—high enough to be different, but not high enough to embarrass himself."

Bennie relaxed again until Lucy spoke. "She's smaller. She should be squeaky like a mouse. One girl in my class had a squeaky mouse voice."

A couple of higher notes satisfied the kid until the faun, Mr. Tumnus, appeared on the scene. "I can't make a *mister* have a high voice."

"But he can't sound like Peter or Edmund. Maybe he has an accent? Like from Texas. Mommy had a boyfriend from Texas."

Noah didn't think this book had any Texans at all. Though he hadn't connected it at first, things felt familiar—especially the snow and the wardrobe. And that lamppost. This was Narnia—like the movie. He'd known there were books in that vague way people often do—like how they knew there was a Joseph in the Bible but only knew he had a colorful coat or that Moses was a baby in a basket.

"I think Mr. Tumnus would sound British."

"Okay." Bennie settled back again, confident in Noah's ability to make a British Mr. Tumnus come to life.

Not fair.

So, using a "British" accent that slipped into a jumble of semi-British, a smattering of Spanish, and an accidental French, "Aid-*monde!*" for "Edmund," Mr. Tumnus came to life—a comical, ridiculous life but life, nonetheless. Bennie sighed, and it sounded more like contentment than disgust, so Noah kept reading. He'd planned to stop at the end of chapter two since the first had been so short, but Bennie turned the page and grinned up at him. "This is good! I thought the witch was going to beat them to the wardrobe."

"We'll see what happens tomorrow night. It looks like Edmund goes in."

"Read it now."

The dad gene must come alive with the proximity of children, because Noah nearly said, "How do we ask?" Instead, he gave his son a look. How many nights had Bennie *not* had a dad read to him? Had Tara? She hadn't seemed the mom type much less the book-reading-to-kids type. *Maybe if you'd gotten to know her in the friendly sense before the Biblical sense, you'd know this.*

It was a common accusation lobbied at self in weak moments. It's also one his mother had, repeatedly, reminded him had been washed clean in the blood of Christ. *"Therefore, there is now no condemnation for those who are in Christ Jesus." Get over yourself, Lampe.*

Bennie stared at the page, waiting. "L says lllll, right? So is that Lucy?"

Noah read. All of chapter three and the first page of chapter four when he realized Bennie had gone heavy. Dead to the world. They'd start over with four the next night.

Leaving the book on the couch, Noah struggled upstairs with his son, decided to skip teeth brushing, remembered the cost of dentistry, and woke Bennie up. "We need to brush your teeth."

Little fists—how had he never noticed how small his son's hands were?—rubbed sleepy eyes. "Was the tall lady the witch?"

He grinned. "You'll have to wait until tomorrow to see."

By the third "reminder" (near lecture) before breakfast, a sickening, uncomfortable feeling had settled into Noah's gut. Hadn't he hated it when his mom left a million "don't forgets" before walking out the door? Wasn't he doing the same thing?

Aaannnd one more thing he needed to apologize to his mom for. He'd been awful about that, and now look at him. He'd save the last remin—um, *suggestion,* that is—for just before he left.

Bennie picked at his eggs, taking one bite to Noah's three or four. He had to do something. "What are you going to do with Megan today?"

The kid shrugged, one side of his Hulk pajamas barely rising over the other.

It didn't take a guy who'd aced parental sensitivity training (he hadn't) to realize something bothered his son. See? There was even hope for him! But knowing what to do now... *that* would be nice.

"Is there something you want to do?"

A quick shake of the head preceded Bennie's close scrutiny of his plate. Noah didn't know what to make of it until he saw a tear splash onto the now dry, rubbery eggs. That was when his heart broke the first time.

Pushing his plate away, Noah moved to his son's side and hunkered down to look into that precious face. And there he went again. Precious. When had he *ever* even acknowledged the existence of that word?

Bennie's enormous eyes looked even bigger full of tears he fought to control. Noah picked him up and plunked them both down on the kitchen chair. "Want to tell me about it?"

The kid shook his head before burying it in Noah's shoulder and sniffling. With his arms wrapped around Bennie, Noah held fast and allowed himself to marvel...even *revel...* in the moment. The kid had made a few small overtures. Tiny little ones, but they'd been real and hinted that he was getting used to Noah. But this...

Those little fists clung to his shirt and occasional gulps hinted at attempts to repress sobs. "Hey, now... it's going to be okay." Noah grasped at anything he could think of. "Missing your mom?"

When his head shook, nodded, and shook again, Noah took it to mean that he did miss her but that wasn't the problem. It was, most likely, the wrong translation. Still, he tried again. "Sick of eggs?"

A single shake.

"Do I stink?"

The giggle broke off in a sob.

"Bennie, I want to help, but I don't know how. You can talk to me. We have…" He glanced at his phone. "Half an hour before Megan—"

But that was all it took. Those sobs burst forth like summer rain showers. Somewhere in the middle of it all, Noah thought he heard, "Don't want you to go," but it could have been, "Dad, you're so slow." And he'd take that, too. Bennie didn't call him Dad much. Once that he could recall. Only once.

A dozen ways to spin this, and Noah didn't have a clue which was best. The money angle? Explain they needed money to survive, or would it make the kid afraid? Maybe money for things like ballet lessons, or did he *really* want to reinforce that? Responsibility and keeping your word? Too heavy for a kid Bennie's age?

What would he have wanted to hear? His father would have gone the responsibility route. His mother would have gone practical finances. Neither would have soothed. Then it hit him.

"You know I don't *want* to go, don't you?" Was it his imagination or did the sobs soften just a smidge? "If I didn't have to, I'd rather just stay here and hang out with you. Go swimming. Tear the flowers from the front yard and put a treehouse there."

This time Bennie definitely quieted a bit.

"But here's the thing. I have a job. I promised my boss when he hired me that I'd be there at eight every morning and I wouldn't go home until five at night. If I don't go, I'm telling him and everyone—even you—that they can't trust me when I say something."

"I know I can!" The kid sounded far too hopeful.

"But you wouldn't—not later. I'd tell you I would do something you thought I'd say no to, and you'd remember that I told my boss I'd be there and then I didn't go. And you'd wonder. Anyone would."

"What if I get sick?"

Who had taken care of his son the last time Bennie had been sick? Where had he been? Foster care?

It still burned his gut that the boy had ever had to be part of that. He'd complained to the social worker that the whole mess could've been avoided if Tara had just told him about their son—he'd have willingly paid child support too. Been a part of Bennie's life so when all this happened it wasn't a shock.

The woman had given him a weak smile and said a lot of women didn't want to share custody with their "baby daddies." She'd actually said that. "Baby daddy." His gut still churned at the word. He, Noah Lampe, had been a *baby daddy*. Ugh.

"Dad?"

Jerked from his musings, Noah squeezed Bennie just a bit tighter. "I would, if Megan couldn't stay. My boss would let me off work for emergencies like that. He's not a mean guy."

But the mention of Megan had made Bennie stiffen—no doubt about it. That's when he remembered that everything had started going downhill when he'd asked what they'd do today. "Don't you like Megan?" He'd seemed to when Megan spent a few hours with them.

"Yeah."

The urge to correct with, "Say yes," nearly overrode basic common sense. *Parenting tip #58. It's more than "pick your battles." It's that "don't exasperate your kid" by picking on* them.

"Did you have a b—" Noah cut off "baby" almost in time. "Um… sitter when you lived with your mom?"

He nodded. "Grannie Jan."

"What'd you guys do?"

"Make cookies… watch her shows." Bennie wrinkled his nose. "I like the games but not the kissing shows."

"You and me both, kid. Okay, did you play games or

go swimming?"

At first, Bennie shook his head but then a sigh followed. "Sometimes we played Sorry. I'm good at Sorry."

"I'll bring it home tonight." Even as he spoke, Noah could hear his mother. *You can't buy the child's affection. It's good for children to wait for things.* And she was right. He knew it.

But sometimes you put aside those truisms (is that a word?) in favor of building bridges. And right now, this bridge hasn't even left the bank. No pilings—nothing.

"I could go with you. I could sit in the car and try to read the book. Then we could get the game after work."

This wasn't good. It really was Megan. Now what? After another glance at his phone—only fifteen minutes now—Noah knew he had to do something. "Can you tell me why you aren't comfortable with Megan? Why didn't you say something? I need to know so I know how to make you feel safe as much as possible."

Dentists have an easier time removing impacted molars than Noah did getting the truth from Bennie, but it boiled down to the fact that Megan smelled like the daughter at the foster home he'd been in before coming to live there with Noah on Wilkinson Street. Once started, he couldn't seem to stop with a sickening download. "She pinched me. And scared me at night. And didn't let me go when I had to. Then I got in trouble for wetting my pants."

They'd have to talk about this. Obviously. But they couldn't now, and Megan would be there in just a few minutes. He first zipped her a text and asked her if she'd be willing to go home, shower with different shampoo and be sure not to use body spray. Then he called his boss and said he might be as much as fifteen minutes late.

"Fine, but you're staying over. This daddy game of yours better not become a problem."

It was the first time Dan had ever been anything but supportive and understanding. *I've pushed all the boundaries, I guess.* Noah assured him that it wouldn't be a continuing problem.

After all that, of course, Noah realized it could be fabric softener. "Was it Megan's *clothes* or herself that smelled like the other girl?"

"Perfume. It's the same. I hate it." The kid sounded like he'd start sobbing again.

Whew. "Okay, here's what we're going to do. I'll come home at lunch. If you're still unhappy, I'll drive you out to my mom's house. I'll get in trouble at work, but you have to feel safe. But you have to do your part."

Bennie sat up, eyes wide and concentrating enough to make him look constipated. "What do I do?"

"You tell me if Megan does one thing to hurt you—inside or outside but…" Oh, how he hated to have to say it. "You can't tell me she did if she didn't. If I can't trust you to tell me the truth, I have to trust someone who hasn't told me a lie. I *always* want to believe you."

A dozen emotions flickered over his son's face. Hope, fear, uncertainty, and disappointment were among them. Then his jaw set. His lips pursed, and he gave a little nod. "Okay. I will."

Noah kissed the boy's head and said, "You don't have any reason to believe me, little guy, but I love you more than I knew it was possible to love anyone. I'll be back at lunch and then after work. We'll go buy that game together. I need you to make sure I get the right one."

After a hug—those spontaneous hugs were becoming more frequent and the best parts of his day—Bennie hopped down, sat in the chair, and forced a bite of food in his mouth. Noah would lay good money on the boy having to still a trembling lip too.

I really do love this kid, Lord. I just don't know what I'm doing with him.

Ten

Book boyfriends don't cheat.

Despite aching to read the next chapter of *Fawkes,* Harper closed the book and reminded herself that the men in the cell would *not* kill him. After all, it was only chapter three, and killing off the main character in chapter three wasn't just illogical, it was stupid. No one needed stupid.

But if she didn't get some sleep, she'd regret it tomorrow. A glance at the clock amended that thought. Later today. The muggy heat had been miserable these past couple of weeks, and with so little rain, even the corn was refusing to grow, or so the locals had been complaining. So, with her little window AC chugging away, Harper rolled over, snapped off her bed lamp, and snuggled under her sheet. If only she could tolerate a single blanket for a hint of weight. Exhaustion consumed her before she had a chance to roll over for the first time.

Sleep dragged its miserable self away from her and went to find somewhere more comfortable to rest. Harper sat up in bed, wondering why she was so warm and why it was so quiet. She turned on the light and blinked around her, determined to solve the mystery and lock the culprit in the slammer.

Perspiration answered the question for her. The AC had finally bit the dust. Furthermore, she absolutely couldn't afford another one, and even more couldn't afford *not* to have another one. How was a body supposed to sleep in this muggy mess?

With windows open and hoping for a cross breeze, she tossed and turned for the next half hour. Not happening. Crawling from bed, she pulled on jean shorts—the ones too short to be seen wearing in public but kept her cool—and grabbed her store keys. She'd walk around for a while and load up some of the little free libraries. Red Wing had one on every corner and half block it seemed. And it was a good way to get rid of the plethora of junk fiction she hated.

At least at dark-thirty on a Tuesday morning, there shouldn't have been much chance of being seen. *Someone* would. They always did. They always called, and some officer *always* wanted to know what she was doing wandering around at… Harper checked her phone again. *One in the morning. I'm going to be dead tomorrow.*

A few die-hard fireflies still beat out love notes in morse code on Myrna's lawn as she crept out the front door. The memory of her latest flora victim sent her back inside for the trowel she kept in the junk drawer and the pot she'd have to hide on the top shelf of her cabinets with the other dozen or two.

Inside five minutes, the last rites had been said and the philodendron or whatever it was had been laid permanently to rest. "And you're *not* a resurrection plant," she hissed. "No coming back to life for you!"

As Harper turned onto 3rd Street, the theme for *The Good, the Bad, and the Ugly* played in her mind. She almost expected a tumbleweed to roll down the center of the road. Pulling out her phone, she tapped the YouTube app, typed in the theme song, and stopped short. The Danish National Symphony had done it? Harper tapped the screen and a recorder played. An elegant woman stood before a microphone and, no joke, sang, "Wah, wah, wah…"

Again with the "wah, wah, wah." Harper couldn't believe her eyes and ears, which upon closer consideration, was pretty cliché of her. But all she could think of was this woman in an interview, giving a list of her career highlights and saying, "Oh, and I was the wah, wah singer for…"

A snort escaped as she unlocked the door to her store. In less than a minute she'd filled her tote bag with the most recent under-the-counter rejects and had headed out again. Jaywalking as free as a bird with no one on the street to judge. Or ticket. Not that Jake the Cop had ever done it, despite his multiple warnings. Other cops didn't even bother to look twice at her, but Jake always liked to push his weight around. The guy had authority issues—as in, he liked to make sure the world knew he had some.

Across the street from her store, she pulled out her phone, used the flashlight app, and sorted the books in the little house-shaped box full of mostly garbage masquerading as books. There was a copy of *A Room of One's Own*, which she'd heard was good, and a couple of the Incorrigible Children books. She liked those, too. The rest were mass market paperbacks—spy thrillers by authors no one had heard of, bodice rippers by the same, and a bunch of brain candy for kids.

Harper might have felt guilty for contributing to the numbing of American minds, but considering there was a bookstore full of wonderful books only a dozen or two footsteps away and a *library* full of more, well… people who chose free junk over free good stuff or to invest in a personal library deserved the garbage they got.

Down the street showed better offerings. She hadn't read *The Night Circus* herself, but she'd heard good things about it. The Crawdad book, oooh… even the Guernsey one. Mrs. Klair must contribute to this one. There was no other explanation. Tammy Statdler would never give up *her* copy of Guernsey. The woman even liked the Netflix adaptation. Travesty. Anyone who thought it was okay to make a cheap imitation of *North and South's* ending scene instead of the real, delightful library scene didn't know what she was talking about.

Not that Harper had opinions on that or anything.

When a car passed on her trek up Bush Street, the peaceful night scratched to a halt. Or maybe it was the mosquito that bit her right about then. All Harper knew was that in minutes, some cop or another—likely Jake with her luck—would show up wondering why she was wandering around after dark. *Like I'm twelve and out to TP someone's yard while my parents sleep blissfully unaware of their daughter's devious deeds.*

She'd planned to go all the way up to South Park Street and work her way back, but she turned on 7th and hoped she could make a wonky loop—or maybe someone over by the Downtown Plaza had emptied out the one not far from there. She could shove a bunch of bodice rippers and some cheesy westerns for the old folks.

Mr. Laffey would have something to say about it. So far, he hadn't figured out she was the culprit on that score. He just liked to come in now and then, sit in a comfy chair, and read without the blue and purple-haired old biddies flirting with him. They did it, too—worse than middle school girls circling a new guy. Revolting.

The street lit up and grew brighter. The sound of an engine… slow-moving tires. Any second now, a bright light would shine and—there it was. Harper sagged and shifted the heavy book bag to her other arm. She really needed to get a backpack for this, but that would only make her look more "sus" like the kids said now. At least when she was in high school, they hadn't yet turned text speak into real speak. And now she was *that* person—talking about how things were back in "her day" as if it were *the* heyday.

The car pulled up ahead of her and parked. For the first time ever, Harper half prayed that it would be Jake. At least she could get away with being sassy with him. And Harper felt decidedly sassy.

A head appeared… was it… Eyes met hers. "Harper Brevig—a one-woman crusader for Red Wing literacy."

Relief did nothing to temper her tongue. "Officer Jake Beasley—protecting Red Wing streets from insomniacs one night at a time."

80

At least he grinned as he came around and met her under the streetlight. "People don't want their gas stolen or their ashtrays raided and coffee quarters stolen."

"Well, I don't do that."

"No, you fill the minds of residents with…" He held out one hand and smirked at the roll of her eyes before she withdrew a book from the bag.

Please let it be a western.

Jake took the book and snickered. *"Steamy Desert Knights."* After another glance at it, he handed back the paperback and shook his head. "Someone likes a play on words and doesn't know a thing about deserts."

"Yeah?"

"They're hot, sure…" Another juvenile snicker followed that statement. "But deserts aren't steamy. They're dry. I've got a cousin in Nevada near Las Vegas. It's like an oven, not a sauna."

"Not sure that's the kind of steamy…" Harper took a look at the author's name and didn't bother to stifle her groan. "Blossom Lovelace. Of course it's *Blossom Love*lace. But regardless, I doubt she was going for that sort of steam or geography when she wrote the book that she probably didn't get to title herself."

"Hmm…" He stared at her and then at her chest. If he hadn't spoken when he did, Harper might have gotten herself arrested for assaulting a police officer. "'*Book boyfriends don't cheat?*' What does that even mean?"

"Well, not to put too fine a point on it…" This was too fun. "But book boyfriends—"

"Which are?" He folded his arms over *his* chest, and much to Harper's disgust, she noticed that he did have rather beefy arms at that—not in the tubby, spend-too-much-time-in-Hanisch's sort of way, but more in the how-much-does-this-guy-work-out? kind of deal.

"Great men in books who, again not to make things too complicated, stay the amazing guys the authors created them to be." *Unlike humans who totally do not stay who their Creator designed them to be.* A sigh escaped while she pondered that thought. *Guilty as charged.*

"So… perfect. Not real. Better to have a fake guy who can't make a mistake than a real one who can?"

She shook her head. "We call characters like that "Marty Stus. No one likes a totally perfect character. But good guys who don't cheat—we like."

Something shifted in Jake's expression. He eyed her for a moment before dropping his arms to his side. "Who hurt you? I'll kill him." A wince followed. "Metaphorically speaking, of course."

Aw, he wasn't so bad. Not really. "Thanks, but no one hurt *me*. Never had a boyfriend, so never got hurt. But I've watched friends go through it for years, and I decided book boyfriends are best. Safest."

"And not real." For just a moment, Jake looked like he'd step closer.

Harper's breathing became erratic. Yep. That flight response had already filed its fake plan with the FAA and was on course to get her out of there—now. No one, not even Jake Beasley was going to—

Jake's arms folded over his chest again, but this time it didn't feel so imposing. "Harper, a 'book boyfriend' can't hold your hand—can't hold *you* when something goes wrong. You can't kiss a fictional guy. You can't marry him and have a family. And…" He grinned as something else came to mind. She could see it. "Why is it okay for girls to cheat on book boyfriends with lots of book boyfriends? Or do you just break up every time you find some guy you like better—some *fictional* guy?"

Well… if Jake Beasley were going to start making sense, she'd have to quit talking to him. What kind of fun was that? But before she could fire back something about that being the beauty of book boyfriends at all—the rules were different, she saw it. He really was concerned that she'd miss out on life. And that was kind of sweet.

"Until I find a real guy who makes me decide he's worth the risk… I'll stick to my non-cheating book boyfriends who don't care if I go out with another guy every night."

For one horrible second, Harper saw something in Jake that made her want to run again. Was that flight plan still valid? Then it faded and a weak smile followed. "You know they do, right?"

"Who do what?" She shook her head. "I mean, who *does* what?"

"Book boyfriends. They do cheat."

"No they *don't!* That's the—"

Jake broke in. "But they do. Thousands of women could be having a 'date' with your book boyfriend at the exact same time you are. So, unless you're the only one who has ever read the book, they cheat too."

She pulled the shirt away from her body and read the words upside down. "You've just ruined my already awful night. Thanks a lot."

An hour later, Jake, having wrestled an AC unit into the hole left by her dead one, waved goodbye at her door and whistled as he walked down to where his cruiser sat parked on the curb. Harper waited until he drove off before she ripped off her T-shirt and pulled on another one.

If it involves books and pajamas, count me in.

Eleven

Introverted but willing to discuss books.

"Hey, Harp."

She scowled at her reflection in the shop door window and decided playing nice wasn't worth that. "Anders. Just the guy I hoped would know some answers."

"Not if you're going to call me Anders."

"Says the guy who just called me Harp. Besides it's your name."

And so began the ticking of a very annoying clock somewhere. Anders caved first. He always did. "Fine, *Harper*. What's up?"

"My taxes and insurance. I'm blowing through the store account faster than seems reasonable."

And so began the story. She denied spending an obscene amount of money on rare editions. That hurt, too. She'd *wanted* to buy a copy of P.G Wodehouse's *The Pothunters* worth four times the two-thousand-dollar price tag, but at the rate she was going, she'd be broke by January. It hadn't seemed prudent. Aaaah… prudent. Now that was a good, solid, underused word.

"Look, Harp-*er*, I'm driving to Hastings today. When I get done there, I'll come look at the books and see what I see, but Aunt Lorene didn't exactly give me a rundown of how she did things. I do know she made a good profit every year—not enough to make me independently wealthy when she died, but…"

There it was—the dig. The reminder that the *favorite* cousin hadn't gotten the inheritance he'd expected. Instead, the aunt who had never liked Harper had left the store and everything connected to it to her. It galled her to do it, but she said, "I'll buy you dinner at Fables."

"Deal." Anders' tone softened a bit. "It'll be okay, Harper. I don't know what's going on, but nothing's irreparable. And I've got savings if that's what it takes."

She loved that he offered, but she wouldn't accept it. If she couldn't keep Aunt Lorene's accounts flush, throwing his money off the business equivalent of Sorin's Bluff (or that's how she saw it) wasn't the solution.

Mr. Laffey came in not ten minutes after she'd disconnected. He found her rearranging the classics section, looking for that collector's edition of *Moonstone* she'd seen on the wrong shelf last week. Should've fixed it then, but "Edward" had made that comment about kings in *They Came to Baghdad*, and she hadn't been able to stop thinking about it.

"My son's coming from Davenport next week. Likes that sci-fi nonsense."

Coming from a guy like Mr. Laffey, the son could like anything from space opera to *The Lord of the Rings* trilogy. What Harper knew, though, was what Mr. Laffey meant. He needed a book waiting for the son so he wouldn't have to talk as much. Mr. Laffey wasn't much of a talker.

"Why don't you go on over to your chair? I'll pull out a few covers to see if any look like the right style for what he reads."

"You can do that?" The man's pale eyes looked even paler than usual this morning. "You're a wonder, Harper Brevig. Lorene would be proud."

"Doubt it. I'm running her store into the ground. She's probably up in heaven giving the Lord an earful for letting her give her least-favorite niece her life's work."

"She was proud of you," Mr. Laffey insisted. "Said

you're the only one she could trust to appreciate what books can do for people. She said you'd struggle at first…" The man rubbed the coaster-sized bald spot on the top of his otherwise full-head of hair. "People not being your strong suit, you might say. But she knew you were the right one for the store and it was the best thing for you."

Strange. No one had even hinted that it had been that well thought out. Harper had figured she'd put all the family's names in a bowl and drew hers. Maybe even put it back and had to concede when she drew it again. But *choosing* her? Weird.

Without saying any more, Harper went in search of those books. She pulled off a Sanderson, the new Andy Weir, *Out of the Silent Planet*, and the indie published sci-fi the author had brought in last week. At the last second, she grabbed one of the Wheel of Time books too.

Mr. Laffey stared at the covers, his confusion growing. "They all look right. He must read more widely than I thought."

As he'd been examining the books, Harper got an idea and decided to run with it. "I'll box them up for you and drop them off on my way home tonight. You can bring them back one at a time after you know which one he wants." She'd made it halfway to the counter before retracing her steps and adding, "And don't you even think about trying to carry them all at one time. I'll charge you if they arrive damaged."

Waiting for Anders was almost as bad as waiting for Christmas. When she'd eradicated all the dust, moved all last quarter's new releases to their general stock shelves, and rearranged a display of "beach reads" in hopes that some poor fool would buy them during the last few weeks before school started, she gave up and went after the project she'd been avoiding.

With a flick of the light switch and a click of the gate

that blocked the stairs down to the basement, Harper descended into what should have been a dungeon. Instead, the bright, welcoming room greeted her. In the corner was that weird Tiffany blue desk with the cut glass knobs and shiny gold accents. Not her style at all.

"I can paint it later. For now, it goes upstairs."

Carrying it up—not possible. She'd topple over for sure. After four tries, Harper went to get the plastic wrap she used to protect books she shipped and wrapped it around the tabletop. It didn't take half the roll, but it felt like it. Then, with that protected, she grabbed the underside of the drawer slides with one hand, the stair railing with the other, and dragged it up the steps on its surface. The plastic snagged a time or two, and one part ripped away, but much to her disgust (although also impressed), the paint didn't even get a scratch.

The desk—small as it was—was a full half inch too big for the little nook she'd hoped to fit it in. A close inspection showed no way to make it work. The back room made the most sense, but putting it back there where the little kids spent all their time meant the journal and supplies she planned to put with it would look like a nightmare in no time.

Great. After spending a fortune on supplies and dragging the desk up there, she wouldn't have room for it anywhere. Just as she started back downstairs with it, a new idea hit her. Maybe...

At the top of the stairs on the second floor, it stood there. A low bookshelf used to hold double-stacked Penguin classic paperbacks. She wouldn't get rid of them, but they would be a great excuse to get rid of other junk. Like those rows of Barbara Cartland Regency refuse.

She was a hot, sweaty mess by the time she got the books moved, the bookcase *re*moved, and the desk shoved into place, but the result... perfection. Even the stupid blue didn't look too bad. The glittering knobs... well, she could replace those. Someday.

The journal was the most important thing, so she laid

it open to the middle and centered on the surface. She'd need a chair, a pen cup, and baskets for the stickers and tapes. Wasn't there a chair downstairs?

There wasn't. This project was turning out to be a bit ridiculous. But she did have baskets at home. Yes, they stored her hair ties and washcloths, but a ramekin would work for the hair ties. She never used ramekins anyway. But a chair… She didn't have one. She had an old barstool, but it was too high.

An hour later, Anders found her up there with a hacksaw, plowing through the leg of that barstool as if sawing off metal stool legs was part of every bookseller's workday. "What're you doing?"

Harper jerked, the saw slipped, and blood poured from the cut on her index finger over the saw blade and onto the floor. For a moment, Harper stared at it, fascinated. "That would be cool on the cover of a book."

"You're an idiot. Where's the first aid kit?"

Aaah… Anders. Ever the sympathetic guy. "Under the counter. To the left. Next to the untouched bank bag."

"Very funny *Hobson*." He stopped three stairs down. "And did my little cousin just make a *movie* reference instead of a book one?"

"Don't get used to it. It's almost the only one I know. Dad…"

That's when the cut began to hurt, and Harper stuck her finger in her mouth. She jerked it back out. Gross.

If she'd known Anders would go all he-man on her and insist on finishing the job, she'd have left the stool until when she saw him pull up to the store. He could have worn out *his* biceps or whatever the muscles were that now screamed anytime she moved them. Wasn't that supposed to be the next day?

"Talk to me about the books."

"I want you to look at them. Just tell me what I'm doing wrong. I don't get it. Aside from the stuff I bought for this stupid journal, I haven't done advertising or bought anything frivolous. I've been careful with new book orders…" She shot him a wicked grin. "And I've said no to ninety-five percent of the junk people try to sell me."

"Says the gal with a stack of that junk all over the floor." He shot a significant look at the Cartlands.

"I didn't buy those. Why did Aunt Lorene let that trash in here?"

"I was joking. What you call trash, other people love. And they have that right. And even at a buck a piece, that's gotta be a day or three's worth of electricity right there."

The books shone in new light. Actually, they didn't shine at all, but they didn't look nearly as much like kindling now as they had. "Didn't think of it that way. I've been sneaking some of the junk out to the book boxes all over town."

The odd, faraway look he got when an idea began to germinate surfaced. Anders stared first at the pile and then wandered around the room picking at different titles before turning back with a smile. "I've got it."

"Let me have it."

The smile transformed into a diabolical grin. "You should *never* say that to me. But I'll give it to you this once…" He swept the room with one more searching look before nodding. "You need to give away *only* the first book in a series. Then, on the last page, you need to put a sticky note that says, *Kathleen Kelly couldn't buy her groceries for just one dollar, but you can get the next book in the series from Twice Sold Tales for only a dollar. Continue the series today!*"

"Genius. I'm totally doing that."

"Now show me the important books." Anders jogged downstairs without waiting for her to answer.

After printing out pages, they closed the store and walked down to Fable's, but the door was locked and a "thank you for your patronage but we've closed" sign had been taped to the window. Harper pulled up the website on the phone and got a similar notice. "But they had good spaghetti!"

"You would go to a restaurant and get *spaghetti*. Whatever. Let's go back. I'll drive us to The Smokin' Oak, but you're still buying."

"And you're still going to help me figure out how to cut costs."

Two hours later, Harper changed into a fresh T-shirt and crawled into bed with *Fawkes*. After the depressing news that she definitely *was* running the store into the ground and needed that guy she'd sent packing last year… That fact still hurt and Anders' triumph as he made her admit it hurt even more. Yes, sales were down, but expenses were up, despite the fact that Harper spent less on stock than Aunt Lorene had.

"You need Coleridge," Anders had said.

"I have a whole shelf of him!"

"*Milton* Coleridge—the Bookstore Doctor, they call him. Look it up on Facebook. It's a group."

"I don't *have* Facebook."

Anders had driven her back to the store, gone into the "bible" Aunt Lorene had created for running Twice Sold Tales, found passwords, and entered it into her phone. All right, he'd downloaded an app first. An *app!* For *social media*. Gag.

But there it was. Twice Sold Tales had its own page and everything, and she could join this Bookstore Doctor group *as* her store. Read through posts. See if she could glean ideas. When she'd clicked on join, a bunch of questions had popped up and she'd backed away again.

Tossing *Fawkes* aside, she grabbed her phone and went back into the app. She could do this. For the store. For her future.

Guilt nudged her. "Fine. For *Red Wing*."

Twelve

Parenting tip #127: "Just one more chapter" means you plow through books faster and have to buy more.

After a week of ballet camp and two weeks of regular classes, Noah had learned how to enter the shop without jingling the bell. If he were honest with himself, he'd admit he felt stupid standing at the window and watching his son all through class, but he'd learned a lot about Bennie in the six weeks they'd had together.

Bennie wouldn't "tell" on anyone ever again. He'd suffer in silence until he died first, and Noah didn't think that was an exaggeration. First it had been Megan. He'd nearly fired the poor girl when Bennie cried every morning before coming downstairs as solemn as a soldier before battle. Only the still-running nose and red around the boy's eyes gave him away.

But Bennie had cried over that, too. Whatever had made him tell everything that had happened while in foster care had now clammed him up tight and had determined that nothing, but nothing would make him "tell" again. The social worker assured him it was all normal.

It had taken his mother to retranslate "normal" to "common behavior in grief and trauma recovery."

So, not willing to risk his son to the potential taunts and teases of little girls who weren't used to boys in what some obviously considered *their* domain, Noah stood at the window every Wednesday night between five and six o'clock and watched for... well, anything that might upset Bennie. So far, things had gone well, but despite his mother making murmurings of him being a "helicopter parent," Noah refused to back down on it.

I'd have been cruel to him at that age. Kids attack what they don't understand. The more he thought about it, the more he realized the same was true of adults. *Probably where kids learn it.*

A sign on the door reminded customers that Twice Sold Tales would have a fun booth at River City Days with book puzzles, prizes, games, and more. Bennie was almost as nutty about books as he was about ballet. They'd planned to go anyway. With a dunk tank, a bounce house, an "archaeological dig," kid's activity tent, mini golf and more, he'd have been a fool not to. But now they'd make a point of stopping at her booth and playing her games and things.

Low, tense voices reached him before he could make it to the stairs. "—don't want to have to ban your children from the store, but they cannot come in and—"

"They're just child—"

He probably should help again, but Bennie... A glance at his watch told him he had just a couple of minutes before the class would be upstairs and in front of the windows. Noah took another step. And another. With one foot on the first stair, Harper's voice reached him again.

"Listen to me, little boy."

"I's Peston."

"Excellent," she said and tried again. "Does anyone ever hurt your feelings? Say things that make you feel bad or push you on the playground?"

Silence nearly smothered the store.

The kid must have nodded, because when she continued, Harper said, "Well, books have feelings too. They get hurt when you throw them on the floor. See..." After another second or two, she said, "This spine is broken. Do you know what happens if *your* spine gets broken?"

"Now wait just a min—"

Noah snickered. The mother—it had to be a mother—had a valid point. Harper did sound like she'd half-threatened to break the kid's spine.

"You can't walk. You have to be pushed around in a wheelchair. Sometimes you can't move your arms either." After a few flips of paper, she continued. "I have to tape this book now. And it'll never be as strong again. Because you hurt it. Books are my friends, and I won't let you hurt my friends. So you have to be *nice* to them, or you can't come back."

Again, the mother started to protest, but the little boy spoke over her. "I's sorry." A sniffle followed. "I don't wanna hurt the books."

The mother offered to pay for the damaged book, and as she rang it up, Harper suggested making him help her tape it up and recommended duct tape rather than packing tape. "It's stronger."

Before she made it to where she could see him, Noah crept up the stairs, hugging the left side at the middle to avoid creaks, and stopped short at the sight of a blue desk where a bookshelf had been. A blank book lay open on the desk, and a small sign sat in a small frame. It said: PLEASE LEAVE A NOTE OF ENCOURAGEMENT FOR SOMEONE. YOU NEVER KNOW WHO IT MAY HELP.

What a cool idea. He'd have to bring his son in soon and have Bennie draw a picture in it. Maybe he'd find a quote from the next Narnia book that they could write with the picture. He had to remember to buy that before he left, which meant he wouldn't be able to sneak out this time. Unfortunately.

There, atop the low bookcase that ran beneath the windows, lay a pair of binoculars. Noah stared at them. He lifted them to his eyes and saw the studio in perfect clarity. So… she'd known all along. Why didn't that surprise him?

The door jingled seconds before the first sob reached

him. Noah's throat tightened. With one quick glance through the binoculars to be certain he could still see Bennie's head as the kid sat on the floor doing his stretches, Noah crept back to the stairs and peered around the wall.

"I can't do this, Lord!" A hand clamped over Harper's mouth—her hand. Another sob followed, then the patter of feet on stairs—leading away. Must be going downstairs to vent.

Poor girl. He thought she'd been brilliant, but this was the second—no, wait. The other day. *Third* time he'd seen kids terrorizing the place. It wasn't right.

The desk called to him. Noah settled onto the stool there and winced at the creak. After choosing a blue pen, he flipped through the pages. Blank. That stopped him. She'd know it was him if he wrote anything.

So, near the back, he hesitated for another moment before scribbling down the first thought that didn't sound completely stupid. The messy block letters looked like they should contain a ransom notice, but maybe she'd find them on another day like today—one when she needed just a hint of encouragement.

That done, he moved back to the window, took up the binoculars, and leaned against the bookcase, half sitting on it. And he watched, because in his mind, that's what fathers did.

As soon as that guy—Noah? Yeah. Noah left, Harper should have locked the door and gone home. But she'd found a row of books high above the counter and behind another row of books, and in it... *Picnic at Hanging Rock*. A quick Google search had unearthed a fascinating tidbit from a reader blog. That woman said the book reminded her of the TV show, *Lost*, but in 1900.

So, with the store quiet, she peeked into the first chapter, and at the author's assertion that the reader would have to decide if the story were true or not, kept reading. Why such narrative that obsessed over "mantlepieces" held her attention, she couldn't have explained. So, it was probably a good thing that no one would ask.

Miranda had just offered Mr. Hussey a caramel, something that made Harper's stomach growl, when the door jingled open and the little ballet boy entered, a wide grin on a newly freckled nose. Harper felt certain she would have noticed those freckles if they'd been there before.

"Hi! Did you finish *Prince Caspian*?"

Bennie nodded. "We need the next one."

"Well, go on and get it, then." When the kid darted a look at his father, and Noah frowned, Harper decided she must have sounded put out. So maybe she was... a little. But that wasn't the kid's fault. She shot Bennie a wide grin. "The next one has my favorite opening line of all time."

That's all she needed to say. Bennie shot her a huge grin and took off for the back of the store. Noah stepped up to the counter and looked at the book in her hand. "Good book?"

"Just trying to figure out why my aunt had it hidden up with the collector's books." She showed him the rather boring cover. "It's pretty good so far, though."

Noah moved as close as he could with the counter separating them and whispered, "Thank you for the binoculars. They're perfect."

"I found them in my aunt's basement on Sunday and asked if I could borrow them. She gave them to me—didn't think they worked, but they do."

"Better than my phone for sure. Anyway, thanks."

Bennie's footsteps pounded—no pitter-patter here— as he raced back, the next book in hand. "This has a three, so it's right?"

Their heads bobbed in unison as Harper took the book and Noah pulled out his wallet. *Good thing I didn't close up. This is more important.*

While she rang up the purchase and slipped the book into a paper bag, she watched Bennie. He stood there at the door, staring out at streetlamps that had just turned on. An idea hit her. With a finger to her lips, she moved around the counter to stand next to Bennie.

"Want to know a secret?" she whispered.

All she received was a silent nod. The kid never took his eyes off that lamp.

"Last winter when I opened the doors to bring in a tree…" She slid down the locking mechanism for the second door and opened them both. "They looked like I was looking out from a wardrobe."

This time, his head swung around, and he gaped at her. "Is that *the* lamppost?"

Harper shrugged. "If you want it to be, it is." Then she leaned close, cupped her hand around the boy's ear, and whispered, "Wait'll you read the story about how the lamppost got there!"

They stood in companionable silent reflection. Then Harper felt his little hand slip into hers, but he never shifted his gaze. She glanced back at Noah, uncertain what to do, but the man stood there, obviously dumbfounded. A sheen glazed over his eyes. He swallowed hard.

It didn't take a genius to discern that Bennie didn't often open up like that.

Cars passed, a few tourists too. After what seemed forever and only a blink, the little guy said in an awed whisper, "That's it then." He gazed up at her. "Isn't Narnia *wonderful*? I just love Aslan."

"And Aslan loves you."

Wide-eyed, Bennie stared at her for a moment before beckoning her closer. Then he whispered, "I think Aslan is Jesus—like at Sunday school. But I think he might get mad if I say that."

Her heart broke for him. "He" obviously meant Noah, but the boy didn't trust him. No one ever talked about a mom. Divorce? Probably. Abandonment too, she supposed. Poor kid. Or maybe just afraid to cross parents or something. Her parents had "enjoyed" (if you could call it that) a drama-free marriage. Passion-free too, from all she'd ever noticed. Now Harper suspected there might be advantages to that.

The boy's belly rumbled. "Oh, someone's hungry."

"She's right, son. We should go. She's probably hungry too. We'll go to Hardee's, okay?"

"Can she come?"

In case Noah felt obliged to agree, Harper shook her head. "Thanks for asking, but I have a lot of work to do. And I have dinner waiting at home." Okay, so dinner was frozen and would take ten minutes in the microwave. So what?

At the register, she scrawled a note. *You should explain how Aslan is a sort of Christophany.* After thinking a moment, she added, *He figured it out. Smart kid.*

Noah said something about seeing her at River City Days. Bennie beamed. They both waved and took off down the sidewalk as she locked the door and got to work setting the place to rights. The memory of Noah thanking her for the binoculars sent her racing up to put them away for the next week and over to the desk.

The page was blank. She fumbled around, flipping a few pages forward and backward before turning off the lights and heading downstairs. It would've been cool if he'd been the first person to write in it—someone she knew. That didn't work. She didn't *know* him. It was more that she'd know he was the one.

Oh, well. Maybe tomorrow.

Thirteen

Parenting tip #131: Parenting is 10% copying, 10% applying advice, 10% sheer dumb luck, and 70% jerry rigging.

Despite pessimistic attitudes about the River City Days weather forecast, it was still in the mid-seventies as Noah and Bennie wove through the crowds at Bay Point Park. Kids squealed, music pulsed, and the scents of differing foods competed as if vying for a prize. With each step, Bennie dragged a bit more.

"Want to go to the activity tent?"

Bennie shook his head—just as he had to the treasure hunt, the car show… Twice, Noah had expected an all-out tantrum, but the kid didn't seem to have it in him. But why?

His mother's warning prior to their week of activities poked at him. *But that was about setting expectations that we couldn't continue. This is just a special day.*

"I gotta pee."

Well, at least it was *something*. "Sure. Restrooms are this way." Making their way to those restrooms wasn't as easy as knowing where they were, though.

While Bennie went inside a stall, adamantly refusing urinals, Noah zipped a message to his mom, explaining the situation and begging for help. Her reply came in seconds. DOES HE WANT TO BE THERE?

Of course! They'd been looking forward to it for a week. Bennie had asked a million questions about all the things they'd do. He zipped back an answer that should satisfy the most concerned "Neena" alive. That's what his mother called herself this week. He doubted it would stick. She'd be Grandma in the end, but with a new friend who was obsessed with what he'd started calling "boutique monikers," she'd tried out a few. Gigi failed immediately. Mimi went too. Neena... no way.

Her reply asked if they'd eaten, and Noah admitted not. LOW BLOOD SUGAR?

MAYBE. BUT I BET HE'S OVERSTIMULATED. GET HIM TO MCDONALD'S OR OVER TO GODFATHER'S. LET HIM DESTRESS. IT'S A LOT FOR A LITTLE GUY. His reminder of all the food there earned him an admonishment not to be stupid and to definitely do Godfather's over McDonald's.

Well... he *had* asked. Bennie appeared in his line of vision, hands up and dripping. "No towels."

"Dry 'em on your shorts. You hungry?"

Panic flashed in the kid's eyes before he nodded.

"Grandma says we should go get Godfather's pizza. Do you mind leaving for a bit?" *We'll never get a good parking space again, but...*

"I like pizza." It wasn't *what* he said but how he said it. The words dripped with relief.

Maybe Mom's got something here.

"If we go, we might have trouble getting a parking space again. We'd have to walk a long way or maybe go up to the bluff and throw Frisbees instead. I've been saving disc golf for later."

Okay, no doubt about it. Mom was right. The kid practically danced for joy. "That's okay."

But the sight of Harper manning a book booth prompted Bennie to dash over and say hi. If only Noah could figure out how to get that kind of enthusiasm when the boy saw *him*. A huge wooden tray took up most of the booth front and on it were wrapped books with squiggly lines on them—stair steps and... fence boards?

"Are you going to try to figure out the puzzle?" Harper grinned at Bennie before shuffling a few of the books around like one of those little plastic number games Noah used to get from the dentist on his trick-or-treat route. He could see three books standing together, their titles now readable. "All you have to do is make them line up without picking them up. Anyone who does it wins a ten-dollar gift certificate to the store."

As if he hadn't been ready to bolt from the place just a minute before, Bennie began shuffling. Sliding down. Pushing back. The tip of his tongue peeked out from the corner of his mouth. Harper stood there with a huge grin on her face, which wiped away the usual pinched look she wore. She caught him watching and grinned even bigger. That crinkle he'd first noticed on her nose when she smiled appeared, and Noah could read her thoughts as if she'd spoken them.

"Isn't he cute?"

Of course, Bennie was cute. But for the first time, Noah noticed that Harper Brevig was pretty cute herself. Bennie ripped that thought from him, though. "Dad?"

His heart stilled. It might have been—most likely was—the first time Bennie had ever called him that in public. He'd said, "my dad." Hadn't he? But to address him?

"Hmm?" There. That was calm and cool, right?

"See that one?" He pointed to a book that had half of *Jungle Book* along one edge. "That goes here." He pointed to a row down and two books over. Then, he pointed out, move by move, what would happen to get it there. "But if I do that, this one…" Again with the pointing. "It won't be where it's supposed to be. What do I do?"

After shooting a questioning look at Harper, he took her nod to mean, "Sure. Go ahead and cheat with your son." So he did. The poor kid could probably do it better without his help, but since he'd asked…

Three moves in, Noah realized "could probably do it better" was the greatest understatement of his day. An older man with a hairline that had receded so much he should be grateful it wasn't his gums stepped up. "Don't be afraid to move them into the wrong places. You need that top row first. And to get that, you want to get the corners right."

A woman about Noah's age started flipping through books to his right. She caught sight of the puzzle and said, "If you move that middle one left, you can slide the top right corner all the way up then."

She was right.

One by one, Noah, Bennie, and half of Red Wing (or so it seemed) moved books around until the last two needed adjusting. Noah could see just how it had to go, but Bennie hesitated. "I don't want to move anything. They're almost perfect."

The older man tapped a cover. "What would happen if you moved that? Think ahead."

Bennie's finger slid sideways. Another finger "pushed" the bottom book into place. A huge grin split the kid's face. "Oh!" And in three swift moves, he had the picture all set. A cheer went up all around them, and Bennie jumped up and down, fists pumping! "I did it!" It was the most emotion (aside from grief) Noah had ever seen from him.

"You did! Great job!" the older guy's voice cut through the victory dance.

All celebration froze. Bennie turned to the man and gave a shy smile. "You helped—a lot. So did my dad."

Noah tried not to wilt at that.

"And her… and her…" At the sight of the enormous group around them, he shifted back, almost pressing into Noah. "Um… thanks. For the help. Yeah." He turned a panicked face to Noah. "Were we going to get pizza?"

Harper broke in, holding an envelope. "Well done, Bennie. I can't wait to see what book you get. I'll stay open later on Wednesday if you guys want to come in for it after ballet class."

He'd have demurred. Going into that store after ballet

meant that dinner was late, their short prayer and devotional time got shorter, and Bennie fell asleep in the middle of reading, so they had to reread everything the next night. But Bennie lit up. "Can we, Dad?"

If Noah didn't know better, he'd have sworn that Bennie knew exactly what to say to get his way. How could he resist when the kid called him "Dad"? *Again!*

"I suppose. Maybe I'll bring sandwiches to eat on the way home."

"Can you bring one for Harper? I bet she likes turkey. With cheese."

Harper would have protested, but something his mother had said about encouraging generosity prompted him to ask, "Lettuce? Tomato? Pepperjack or cheddar?"

The woman gave Bennie a weak smile before turning to him with a wrinkled nose and saying, "No… um, just cheddar and turkey is fine. Thank you."

If his translation skills were at peak performance, he'd say that meant, "Don't put any nasty veggies on *my* plate!"

"Yay! Dinner with Harper!"

A few people around them chuckled, and only then did Noah realize the audience had hovered through the whole thing. A few knowing looks told him everyone had misread the situation. Harper Brevig would no more go out with him if he asked (which he wouldn't) than he'd go out with her. Nice girl. Mostly. But really…

Besides, I'm too busy learning to be a dad to start dating again. Ugh.

If only he'd been able to get that through to Bennie. All the way to his car, the kid chattered about it. Apparently, Megan had a "date" with her boyfriend that night and had told him what it meant. "We have a date with Harper on Wednesday. We can't forget!" He waved the envelope in triumph. "Do I have to get the next Narnia book, or can I get something else?"

"Get whatever you want. The Narnias are my contribution to the Lampe Family Library. By the time you have kids, we'll need another house just for the books."

He'd thought to shock Bennie, but the kid just beamed. "That'll be *cool!*"

Great. He'd already created a bookworm. Not bad for six weeks of parenthood.

If one more person said, "I didn't know Lorene's store was still open," Harper would commission T-shirts that said, "Lorene's niece. Buy books." or something. Several older folks nearly cheered to discover her there and asked if she'd made many changes in the store. It felt comparable to someone asking if the Catholic church had decided to do away with the pope in modern times or something. After the third time someone asked, Harper concocted a reply that she hoped would "spur them on to love and buy books."

"Oh, not yet. But if business doesn't pick up, I'll probably have to try something drastic. I really don't *want* to, but maybe I need to start carrying magazines and phase out the used books. People seem to want all the latest bestsellers and more self-help stuff these days…"

The man staring at her went from polite inquiry to insta-panic. "That would be—but you can't—I mean, I don't think—" The guy's Adam's apple bobbed. Twice. "Now that I know you're still open, I'll be sure to let everyone know. Give it another month or two—Christmas is coming…"

He must be a businessman himself. Only a businessman would say "Christmas is coming" at the beginning of August as if the year were nearly over. Harper nodded. "I can try. I just can't keep going like this. Pretty soon I won't have rent money."

And her heart sank all the way to her toes. It was true. She had almost blown through her whole business account. And if tax bills started coming monthly or something—and it seemed like they might as well—she'd really be in trouble.

By three o'clock, she'd handed out three gift

certificates. By four, folks just gave fake interested glances as they sidled past on their way to food stuff and the music. Harper took the moment to refill her insulated tumbler and call Anders at the store.

"How's it going?"

"Great. People are buying tons of those paperbacks upstairs. I bet you've cleared off a shelf or two's worth. Sold out of that new magical realism book you have, six people ordered the Mrs. Kip book, and some author came in and said she wanted to hold her book launch here. She's writing about the Sea Wing disaster—something about a split-time book? Whatever that is."

"Two periods of history whose independent stories manage to converge into one by the end. Sort of. Depends on the author."

But despite the evenness she'd managed to keep in her tone, Harper wanted to tear out her hair. She always sold books on the weekends. Always. But it sure sounded like Anders got more people to come in… or at least to *buy* than she usually did. Two shelves of those cheesy, junk books? Wow. If she could sell them out, she could totally put some of the other stuff in that area. It would be so much better.

The truth glared its fiery eyes at her. She'd have to call the book guy. Swallow her pride. Apologize for kicking him out of her store—basically. And… Harper sighed.

"Get help before it's too late."

"Want me to call Milton?"

Oops… she hadn't meant to speak aloud. "I'll do it on Monday. I guess it's time."

"Past time. I still don't know where all your money goes."

"Insurance and taxes. They'll be the death of me."

Anders snickered. "More like of your store."

104

Fourteen

Books: your best defense against unwanted conversation.

Harper did not call Milton the Bookstore Doctor on Monday. Or Tuesday. Or Wednesday, Thursday, Friday... Nope, for nearly three weeks, she rearranged bookshelves and tried to be more like Anders with the customers. That one still got to her. Apparently, people expected her to interact with them. Whatever happened to book people being more interested in reading than small talk? Even that morning's T-shirt had gotten that right!

The Tuesday after Labor Day, the door opened, and a kid appeared. She'd seen him every two or three days since River City Days. Sandy hair, gray eyes (who knew gray eyes could be so startling?), and a lanky build that probably hid serious muscles. Why she thought that, Harper hadn't decided yet. But she did—think it, that is.

Though she hadn't been able to prove anything, Harper had suspicions about the boy. He probably wouldn't notice, but she'd purchased three mirrors at a garage sale across from her house that weekend and had arranged them so she could see anywhere if she just moved into the right place.

The kid favored classics in nearly every genre. She'd swear he'd stolen *Persuasion* just a few days before. And yes, he'd stolen it. Harper felt confident of that, and today she'd prove it. Sort of. Technically speaking, today she'd prove that he stole one... today. Would it be Ray Bradbury? Zane Grey? Marcus Aurelius? Dumas? Gaskell?

Actually, she'd love to know what he thought of *North & South*. She was still of two minds about it herself. One reading she'd love it. The next, she'd find it tedious, depressing, and such a Mary Sue nightmare that she couldn't stand to think about it ever again. And she'd really love to come to some conclusion about it so she could rewatch the BBC mini-series. Thus far, she'd held off so it wouldn't influence her decision.

Steinbeck. Interesting... She wondered which book he'd take. Of course, she'd feel like an idiot if he brought something to the counter and paid for it. But with all the times he'd come in and left without so much as a nod her way (he had his virtues), she doubted it.

The minute the book slid into his coat, Harper nearly cheered and did a victory dance. Only a quick flash of remembrance that The Kid (she'd begun thinking of that as his name now) didn't know she knew he was stealing from her kept her from it. And the moment he sauntered out the door, she dashed back to see what was missing.

Travels with Charley. Interesting... An undervalued book as far as she was concerned. Not what you'd expect from a kid whose peers probably didn't know that Steinbeck wasn't a linebacker for the Vikings. Half the kids she listened to didn't seem to know how to read much less like to.

Maybe someone should raise the legal reading age to twenty-one. Then maybe kids would give it a shot. That thought prompted a snicker. Too true. Wasn't there a quote in *Travels with Charley* to that effect? A quick search on her phone brought it up. "I think today if we forbade our illiterate children to touch the wonderful things of our literature, perhaps they might steal them and find secret joy."

Her favorite quote hovered in her mind. Though she could always remember them clearly, rarely did Harper manage to accurately quote things. *"We value virtue but do not discuss it. The honest bookkeeper, the faithful wife, the earnest scholar get little of our attention compared to the embezzler, the tramp, the cheat."*

Oh, so many good quotes in that one. The one about Texas, for instance. One of the girls in her dorm at college had been from Texas, and when Harper had asked if it was true that *"Texas is a state of mind, but I think it is more than that. It is a mystique closely approximating a religion,"* the girl had just stared at her. Harper decided that it must mean it was.

The Stadtlers burst through the door, chattering away and interrupting her philosophical introspections. Dalton and Emily argued over the merits and demerits of manga while Sophie chattered to her mother about a book Harper didn't recognize but became intrigued about. *Epistolary and in the twenties? Sign me up!*

"Afternoon, Tammy." Harper offered herself a pat on the back for remembering to greet the customer.

"I have my list for October." Tammy let Sophie go explore the kids' section while she dug through a planner thick enough to manage every second of every day for at least half a dozen people. It probably did. "Got it!"

While Harper read over the list and began finding several of the books on the shelves, she asked about the book Sophie had been talking about. "Sounds great."

"Oh, it's lovely. It has the feel of *Understood Betsy* and in the style of *Daddy Long Legs*."

That was great… except it didn't tell her the name. "And the title? Author?"

"Right." Tammy shot her a sheepish look. "I'm still lost in the world of Maisie Dobbs. The kids interrupted my afternoon read to bring me in. Anyway, the book is *Love, Mary Elisabeth* by Christy Martenson. You'll love it."

"I'll get a couple for the store." She turned back to the computer before she forgot it. "Maybe Bennie will like it."

"Bennie?" Tammy stared. "You have a… little brother?"

Lost in the computer system trying to find the book,

Harper just shook her head.

"A... son?"

Though not in the habit of using God's name flippantly, the words flew out before she knew what she'd said. "I mean, no. Sorry." She offered an apologetic look to go with her flaming cheeks. "Seriously. Sorry. Not sure where that came from. But no. No kids. Probably ever."

Tammy had started to turn back to her perusal of the discounted shelf, but she paused at that. "But... you're so good with kids. Kids love you."

"Kids get older and become adults. I might like having kids, but I know I wouldn't like adult kids, so... no."

Only after Tammy had paid for the books they bought, the books she ordered, and the "super-cute" sticker that Sophie was "obsessed" with, *and* after they all traipsed out the door, did Harper realize she'd effectively said that she didn't like Tammy. And that wasn't true. Tammy and her husband were two of the few people between the ages of sixteen and fifty whom Harper actually liked. Oh, well. She hadn't seemed offended.

As if a ticking bomb, the schoolhouse-style wall clock inched closer and closer to the end of the day. If she didn't call soon, it could be too late. What if he were in Maine or something? Then again, he could be in California or Washington!

The ridiculousness of her procrastination struck hard and fast. Harper picked up her phone, found the number her cousin had sent and called it before she could stop herself. When it went to voicemail, she sagged in relief. "Hi, this is Harper Brevig. We met last November when my cousin called you? Yeah. He was right. I was wrong. I was also probably rude. I was wondering if we could talk about my store..." Not knowing what else to say, she rattled off her number and disconnected. There. It'd probably be a week—maybe two—before he got back to her. Maybe by then, she'd have an idea or two of her own.

Her phone buzzed before she even set it down. The

name on the screen sent excited, dread-filled shivers through her. Forcing confidence into her tone, she swiped the answer button and said, "Twice Sold Tales. I should say 'How may I help you?' but I think Steinbeck said it best. "'I suppose our capacity for self-delusion is boundless.'"

Milton Coleridge laughed. "I think we're going to get along great."

For the first time since Bennie had started his ballet classes, Noah burst into Twice Sold Tales and didn't make for the stairs. Instead, he wandered through the cubby holes and mini-aisles until he found Harper on the floor, surrounded by mini-stacks of books.

When she didn't notice him, Noah took a moment to really look at her. Harper's hair hung down in waves— natural ones. She hadn't created those with a curling iron or whatever girls used these days. The ends frizzed, and one wave fought hard to twist into a curl. That's when it hit him. Harper never wore makeup. Never "styled" her hair. In fact, if he had to guess, he'd assume she got it cut once a year "whether it needed it or not." A pointed chin and tiny ears that did little to hold back the hair she kept tucking behind them gave her round face interest. If she wore oversized round glasses, she'd be adorable.

Without looking his way, her hand reached back and nearly touched his foot. When she found nothing, she reached further and jumped back as her hand landed on the top of his work boots. "Oh!" Her gaze shot up and glared at him. "You scared me."

"To be fair, I've been here for a couple of minutes..."

After another sour look, Harper shrugged. "Fine. Make yourself useful. Hand me that stack beside you." Then she froze. "Why aren't you upstairs?"

Noah felt his neck flame, but he fought to calm himself. "Um... just..."

"If you're asking me out, the answer's no. Does that help?"

This girl! Though he tried to restrain his amusement, he failed. A strangled chortle escaped. "Um… sorry. That's not what I wanted, but…"

"Good."

The girl didn't even look embarrassed that she'd misread him. Should he be impressed or insulted?

"So what is it?"

"Bennie." The name blurted out before he could stop that one too.

That got her to her feet. "Is he okay?"

Any doubt that he'd made the right decision in asking her opinion fled. Harper might not be pining away for him, but she most definitely cared about his son. They agreed on that one anyway. Noah tried to say something cautiously optimistic, but his voice caught, and he shook his head. The words spilled out after that. "Yes. No. I don't know. I don't know what to do." Did his voice break? Noah grimaced when he realized it had.

"Is one of those little tutu-divas messing with him?" Fists formed at her side. "Let me at her."

The sincere ferocity in tone, stance, and flashing eyes settled his nerves, as embarrassing as that might be. Maybe he wasn't overreacting. But Noah shook his head. "Not them. At school."

And the story tumbled out. The mom who had come into his work to tell him she'd seen two boys picking on Bennie—taunting him. How Bennie had stayed firm until they'd seen her storming away from the car line. How he'd crumpled when she'd asked his name and if he was hurt. His voice broke. "He told her he didn't have any 'Band-Aid hurts.'"

Harper blinked at him. "What does that mean?"

"That his heart hurt. His feelings."

Did tears—? They did. They filled her eyes. "Why do kids do that? They're horrible. I hate kids."

That prompted a smile. "No, you don't. You love

110

them. Can't fool me."

"But he's been through so much already."

How'd she know that? How much had he told her? Then again, Red Wing was a small town. And if his mother ever came in, all hope of privacy was gone. So… there was that. But the mention of his mother reminded him why he'd chosen to talk to her. "Speaking of Mom…"

"Were we?" She shook her head. "I thought we were talking about—oh, you mean the mom at the school. Gotcha."

He didn't mean that, and he couldn't create a smooth segue, either. "Actually, it was in my head. Anyway. My mom thinks I need to find out who the kids are and ask the principal to call in the parents for a discussion."

It gratified him to see her wrinkle her nose. "So things get worse when the kids find out he told on them? Yeah. That's smart."

"My thoughts exactly. But… He won't stand up for himself. I *have* to work, so I can't just stay home and try to teach him the half dozen things I remember from school. I can't afford a private school. So he has to go."

He saw it. For one flash of a second, Harper had been tempted to offer to teach him herself. He'd have to remember to thank the Lord later that she'd stopped herself. In his desperation, he might have agreed, and *that* would not be a good idea. He needed a solution, not a different problem.

"I was—" She broke off and picked at a cuticle. "Look, our family sticks together, okay. So when one of us was picked on, all of us came around and made sure that we were never alone."

"And Bennie has no cousins in town. They're scattered around the county—mostly in Hastings and a couple in the cities."

As he spoke, Harper froze, stared at him, and took off for the stairs. Noah followed. "What's—?"

"We should be talking up there where you can watch him."

111

Sometimes he'd thought Harper Brevig could be a bit... brusque. Rude, even. But man... when you wanted someone in your corner, you wanted her. "Thanks."

At the window, he picked up the binoculars and Harper picked up the conversation as if she hadn't even interrupted it. "Bennie doesn't need cousins. He just needs someone he can trust. A friend or two. Someone to ensure he's never alone. It's especially good if that kid is a bit older. Who goes to your church?"

Before he could answer, the door opened downstairs. An exasperated look splashed across her face. "Be back... someday."

When she greeted someone downstairs, Noah set down the binoculars and hurried over to the journal on the desk. There was a smiley-faced picture of a flower with the words, "You're nice," written in chunky writing. Though he agreed with it, Noah thought she needed a bit more. He flipped back a way and found a blank page not too far from his last one.

Just in time, he pulled the pen away from the paper and hesitated before finding that other page. There were the words. YOU'RE DOING A GOOD THING HERE.

This time he wanted something... more. How did you tell someone she was amazing without making it sound romantic? That was the *last* thing he needed. She'd kill him anyway—if she ever figured out it *was* him. Then it came to him. THE WORLD NEEDS MORE HARPERS IN IT.

There. A smile formed. He hadn't solved anything, but he had. And that was pretty cool.

Fifteen

Book recommendation: The Little House Books. A great first glimpse into pioneer life through the eyes of one who lived it.

Green trees and short corn greeted Milton Coleridge as he neared Red Wing from the Wisconsin side. Some might consider a guy in his forties to be too old to get a thrill at the idea of driving over Lake Pepin just as Laura Ingalls had in *Little House on the Prairie,* but Milton didn't care. He'd driven south of Red Wing just to see the Laura Ingalls Wilder Museum and cross the Mississippi south of where she would have. Too bad they didn't have a bridge across the lake.

He shot a glance at his sidekick, a little blue parrotlet who (sometimes) answered to the name Atticus (not Finch). "What do you think, Atticus? Does the trailer count as our covered wagon?"

The parrotlet didn't have to chatter at all to make his opinion known. Mango. His answer to all dilemmas was mango. "Fine…" Milton pulled a piece from the baggie in his pocket and offered it to his "traveling buddy."

They drove up Main Street and past the adorable Scandinavian gift shop he'd fallen in love with the year before. Past the St. James Hotel with its beautiful decor, history, and view of old town. Driving down the streets of downtown Red Wing pulling a travel trailer would never work. He'd have to drop it off at the RV park he'd found and return. He might just park behind the store and walk around the other streets before heading over to Twice Sold Tales.

That name still brought a smile to his heart. And it had offered an excellent and diverse selection of used books. Too often these days, store owners went for catchy over relevant. At least it was one thing he wouldn't have to criticize. And the bright interior... but no. He needed to take a fresh look when he entered. Much could've changed in the past year.

Despite every effort to hurry, it was an hour before Milton left Atticus to rest in his cage as he shot back up the highway to East Avenue. Past the grocery store and library, past the post office and theater, around the corner and down 4th Street to the small parking area behind Mandy's Cafe, Twice Sold Tales, and... well, he couldn't remember what else. A jeweler's? A vague recollection of pieces displayed on birch "logs" prompted a nod. Probably.

The amazing bakery, the church that had welcomed him as if he'd belonged there all his life... Yep. The town was just as wonderful as he remembered, except that right now flower baskets hung from the streetlamps. Those hadn't been there last November.

As he started to push open the door to the store, Milton took a moment to absorb the experience. He backtracked and examined the display windows. One featured autumnal reads—*The Night Circus* stood on a small bale of straw with a pumpkin next to it. Behind it, a stack of crates with several of Jaime Jo Wright's spooky reads. On the opposite side a mask dangled from the corner of a thin pedestal table. On it, a hardback copy of *Fawkes*.

Nadine Brandes... interesting.

On slat board, a few other books had been showcased, including a few classics like *Wuthering Heights* and that new Mrs. Kip book. Excellent. The display offered everything you wanted—something for everyone and arranged in an appealing display certain to draw the eye of passersby.

Milton moved to the next one and grinned. Someone was a BookTube enthusiast. Here a dark academia vibe had been attempted and with reasonable success. A stuffed crow—fake, he hoped, or Atticus would never forgive him—perched atop a thick volume of *The Complete Works of Edgar Allen Poe*. Another copy of *Wuthering Heights*, Gaskell, Dickens, Wilkie Collins, Rudyard Kipling, Thomas Hardy…all the Victorian greats appeared to be represented in the dark, glassless barrister bookshelves. A sign had been tented on top of the bookshelves. GET READY FOR VIC-TOBER TODAY!

A slim volume of Emily Dickinson's poetry lay atop a pair of ivory lace gloves, and showcased amid a sprinkling of silk fall leaves… Milton nearly gasped. Was that a…? He peered closer. It sure looked like it.

If that's a first edition of At the Back of the North Wind, *I'll throttle her myself.*

Jerking the door open, he stepped inside, instantly irked at the placement of the front counter with its iPad "cash register." It was the most logical place to put the thing, but it broke the aesthetic of the whole store. The brightness of the rooms still delighted him. Most bookstores didn't try for a bright atmosphere, and those who did rarely managed to maintain it. But this one had—and without turning it into a sterile environment.

He'd made it to the staircase before he saw or heard a soul. Muttering… was that swearing? No… just the rants of someone who wished she could, he suspected. The moment he took a step up, Milton realized the woman—it had to be a woman—was actually *downstairs*. He kept moving, pausing now and then to admire a display or adjust a title on a shelf.

If this store isn't making money, it isn't for the usual reasons. A challenge. Milton loved nothing more than a challenge unless it was a challenge with books involved.

Peering down the stairwell, Milton saw someone move into his line of sight and out just as quickly. An

"Argh! No! Okay. Fine. Who needs lights?" reached him. Since there weren't any, "No customers," signs anywhere, he jogged down the steps, his Tom's loafers not making a sound until he hit one that creaked.

The woman squeaked and jumped back. "You scared me!" Rather than a start of surprise, the expression she wore informed him it had been the accusation it sounded like.

"Thought I'd come see if you were all right."

This time she paused and stared. Milton took inventory as well. Build: slim. A Victorian author would probably have called her "willowy." Features? A fantasy author would have called them elfin. Hair? Well some might think she could use a good stylist. Frankly, he agreed, but there was also something refreshing in a woman who didn't look ready for a stint on the six o'clock news.

But the T-shirt she wore… Genius.

A book a day keeps reality away.

He couldn't help it. "Great shirt."

The color drained from her face. Without looking down, she closed her eyes and whispered, "T-shirt?"

"Yep."

The groan had probably been heard as far as Rochester. "I got so busy I forgot to change."

That made no sense. "Why would you?"

She made a sweeping motion that would make Vanna White proud. "Not professional. I'll go change. Look around." She paused and added, "But probably upstairs. There's not much to see down here."

Though he shouldn't allow himself to be distracted from a good idea, Milton swept the room with a quick gaze and landed on a tower of books with lights sticking every which way. Just in time, Milton adjusted his question from "what on earth are you doing?" to "book Christmas tree?"

Harper—it had to be Harper Brevig, although she didn't look how he'd remembered—nodded. "I thought I should practice on a slow day so I could do it quickly on Thanksgiving night." She eyed him. "I was kind of thinking about doing one of those 'date with a book' things. Wrap them up with a clue on the spine and people can just slide a new one into a spot if they want one that's there. What do you think? Would you buy one like that?"

"Definitely." He offered a cautionary smile. "But put a sign up that says to ask for help, or you may find someone buried in books and your insurance company howling at a payout."

"Ugh! No way. The insurance company is bleeding me dry as it is."

That was one question answered. Good.

"Oh, well. Come on upstairs. I'll help you find what you need. Then I'd better change shirts."

He followed her upstairs and smiled when she asked what he liked to read. "I'm pretty eclectic, but after driving across Lake Pepin, I'm feeling the Laura Ingalls Wilder vibe."

Harper cocked her head, watching him for a moment before asking, "Adult or youth?"

"What've you got for both? I read a lot, so I've probably read much of what you might throw at me."

"*Letters of a Woman Homesteader?*" The girl read him well because she shrugged and changed her tune. "What about *Prairie Lotus*? It's about a Chinese American girl on the prairie and takes place at about the same time as the early Little House books."

"Perfect—and I'd like one of those T-shirts too."

Harper winced and turned toward the back where he remembered the children's books being. "Sorry… we don't carry T-shirts."

"You should. That is genius. You should get Twice Sold Tales T-shirts made up with that on the back. Or vice versa. Great uniform."

Her nose wrinkled. "I can't wear a T-shirt to work. It's unprofessional."

If she'd added any emotion into her words, he might have made a different reply, but the girl sounded positively robotic. "Says who?"

"My mom, my cousins, my aunt..."

"Your boyfriend's next-door neighbor's great-aunt's cat's vet?"

He got half a grin before she frowned. "If that's a lead-in to a pickup line, don't bother."

"It's not." Milton grinned as a new thought occurred to him. "But you've got to admit, it would make a good one."

With a shrug so slight he almost missed it, Harper scanned a shelf and pulled a book off. The cover looked sweet, and now that he thought about it, he'd seen a few BookTubers mention it, but none had actually read it. Instead, it appeared on TBR lists month after month. He'd read it and maybe leave a comment or two if it turned out to be something worth recommending.

"Anything else you're looking for?"

Maybe it was cruel—actually, there was no maybe about it—but Milton couldn't resist. "Yeah... a good place for my cage and a good restaurant—one that won't mind if we sit and talk for a long time."

Her scowl—priceless. If she only could see herself. With a huff, she marched off to the counter. "I told you not to bother." And before he could respond, she stopped and stared at him. "Did you say cage?"

"It wasn't a pickup line. We need to talk about the problems with your store, and I'm going to be hungry by the time we get that book tree assembled."

"We—?" The girl's large eyes grew even larger, making her look like one of those anime dolls. "I didn't recognize you. You're Milton Coleridge, right? Great name, by the way."

"Thanks. I'll pass the compliment on to my mother."

She slipped the book into a paper bag with TST intertwined on the front and popped a bookmark inside before sliding it all across the counter. He offered his card, and she shook her head. "I don't know what you're charging me, but if you can save me, it's worth all that and a good book."

Part of him thought he should argue, but instead, he asked her to put it under the counter and lead the way to the book tree. "I've always wanted to make one."

"I found it on Pinterest. I'm great with creativity plagiarism. If someone can do it, I can copy it. Until now. It's like trying to rewrite *The Brothers Karamazov* or something. I just can't get it right!"

"You've got help now. Let's check this out."

The first day of autumn. Surely Milton arriving on the first day of autumn held some warm and beautiful significance. Harper stepped out of Kelly's Tap House with a spring in her step and delighted in air so crisp and cool it reminded her of a perfect apple.

Milton had offered her a ride home—twice, even— but two things cautioned her, and one stopped her. First, getting into a strange man's car—not exactly a brilliant move. Letting that strange man know where she lived? Equally stupid. And though she did her best to convince herself that responsible reasons like those had her meandering along the sidewalks of downtown at nearly ten o'clock, the *real* reason had everything to do with a moonless night, leaves crunching beneath her feet, and a backpack (she'd gotten smart about that) full of books for the little free libraries on her way home.

That Milton agreed there should be no reason she wasn't making a reasonable profit didn't hurt. He'd go over the books tomorrow, but much to her surprise, the whole day had been full of comments like, "beautiful display" and "great selection." When he'd heard about Anders' little free library marketing plan, he'd given wholesale approval.

Of course, the minute he saw her taxes and insurance and everything, she just knew he'd tell her to move to a less expensive building. But downtown buildings didn't come cheap, and she needed that tourist trade that came with it. Besides, she *owned* the building. Shouldn't that matter for

119

something? Maybe he'd tell her to rent out the basement or the upstairs. She could do that maybe… open one of those workspace places? Charge people five bucks an hour to come use her wi-fi and get work done or whatever?

But why should they? They could go next door to Mandy's for free.

The first book box was stuffed. She flipped through to make sure there wasn't anything she wanted to read and moved along. The next one across from her own store held a familiar book… *Travels with Charley.* A peek into the back cover showed her inventory mark. The one The Kid had taken. Interesting. Harper felt no qualms whatsoever about taking it back. And still in excellent condition.

A copy of *Dear Enemy* taunted her. She'd been holding out for a couple of used copies of it. Getting new ones of that were rare. People didn't read the good old stuff much. After hesitating again, she snatched it off the shelf and put five of her own books in there—including the first book in the Nedé Rising duology. That book ought to more than make up for taking a book for the store. It's not like some of her regulars didn't do it. She couldn't say anything about it, but she knew what was in those things better than anyone.

The next box—stuffed. She pulled out a book she thought Mr. Laffey would want for his son and added a Danielle Steele. Guilt prompted her to add a Debbie McComber too, although she had to wedge it sideways on top of a few other books. Her backpack hung heavy still, so she passed her own house and headed up East Avenue toward a few more. Might as well. She wouldn't sleep for hours.

A car slowed as she approached the next box. When she opened the door, she saw a dome light come on. Great. Someone else calling the cops. Maybe it would be Jake. But it wasn't. Just as she reached the next, Lauren Ehrlich flicked the spotlight on her and nearly blinded her.

And the hits just had to start coming. Hey… that was something to revel in. They couldn't "keep on coming" because they'd just started. Something to add to the gratitude journal she ignored half the time.

"What are you doing? Those are meant to be a trade basis, not fill-your-bookshelf."

Stepping out of the glare of the light, and nearly wrenching her ankle in a gopher hole, Harper held out her backpack. "I'm filling. Harper Brevig. I own Twice Sold Tales."

"Oh! Jake's book lady. Got it. Have a nice night."

All that and she didn't even get out of the car. Maybe Jake wasn't best. This was awesome. "Night!"

Less than three minutes later, another floodlight lit the sidewalk ahead of her. Drat. It would be Jake this time. Keep walking? Submit to the inevitable? If only she had a choice. Harper turned to face her latest tormentor.

Jake stopped and parked. Light still shining, he stepped out and ambled up the walk. "Heard you were out."

"I saw Lauren. Now you guys are telling on me? What is this?"

"She knew I'd want to know you were out. AC still working?"

"Yeah, but I haven't needed it much lately. Want me to bring it somewhere?"

He watched her as she shifted her backpack. "Um… nah. I can come get it. Just tell me when."

"Sundays are best. No work. But after church. Otherwise, just stop in and get my key."

This time Jake stared rather than watched before saying, "You'd give me the key to your place." It might have been a question, but it didn't sound like one.

"If I can't trust a cop, who can I trust?"

Leaves rustled, a cat yowled somewhere, and that set off a series of dogs barking. Jake stepped a bit closer. "I see you finally found a shirt that says what you really mean."

Had she ever *not* meant she wanted to avoid conversation? But as expected, she glanced down at her shirt. It was yellow. What happened to her gray? Oh…

121

yeah. She'd gotten lunch on it and changed into her *Books before dudes* shirt before dinner at Kelly's.

"Well, it's true."

"I'm starting to think you haven't met the right dude."

Harper shrugged. "Probably not. But even the right one means that much less time with my TBR. So... still not worth it."

And before he could argue with her, she took off for home.

Sixteen

Book recommendation: 84 Charing Cross Road—a wonderful picture of the relationship between booksellers and book buyers.

Milton had (understandably, in his opinion) been just a little uncertain about helping Harper Brevig. After all, she'd pretty much kicked him out last year the moment she'd returned home to announce that her dying mother would live to fight another day. That's how she'd put it too. Anders Brevig had stared slack-jawed and then asked how the woman had gone from near hospice to "on the mend" in one month flat, and Harper had said, "Misdiagnosis, and you can go" in nearly the same breath. Milton hadn't realized she meant him until Anders had begun arguing with her.

Still, if she hadn't sent him away, he'd never have wound up in the tiny town of Noel at Christmas last year. That had been a job well done if he did say so himself. Not only that, but in his laptop case, a wedding invitation ensured that he'd spend Christmas Eve in Noel again.

And now… now she was ready. With Atticus in his carrier and the bird cage at his feet, Milton opened the door to the store and winced at the lack of security system. Locking the door behind him, he carried the cage to a spot behind the counter and set it in place. Atticus protested. In fact, the little bird had started chirping, "Freedom!" or something close, every time Milton put the cage door up. Then again, the bird was known for his mocking attempt at a cry of "Sucker!" Maybe whatever he said was "freedom" in some other language.

"For later. You can fly around the store for now." He unzipped the tiny dog carrier and Atticus flew to the top of an old Chippendale secretary that showcased a few rarer editions. "Just don't leave any packages."

Atticus promised not to sully the pages of any of the books by landing on Milton's shoulder and doing his business there. First stop, the restroom to remove the unsightly splotch on his shirt. Then to see what the store might need. First of all, he really needed to figure out a better use of the up and downstairs rooms.

Upstairs would be an amazing place for the children's room, but Harper had wisely nixed the idea. *"Kids falling down the stairs is the last thing my never-ending insurance bill needs."*

And then to sort out why she paid so much in taxes and insurance. Maybe a trip next door to ask about their taxes would be in order. Rude? Probably, but if he wanted to salvage this business, the first thing he had to do was solve the mystery of the obscene expenses and stop the hemorrhage.

Might need to ask to look at the books for the last five years. Did they borrow against the building? A new assessment making everything huge? Behind on taxes so now having to make them up or lose it? Harper hadn't said so, but she could be embarrassed about it—ignorant, even.

By the time Harper entered, he'd decided the basement room could be a classroom that she rented out to book clubs or crafters or even small parties. Or she could use it for the mass market paperbacks and use the upstairs to expand a rare book sideline. She had a few—including the now moved copy of *At the Back of the North Wind* and a pristine collection of twenty Blackie & Son G.A. Hentys.

"Find anything interesting?"

He gestured to the complete set of *Maxie: An Adorable Girl* series on the counter. "Those were in the kids' section."

"They're kids' books, aren't they?"

"Yes… and they're also pretty rare. You want those up with the rest of your pricier books. And yes," he added before she could break in, "they are now *pricier* than they were yesterday. Four bucks apiece is nearly ten times less than they should be." He stopped when she came into full view. "That shirt."

"I'll change! I just wear what's comfortable until I open!"

"No. Don't change. You need to make this your brand—Harper's snarky shirt of the day. And you need to sell them."

Of course, the best place to have them was where the counter stood. But if they moved it, where would he put it? The memory of Olemann's Books in Rockland told him. That awkward center of the store where two mismatched tables stood back-to-back and created a surface to display books that didn't really need to be displayed.

"We don't have anywhere to put T-shirts." She hesitated before asking in an uncertain tone, "Unless downstairs?"

"No." He made a judgment call he hoped he wouldn't regret. "All the mass market and low-priced books. The bulk of the cookbooks, for instance. Only a small section up here with the most interesting and up-to-date titles. The rest go down there with a sign by those up here telling cookbook-loving customers where to go."

She nodded. "Yeah… so what goes upstairs?"

"The rare editions. We give them a showroom. You're going to become *the* place for Midwesterners to find the best out-of-print and rare editions."

Pointing to her shirt, Harper added, "So that I can sell T-shirts that say, 'I like books and maybe three people. Maybe'? Really?"

"Yep. Find a favorite book. I'll show you."

Milton should not have been surprised when Harper plucked a copy of *Fawkes* off the shelf and held it up. "This one was great."

With a glance around the store, he pointed her to the

secretary. "Over there." Then after a moment's thought, he shook his head. "No, YA. We need it by that shelf. Show readers what else you have."

About then is when Harper figured out she'd be the subject of the photo. Her demurring became a protest that turned into a flat-out refusal. Milton was undeterred. "Do you want to save your store or not?"

"Isn't there some other way to do it without throwing me in the swimsuit competition of a beauty pageant?"

The words made no sense… until they did. "Good one. But no. Stand there, hold up the book, and smile."

Bad order. She looked like someone must be pointing a gun to her head or had a knife in her back. He'd have told her to pretend to read it—or even actually read so he could get a relaxed photo, but one thing stopped him. No one would be able to read the T-shirt.

"No one wants my snarky face *or* my snarky shirt. I'll just bring one on a hanger or something."

But "snarky face" did it. "I want you to hold up that book and think about how annoyed you are that I'm taking a picture. Make sure I can read your shirt. And *go!*"

It wasn't great, but Grumper—that is *Harper*—managed to at least give him an interesting look.

A thought occurred to him. "How many snarky shirts do you have?"

She peeked into *Fawkes* as if hungry for just a few words before sighing and sliding it onto the shelf. Turning to him, she shrugged. "I don't know. A dozen? Most of the ones I want don't exist."

"Then we'll make them." Decision made, Milton pulled out an envelope from his pocket. "Seed money. I didn't think we'd need it for you, but until we get your bills squared away, we're going to assume we do."

Harper didn't even reach for the envelope. "What money? I don't garden. I kill things."

Literal. Keep things literal with her. "I'm investing in your T-shirt business. This is the money we'll use to buy T-shirts."

126

Her lips stretched into a scowling line. "I don't have room to become a clothing store. Sell them at the Uffda Shop."

"No." Milton held her gaze and refused to back down. It was a gamble, but he suspected she'd handle straightforward opposition best. He'd better be right.

Atticus piped up, "Sucker!"

That broke Harper's concentration. She whipped her head around and stared. "Does he talk? I thought I heard—"

"Sucker!"

"That." Folding her arms over her chest, Harper focused back on him again. "Did you just tell me no?"

"I did," he said in an attempt to avoid the "yes/no" confusion of answering that question. "We need to sell them here. We're going to create a market for them, and folks are going to want to buy them from *you*."

"We don't have—"

Milton beckoned her to the tables in the center of the store. "Here. We're moving the counter here. We'll put the T-shirts there. That shelving behind it is great for overstock and we'll hang the shirts on cardboard cutouts of popular book heroes and heroines."

The girl stared at him as if he'd left pages of his mind scattered in the wind. "So... print out Anne Shirley in her pinafore and tie a 'Reading is Lit' shirt at her waist?"

The idea couldn't have been more perfect. "I was going for Laura Ingalls Wilder, considering the area, but that's perfect. Definitely want that. We need Darcy too. Maybe..."

"'Book boyfriends don't cheat.' Although Jake the Cop proved they do. The jerk."

"How do you figure?"

When she explained about the guy "dating" thousands of readers at once, Milton couldn't help a grin. "I love it. Wish I had been able to record that conversation. It would be great for a reel."

Her forehead created furrows that became more

127

pronounced the narrower her eyes became. At last, she shrugged and said, "Does what you just said make sense to you?"

"Yep."

She turned away with a huff, muttering, "Lit, woke, Gen-somethinger."

Twenty minutes earlier, he wouldn't have known it, but Milton recognized defeat now. She'd agreed. "I'll put the tables upstairs to display some of the best books."

"Don't. I think my aunt wants the one with the trestle legs, and I bet we can trade the other one at Boxrud's for something that will fit the aesthetic up there. If I have to, I'll sacrifice my secretary at home, but only if I have to."

She'd hate him, but if she had a secretary, he wanted it. Another one would mean he didn't have to move the one near the stairs on the main floor. Before he'd even moved a step, she sighed. "You want it. Fine. I'll see if Jake the Cop will bring it over when he goes to get the AC from my window."

Interesting… Jake the Cop. Boyfriend? Someone she wants to be her boyfriend? This could get interesting. He'd already had one successful cop/bookseller matchmaking effort under his belt. Just call him Milton-Emma.

"See if he can do that. It would be helpful, unless me putting my seats down in the Land Rover means I can fit it in. Then I'm happy to do that."

"Jake can. He owes me." She frowned as she turned back to him looking confused. "If he loaned me his AC, then he doesn't owe me anymore, does he?"

Atticus piped up, "Sucker!" and Milton shrugged.

After another moment's thought, Harper snatched a rom com off the mystery shelf and moved to put it where it belonged. "Well, I'll tell him he does anyway. He probably won't figure out it makes no sense. He's not very bright."

Considering his theory on book boyfriends, Milton doubted that—doubted it very much. Still, he kept his opinion to himself.

"Well, I think I'll go get me a coffee next door. Want

anything?"

"No. I'm having tea." She froze and stared at him. "Um… I got you a sandwich. It's Wednesday, so I got bacon, egg, and cheese on English muffin bread."

There had been hints that she resented the need for his presence, but this thoughtfulness told him that if she did, she didn't hold it against *him* personally. That would make working with her easier.

Mandy's was just as welcoming as he'd remembered. Milton stood in line and watched the room, taking note of how the employees interacted with the customers, how the customers used the rooms, and what he'd change if he were in charge. There wasn't much, but one thing stood out. Too many tables. And was that even possible for food service?

But he sensed it… two of the tables *felt* as though they blocked the entrance—as if you were intruding on the people sitting there. Not something anyone would want to do. He saw three people start in, turn, and leave. Never a good sign. *At least my instincts are still sharp.*

By the time he'd left, a wisp of an idea had begun to curl about in his mind. It just might work too. It would be a better lead in to asking the owner or manager about rent as well. But first, Harper. He couldn't start making those kinds of changes without at least talking to her about them. They'd do things his way whenever possible, but this was convenience, not essential. He'd pick his battles, and the store would win.

Seventeen

Parenting tip #143: Every good idea won't work for every bad situation. Improvise.

A weighted blanket filled with lead couldn't have crushed him harder. Noah lay with the back of one hand flung over his eyes in an attempt to hide his tears from even the darkness. Just a few days until October. Three months of parenting and he'd already failed his son beyond reason.

Asking Megan if she had a little brother in Bennie's school had seemed like a genius idea. She had… just one grade above, although the kid had been held back, so he was just a couple months past nine to Bennie's almost seven. Perfect for protecting Bennie by just *being* with him to and from class when the worst of the bullying had been.

If they'd only known he was the biggest perpetrator. And Bennie had tried to tell him. He saw that now. The minute Noah had mentioned Gage Hansen, he'd shrank back and promised he'd "be good."

Be good. It had taken a few months to learn this was Bennie-speak for "do whatever I have to in order to save my skin." Noah still couldn't tell if whatever abuse he'd endured had been in Tara's home or a foster home— caused by Tara herself or one of her (many, it seemed) boyfriends. But that he had been abused or at least expected to be (and didn't that mean he must have been in the past?) couldn't be denied. Even his perpetually optimistic mother had agreed to that.

If only he'd realized what it meant sooner. It took a special kind of dad to solve a problem by making it worse. *I would be that dad.*

Tomorrow was Wednesday. Maybe Harper would have another idea—some kid who went to her church that he could trust? Maybe a way to convince Bennie he should do taekwondo instead of ballet? Wouldn't *that* be a relief?

Twice he got up to check on Bennie. The third time he quit pretending and crawled into bed beside the boy and pulled him close. It said something, didn't it, that he could *feel* his son relax. If the kid had been that tense in his sleep…

Still, the gray skies at dawn told him he might as well give up on sleep. French toast. He could do that. And… maybe he'd go in with the kid this once—ask about homework or something. Or maybe… allergy medication? Would it hurt Bennie to have it when he didn't need it—just this once? Keep the kid home and take him out to Mom's until he had a plan?

Nothing prepared him for the water works that ensued when he asked Bennie which one sounded best. So, just before the bell rang, he dropped Bennie off and watched the little Avengers backpack bob as his little guy trudged up the walk to Sunnyside Elementary. Strange how living on this side of town made the building look too modern to him. After spending so much time downtown, he missed the old-style brick buildings with their framed windows and cornices.

And musing about architecture wouldn't change the fact that his son had just entered a lion's den without the protection of angels. Or did he? That thought filled his mind all the way to work, all the way through replacing a solenoid in twice the time it should have taken him, all the way through the lunch he *didn't* take to make it up to his boss. Christians had angels waging war for and with them. Michael the cool dude who could wipe out armies with a single swish of his sword. He needed that one on his son's side. But what about little kids? Were they protected too?

Well, there wasn't any reason not to ask for it. God knew what He was doing, even if right now, Noah wondered if maybe He'd gotten fed up and left him to his own mistakes. *But I wouldn't do that to Bennie. And God's a much better Father than me…*

By the time he met Megan outside Cornerstone Community Church, Noah knew one thing. He didn't know anything. That's it. And the sight of his son's resigned expression instead of the familiar excitement at another day of dancing broke him. "Love you, kid."

Bennie didn't even look back to acknowledge it. Megan gave Noah a strange look. "What's up with him? He's been moody all afternoon."

How did he tell her that her brother was the cause of it all? If he did, and if she dragged Gage in, things could get nasty. But…

"Gage is the problem, isn't he?"

As much as he wanted to for Bennie's sake, he couldn't lie. "Yeah."

Her shoulders slumped. "I'll come tomorrow and Friday, but then I have to quit."

"What?" His heart pinged around his chest like a pinball. "Why?"

She shook her head. "Sorry. I really like Bennie, but I have to tell Mom and Dad. And when I do, the only thing that'll save Bennie is if I quit. Gage is… well, I think he needs help, but they won't listen. I should have known. I'm so sorry."

With that, she fled down the street. Several passersby scowled at him as if he'd tried to abduct her or something. He should go after her—talk to her parents for her. Stop the craziness. But Bennie stood alone up in that classroom of giggling girls in sheer pink ballet skirts and needed to know that despite his father's recent failure… he was still safe. Because *his* father would be there for him. Always.

How do other dads do this?

Noah slipped through the door to Twice Sold Tales and would have headed straight for his usual place by the second-floor windows if the counter hadn't been shoved over to the middle of the store—just a few feet from the stairs. A glance at the corner it had been in showed empty shelves and… nothing but a bird cage. He couldn't argue that the new place allowed Harper to see everything in the store at once, but why? And what was up with the bird cage?

With no sign of Harper anywhere, he crept up the stairs, hugging the wall on the creakiest step, and hurried to the window where the binoculars waited. A quick glance through them showed the top of Bennie's head only. His back must be to the window this time. Noah preferred when the boy sat facing it so he could read expressions as well as body language.

As they rose, the little girl next to him said something, and Bennie threw back his head and laughed. Miss Courtney leaned forward to say something—probably admonish them to be quiet and pay attention. But no, a moment later, she laughed as well. One by one, the others caught a good case of the giggles. Bennie beamed, and it took Noah a moment to realize that his son fit in somewhere for the first time. He'd been included.

He hadn't meant to sigh, but it escaped and wrapped itself around him like an old woman's shawl. In that moment, Noah had to make a choice. Fully accept that his son loved something he didn't understand or risk alienating the kid that had made the phrase, "loved more than life itself," make sense.

In his peripheral vision, Noah sensed movement. That's when he noticed that the bookshelves were different now. One of those old-fashioned drop-face desks—they had a name, but he couldn't remember what it was—sat between the two doors on the side wall. The writing surface was down, and a few books stacked on it. The hutch doors had been left open and books lined those shelves. All old. All probably valuable.

Scanning the room, he saw a chair in one corner with a small occasional table beside it. Oddly enough, the seat of the chair had been used as a bookshelf and it didn't look ridiculous. It should have, but it didn't.

But when he got to the corner to his right, the white tip of a pair of Converse tennis shoes caught his eye. A close inspection showed a lock of hair over the corner of a bookshelf. Harper's. Just in time, he stopped himself from speaking aloud. If she were hiding... surely not from him! But if she were hiding, speaking might reveal her place.

After another glance out the window to see that the group had moved to stretches at the barre, Noah set down the binoculars and moved to Harper's side. Seating himself at her feet, he peered into the corner and smiled at her as she pressed one finger to her lips.

"Who are we hiding from?"

"Milton."

He didn't know that name. Boyfriend? Asking seemed rude, so he took the moment to ensure she wasn't hurt. No bruises, no cuts, no traces of tears. She might be upset about something, but she didn't look injured. She held a dark book to her chest as if protecting it from marauders. More destructive children? Maybe the book had been damaged.

"What are you reading?" He still spoke in whispers, and if the way her shoulders relaxed meant anything, he'd made the right choice. She held it out to him. *The Dictionary of Obscure Sorrows.* What an odd title. Noah flipped it over and read the back. "The Dictionary of Obscure Sorrows *defines new words for emotions that we all feel but don't have the language to express.*"

"You're that girl?" he whispered. "The one who reads the *dictionary* for fun?" He didn't bother to mention that the world had enough unfamiliar words without some guy creating his own. Noah knew when he'd lose a battle of word-wits.

This time a tiny smile appeared, and she held out her hand for it. When he handed it back, he noticed something that he'd seen before but hadn't fully registered. The reverence with which she held books. It reminded him of how people held phones before their new cases arrived or even carried a cake to the table. Careful, deliberate, but also with a touch of joy.

Harper flipped to a page and read, "'Looseleft— feeling a sense of loss upon finishing a good book.'" She went on to describe how the covers locked new friends away and... was that a tremble in her voice as she said it? "Any book that seeks to define things I didn't know I felt until I read about them..."

Giving her toe a nudge, he asked, "What has you hiding out here? And who did you say you're hiding from?"

"Change. And Milton."

"Who's Milton again?"

Her eyelids closed—eyelids he realized hadn't been accentuated by... smoke? No... Shadow. Eye shadow. Man, she had him thrown for proverbial loops. Eye shadow. His cousin was "obsessed" with it. And here he'd forgotten what it was called.

"The guy making all the changes." Her voice broke as she added, "I'm not good with change."

"Why's he making changes, then?"

Tear-filled eyes opened and met his gaze before shifting almost as quickly. "I hired him to help me save the store."

Save the store? It was in trouble? And if she'd hired him, why hide? Oh, right. Change—even if you needed it, and if you weren't good with it, you wouldn't want it no matter why. "It looks good up here."

She nodded. "And I don't have to see those awful books every time I go to the office but..."

"But change. I get it." Well, he couldn't ask for help with Bennie now. Not with her in her own crisis. It might be silly, but Noah felt the overwhelming *need* to try to cheer her up. "Bennie's doing okay in class right now, so I was going to go over to Hanisch's for a donut." He stood and smiled down at her. "What can I get you?"

"They close at four."

They did… but he'd seen Jamie over there when they'd walked to the store, and she'd open for him if he begged. Surely, they hadn't tossed the old donuts yet. "Let me try. What do you want?"

"Fruity Pebbles donut."

"Bennie's favorite."

Harper crawled out of her hole, moved to the window, and picked up the binoculars. "He has good taste. Get something for Milton, would you?"

"Sure. Know what he likes?"

She shot him a pointed look. "It's after closing at Hanisch's. We'll get whatever's left, and you know it."

He'd gone two steps down before he heard her call out, "Thanks, Noah. I needed a friend."

Odd how she said that and also sounded surprised.

Eighteen

Books > People

Friend. She'd called Noah a *friend*. Was that overstating things? Probably, but then again, maybe not.

Harper first watched Bennie do his squats and tiptoes. There were probably fancy names for them. Ballet seemed like a fancy name kind of thing. The funny little kid looked so serious as he watched Courtney Madsen, checked his own feet, looked back... This kid really loved ballet. Anyone could see it.

Noah probably prays for a sudden love of hockey every night.

At the thought of Noah, she swung the binoculars to the right and watched as he covered his eyes and peered through the glass doors as he knocked. She knew the moment someone came to the door when he stepped back, hands shoved in his pockets. She might not be able to see his face, but Harper knew he looked sheepish. A few seconds passed before he disappeared into the building.

She swung the binoculars back over to Cornerstone's upper classrooms and scanned for Bennie. But the kid was gone. One by one she looked at every person there... nothing. She counted to five. To ten.

Tossing the binoculars onto the bookcase below the window, she dashed for the stairs, clamoring down them with a racket to wake the dead. Somewhere below, Milton called out to see if she was okay, but Harper ignored him and raced across the street. A car horn blared, making her wonder for half a second if maybe she'd run in front of one. She'd forgotten to look. Again.

Inside, she took the stairs up to the classrooms two at a time and burst into the ballet rooms panting. There Bennie sat on the floor working hard on his shoes. Courtney Madsen glared at her. "We don't allow—"

Without acknowledging whatever else the dainty little woman said, Harper marched over to Bennie, knelt, tied his shoe for him, and whispered, "Sorry, kid. I didn't see you anymore and got scared. Make fun of me when I leave, okay? Trust me."

But when she stepped out of the room and the little girls began to giggle, she heard Bennie say, "I don't think it's nice to laugh at someone being scared."

One little girl laughed at that—laughed loudly and said, "Bennie's *scared!*"

Before she could decide what to do, another voice, quiet but firm, said, "I don't think he meant him. I think he meant Miss Harper. She was scared."

Courtney informed them all that the interruption was over, and no one would say unkind things to others in her class. "And if I hear of it *outside* class, you'll be excused from all future classes. We don't tolerate bullying at River City Studio."

Those words were followed by agreement from a choir of little girlie voices. That's all Harper needed to hear. She might have made it upstairs two at a time, but sense told her she'd land on the floor in a heap if she didn't take sensible single steps on her way back down. Outside, she started across the street, but someone called her name. A horn blared as she stopped short of stepping in front of a car.

Thudding footfalls followed. That voice. "Are you trying to kill yourself?"

She turned. "I just wanted to get back and forgot to look."

Box in hand, Noah stared at her. "What are you doing out here?"

Harper gave the street a quick glance and started across it. "Making sure Bennie is okay."

Milton stood just inside the doors, watching. She jerked one open and held it for Noah. He entered, shook hands with Milton, and even passed over her Fruity Pebbles donut, but he did it all, watching her.

Harper huffed. Meanwhile, who knew if Courtney Pedersen had just been saying what she thought Harper would want to hear. On the sixth step up, she decided. "I want *The Haunted Bookshop* for stair number four," she called back without pausing.

"Only if we do *Fahrenheit 451*," Milton countered.

"Deal."

She heard Milton tell Noah that he'd insisted they finish the risers and soon. "—and get rid of that *Hundred Years of Solitude*. It fits the theme well, but not her."

"Theme?"

"She's using titles that fit with books. *Great Expectations*... what you might have about the book you're reading." Upstairs, Harper grinned. What would he say about *One Hundred Years of Solitude*?

"How does solitude fit into the scheme of things?"

At the top of the stairs, Harper was tempted to sit down and listen, but first, she needed to check on Bennie. The boy was fine. He stood at that stupid barre, sliding his foot forward, sideways, to the back, and next to his other foot again. Over and over. Courtney Madsen nodded... and smiled? She thought so. But then Courtney tapped Bennie's toe and the boy repeated that move.

Boooring. Still, he was safe, so she hustled back to the stairs and sat. Waiting.

"—seen her T-shirt today?"

"Books and people?"

"It's the greater than sign." Milton sounded thoughtful. "Harper! We forgot to get your picture du jour!"

I'll du jour you! But instead of voicing her true thoughts, Harper just called back that they still had time.

"It's almost closing time. I'll come up there."

Though she sighed, Harper didn't move until they'd nearly reached her. "What's the point?"

"You're creating anticipation. People will begin to look forward to the daily photo. Oh, and we need to order some of that one for the shelves."

"We're almost out of your money."

That didn't seem to deter him in the least. Milton pointed to the window and would have had her hold, but when Noah opened the box and pulled out a donut, his eyes lit up. "Hey, can she use one of those?"

Noah handed over a Fruity Pebbles donut. "They had two of these nasty things left." To Milton he added, "I got us maple bacon—like normal people eat."

After a picture of her in her shirt eating a donut and confirmation of the spelling of Hanisch's, Milton disappeared. Noah stayed there, staring. "You went to check on Bennie."

Perhaps it was a question, but it didn't sound much like one. "He disappeared. I waited half a minute or more. Just *gone.*"

Of all the responses she could have anticipated, defeat wouldn't have entered her consciousness. No one would doubt it, though. The guy looked ready to quit... something. "Thank you."

"He's really okay. He just needed to retie his shoe and couldn't get it. I think he was rushing too fast or something. I did it for him and told him to make fun of me so the girls wouldn't tease him." She went on to describe his defense of her, of the one mocking girl and the other who'd stood up for him. "Courtney said she'd kick anyone out who was mean about stuff like that. A zero-bullying policy."

"That's what his school claims to have, but it's getting worse there."

That didn't make sense. He had found someone to be

in Bennie's court. "But—"

"I managed to choose the kid who had been tormenting him in the first place. Apparently, it's a jealousy thing."

Something she hadn't realized had been arranging itself into a coherent thought finally clicked into place. Harper beckoned him to follow and led him into the office. With the door shut behind them, she turned. "I was wrong."

He blinked at her. "Pardon me?"

"I said you shouldn't go to the teacher or the principal because it would make things worse. That was wrong. I was thinking like a kid." She stared at the calendar on the wall—the one that said February two years earlier. "I was remembering how I felt as a kid—not how I would have wanted things to be. I would have *wanted* teachers and administration to protect me. That's their job. Instead, the *kids* in my family had to."

She chanced a look at Noah and found him watching her. The nod came much slower than she'd have hoped. "You wanted someone to be a Miss Courtney."

Well, technically, sure. But admitting that? To *him?* Cruel. "Basically. If parents don't insist on protection for their kids, this kind of garbage will keep going on—indefinitely."

"Makes sense, but…" The guy looked bullied himself.

"I just think," Harper began again. "Maybe sometimes speaking up is better than enduring. Things get worse because we submit when we should keep fighting."

Jake the Cop could forget it. Milton shot a look at Atticus when the little guy said something like, "Uh, huh." Could the bird read his mind? Did that make him or Atticus the bird brain?

Irrelevant and immaterial. Dr. Praetorius would approve of that assessment.

But back to the original idea. Jake was a good guy, and he was obviously intrigued by Harper—definitely attracted to her. But while Noah and Harper didn't exactly have chemistry yet, they had the promise of it, and he'd seen just the thing to spark more.

That certainty wavered when a pretty young woman brought over a little boy and went in search of Noah. Yes, he should be trolling eBay for sellers who didn't know what they had or considering how else to make Twice Sold Tales unique. But instead, he crept upstairs behind her and listened from halfway as the woman both put Harper in her place *and* reassured Noah that Bennie was safe in her studio. When the conversation switched to the possibility of adding Friday classes so he could be a mouse in *The Nutcracker*, Milton crept back downstairs and went to see how the boy—Bennie, presumably—was faring.

Bennie snapped a book shut when he saw Milton headed his way. A glance at the title as he picked up a different book answered everything. A struggling reader. Maybe that's where the bullying came from. "Find anything good?"

Holding up *Poppy* by Avi, Bennie said, "Miss Courtney said to find it. She said I'd like it."

Despite the confident words, the boy looked uncertain. After watching Bennie's face screw up as he concentrated hard enough to conjure a new book out of thin air, Milton decided he understood. "I think you're right. *Poppy* is a great book. Avi is one of my favorite authors."

The way Bennie relaxed told him he'd gotten it right. Now, to let it go or let the boy know he was a safe place to "land." He chose the latter. "Bennie? Is that your name?" Bennie nodded. "I just want you to know that there's no shame in having trouble with reading. Many people do—sometimes even as adults. The shame only comes if you don't try."

With each word, the boy's jaw hung lower. "How'd you know?"

Milton pointed to the abandoned book. "That was my first clue. First readers often have great stories. I like to read them sometimes."

"No way."

Milton nodded. "Picture books, early readers, middle grade… and even *The Brothers Karamazov*."

The look Bennie gave him prompted Milton to go retrieve a copy of the thick tome and show him. "If someone puts words together in such a way as to make them beautiful, I love it—whether a sentence, a poem, a picture book, or a classic."

"Harper calls the books on that shelf the "Old Fogies." He leaned close and whispered, "But I don't know what that means."

"I think," Milton suggested, "it means books that are old enough to feel self-important." A spark of something prompted him to ask, "Does she have names for other shelves?"

"Lots of them, but I only know a couple."

Milton said, "Can you show me?"

Bennie shook his head. "I don't know you. I'm not supposed to be talking to you. Sorry."

It was pushing things, but this is why he'd come. "How about you go ask your dad or Harper if you can talk to Milton—see if I can introduce you to Atticus."

After hesitating for just a moment, Bennie dashed for the stairs. Milton picked up *Poppy* and smiled. Great choice for a little boy who obviously knew bullying firsthand. He carried it to the middle of the store, paid for it, slipped it in a bag, and set it on the counter. It would be beyond Bennie's reading ability, but if Noah were half the father Milton thought he was…

Bennie raced back downstairs a moment later, followed by the women and Noah. "Dad says yes. Harper said you're okay. You're helping her keep the store open. We're not done with Narnia, so you *have* to save the store. I *have* to know what happens."

"Well, we're going to do it if we possibly can, but

143

even if we didn't, there's always the library."

The boy's head already swung from side to side. "Dad says we're starting my *own* li-berry."

It wasn't kind—and yet it was. Just not the kind of kind a kid usually understood, but Milton couldn't help himself. "It's li-brrrr-ary. Like 'lie' and 'brrr' and 'airy.' I won't lie but brrr it's airy out here."

At first, Bennie looked confused. Then it clicked. "Li-br-ary. Li-brary. Library."

"Excellent."

"Anyway, he says by the time I'm grown up, I'll have a great li-berry for when I have kids." Bennie leaned close and whispered, "I want to have a *lot* of kids. Nice ones."

That "nice ones" ripped at his heart and softened the blow of "li-berry" again. Oh, well. Baby steps. "Want to meet Atticus?"

"Yes!" as they passed the fantasy shelves, Bennie said, "Harper calls those, 'imagination gone wild.'"

That confirmed his suspicions. He *knew* she enjoyed fantasy and other spec-fic, so they'd do it. They'd give shelves new titles just as soon as he could secure a stack of black cardstock and a white pen.

The teacher left with a call to see them on Friday, and the way Noah didn't look at all interested settled everything for him. "Oh! Friday. That reminds me. I found this ghost walk thing they're doing. I want you to go—see what books we can promote for it. They go right past here on the way to the Sheldon Theater. It'll be perfect." He pretended to pause and think while Harper sputtered out an objection.

"Ghost walk? What does *that* have to do with anything?"

"Halloween is coming, they have this local event, and we need to capitalize on it. You should probably take someone with you, though—so it doesn't look like we're scoping them out." Harper frowned.

"What? That doesn't make sense."

His acting skills were taking a beating, but Milton plowed onward. "Actually, a date would be best." He turned to Noah. "What are you doing on Friday? Have a couple of hours to spare to help save the store?"

"I—no, I don't think—"

"Why do I have to walk around in the cold listening to ghost stories again?"

"You should do it, Dad! It'll be cool!"

The votes blurted out in near unison. With him and Bennie in the yay camp and Noah and Harper in the nay, the votes were tied. He had to come up with something fast. "They'll be walking right past. We need a display that'll appeal to them. And you'll get the best choices if you actually listen to the spiel and everything." To Noah, he added, "And even if it wouldn't look less suspicious with her having a date, I'd feel better knowing she wasn't out with a bunch of strangers at night."

Please don't ask why I can't go.

"I just don't know if I can find someone to watch Bennie. I lost my sitter today." Noah was scrolling through his phone. "Yeah. Look. It says to leave kids at home—not friendly. I don't think I can do it, but—"

"Granny can watch me!"

All eyes turned to the boy. Noah found his voice first. "I don't know, bud. I—" He swallowed hard at the pleading look in the boy's eyes. "How about I ask?" he conceded. "If Mom can come, I'll do it." He didn't add, "If I have to," but his tone said it all.

And I'll pray she says yes and that no one thinks to ask why I'm not going. "Because two book people looks suspicious" is weak at best.

"Great. Now, Atticus wants to meet Bennie." He pulled the paper bag from the counter. "And I have a gift for Bennie if that's all right."

When Noah shot Harper a look, he knew he'd made the right decision. Noah trusted her. *Excellent.*

Nineteen

Book recommendation: The CafFUNated Mysteries by Angela Ruth Strong. Combines coffee and tea with books and mysteries. What more could an avid reader want?

While Atticus exercised in the "Dregs" as they'd secretly begun to call the lower level, and Harper poured out her woes about the ghost walk to him, Milton slipped next door, hoping for a chance to talk to the manager, if not the owner. He had his proposal all ready and had opted not to tell Harper about it. She'd balk. Yes, she'd agree and do it, but she'd balk. But if it were all settled before he talked to her, she'd just scowl a bit, sigh a bit more, and start choosing books.

It's how she rolled.

At nine-thirty, Mandy's Cafe was still hopping, but nothing like they had from seven to nine. With the sounds of steamers doing their thing, and the tantalizing scent of coffee beans nearly making him salivate, Milton ordered his white mocha. As the girl behind the counter counted back his change, he pounced. "Is the owner in, by chance? Manager?"

The girl fumbled. Wide-eyed, she swallowed hard and asked, "Is there something wrong? I—"

"Oh, nothing like that. I've been impressed with the service and the friendliness of everyone here. I'll be sure to tell her that..."

"Well…" She dumped the change in his hand, hers trembling just a bit, and shoved the drawer shut. "I can ask."

He pointed to the tables and said, "I'll be in there. My name's Milton."

"Okay…" She glanced back behind her and looked at him again. "You're sure everything's all right?"

"Perfect. I'd prove it and take a sip, but we both know I'd burn myself."

That earned him a weak but genuine smile. "I'll just see if Mandy can come out."

He chose a table near the window—one that allowed both occupants to see the awkward table positioning. Of all the times he'd been in and walked past the coffee shop, only once had he seen anyone sitting there, and it hadn't been for long.

Mandy appeared in a black apron and a smile. She scanned the room through large-framed glasses and paused at the sight of him. He nodded. At least she looked pleasant enough. Smiling, eyes bright… Milton hated himself for looking, but while he didn't see a wedding ring, he saw that she did wear one. Often. Must have been working with food this morning.

Milton rose and held out his hand. "Mandy?"

"Milton. Addie said you wanted to speak with me?"

"I do… do you have a moment to sit? I have a proposition for you—one I don't think your husband will mind," he added as her eyebrows began to draw together.

That smile widened. "Nice…" She sat. "Addie's convinced you're ticked off about something."

"If I were, I wouldn't be here with a proposition."

That earned him a nod. "Right." She just sat there… watching him.

After hesitating… was it really the best move? Well, it would get him into the discussion about the buildings, so it was worth it. He pulled out his wallet and passed over a business card. Mandy took it, a frown appearing.

"The Bookstore Doctor? Um… we're a cafe." She'd

147

have risen, but Milton stopped her.

"I'm here to help Harper next door."

The woman's eyebrows shot up and her eyes widened. "She's in trouble? How? People are over there all the time."

"That's what I'm here to find out. Everything looks great except the crazy taxes and insurance she has to pay. Do you find yours going up all the time?"

Mandy shrugged. "I have a lease—that's all covered by the management company, I assume." After a moment, she amended that. "I mean, I have my own insurance, too—have to. But not for the whole building."

Great. Another dead end. Then again, maybe the management company knew about taxes on it—or would put him in contact with the owner. "So… you don't know the owner's contact info, I assume."

She shook her head. "Sorry. But maybe if you talked to Rivertown Management, they could help you. They're always great whenever I need something."

Again, Mandy might have risen, but Milton pointed to the tables. "And I wondered about your placement of those tables."

A wince told him she didn't like it any better than he did. "We had a different arrangement at first, but with people bringing in laptop bags and stuff, we discovered we wanted more space between tables—less spilled coffee that way." The rueful smile told him they'd learned that one by experience. "Just didn't have anywhere else to put them."

"How would you feel about removing them? That's my proposition."

"I could, but why? They *do* get used from time to time, so they're not really hurting anything." Despite her words, he could hear it. Interest. She didn't like those tables any more than he did.

From his black T-shirt pocket, he pulled out the sketch he'd made of her floor plan and unfolded it. "This is what I had in mind…" While she examined it, he described the "buddy businesses," as he'd begun to call them, in

148

Noel, Missouri. "You're in a better position than Josh and Honey are. You're next door, which makes it easy for people to just go to the next place. With that bookshelf there, people are likely to buy a book and linger. A card in the book will give them a discount off books at Twice Sold Tales. A sale at Twice Sold will get them a coupon for something here. Books and coffee go together."

"She's not Barnes & Noble. I'm not Starbucks." The woman may have protested, but he saw it. Interest.

"No... you're much better. You retain autonomy. But people reading at your tables means they may decide on something to eat or another coffee. Also, having her sending people this way means that someone deciding between you and Hanisch's has another reason to come here."

That caught her attention. "Okay, how would this work? We can't have two tills. That's not going to happen. And what would the shelf look like? Bookshelves can be unsteady—top heavy."

"You can't tell from the drawing, but that is about counter height. It's two three-foot shelves on one side and two two-foot shelves on the ends. A top added. I found everything at Ikea. I can have it ready to install tomorrow night if you agree."

Mandy blinked—first a couple of rapid movements and then a slow, thoughtful one. "That fast?"

"Definitely. And as for payment, I think we have two prices—all 'like new' condition so it remains upscale for you, but hardbacks at ten dollars and paperbacks at five is still a good deal for the customer and easy for you. You'd get twenty-five percent of the book's price sold on commission, so you aren't paying income taxes on full price. I was also thinking Harper could sell gift cards for people to give with the gift of a book. It would work the same way, except that instead of a percentage of the gift card, a certain dollar amount in gift cards would earn her a small card to slip into a bag now and then. We'd use it for marketing."

That's all it took. Mandy's hand shot across the table, ready to shake on it. "I'll get an agreement drawn up."

She'd agreed… and to Friday night. Perfect. He rushed back to Twice Sold Tales in time to see Mrs. Klair decide to take home *The Hunchback of Notre Dame*. The last book she'd taken had been *Breaking Dawn*. The old gal had taken four years to read the whole series. *"It's a guilty pleasure. I like some parts of the series, but others just make me squirm, so I read one followed by a classic every fall."*

Apparently, that classic had been Victor Hugo. Interesting choice, though. After all, the melodrama of the Twilight Saga would only carry over into the story at the great cathedral.

When he asked if he could leave Atticus to go buy the bookshelves he needed, Harper didn't even look up from her book. In fact, she didn't seem to realize she'd been caught reading rather than rearranging "the dregs." With a "Go ahead. Cash is under the drawer," she flipped the page of her book and kept reading.

Milton couldn't help himself. He knelt in front of her and tipped up the book to read the title. *Spotted Hemlock*. The Gladys Mitchell mystery did *not* belong among bodice rippers and alien invasion stories. "Good book."

"Doesn't belong down here. I—"

What else she might have said was interrupted by Mrs. Klair calling down, "Mr. Laffey has a request for you, Harper. Can you spare a moment?"

Without taking her eyes from the page, Harper hopped up and made her way up the stairs. Only when she reached the counter did she stuff a bookmark in her place and smile up at a kindly-looking old gentleman. "Good morning, Mr. Laffey. Did you decide to bring me any of those sci-fi books back?"

The old guy actually blushed. "I started reading them. I'll just pay for them. But… I need a… well, a palate cleanser. Something wholesome but not insipid. Think *Anne of Green Gables* or *Lassie*."

"Oh, I have just the book for you."

Though Milton should have taken that moment to put Atticus in his cage and take off for the cities, the temptation to see what she'd recommend demanded he yield. And who was he to ignore the demands of book tempters?

From an upper shelf at the back of the children's area, Harper pulled a book. He couldn't read the title from so far back, but something about it felt familiar. A light creamy cover… orange filigree… An image in the center— a vignette. It maddened him that he couldn't place it.

Harper handed the book to Mr. Laffey who said, *"Emily of Deep Valley?* What's it about?"

Good choice, Harper. He'll enjoy a book that takes place near the cities and has more depth to it than "playing the glad game" or a rags-to-riches "Optical delusion," as Louisa May Alcott called those books.

With Atticus safely tucked away, Mr. Laffey enjoying getting to know the little bird, and Mrs. Klair off to read her Hugo, Milton took off for the labyrinth otherwise known as Ikea.

Twenty

Reading is Lit

Sirens wailed somewhere as Milton detailed his discussion with Mandy. Perhaps it was melodramatic, or maybe it was the Victorian literature she'd been skimming for Vic-tober, but the wails felt as if they had been ripped from her soul. More people... *coffee* people, no less.

"It's great marketing, and you'll find that readers linger longer when they think they might want to read a book right now. The longer they linger—"

"The twitchier I get," she put in.

She didn't have to be told that the point of her store was to invite people into the place and make them want to spend money. And she *did* like it when people found just the right book. But...

"Care to tell me what that wistful look is all about?"

Another siren wailed as it neared. Weird that. Ocean sirens led sailors to their doom. Land sirens rescued people from it. There had to be a metaphor somewhere in that.

"Harper?"

"I had a friend back in seventh grade. Foster kid. Her mom was amazing. And when they moved her from the home, the mom was devastated. She said, 'I know Anna wasn't my forever child, but it still hurts. I worry about her. Will she feel safe? Will they treat her well? Will she be loved?'"

Milton nodded as if he understood. A closer look hinted that he probably did.

After a moment of reflection, he said, "When I'm standing in line behind someone talking about how good a book will look on her shelf or he says he 'has' to read a book so he doesn't look stupid, I always want to grab the book and run."

Atticus flew to his shoulder and seemed to nod. The little bird then squeaked out, "Read it" as if singing that old Michael Jackson song.

The door pushed open, and Mrs. Klair entered. The woman looked ready to collapse. Harper rushed forward. "What's wrong? Do you need—"

"Fire." It's all the woman could gasp out.

"I heard sirens. Hope everyone's okay."

Mrs. Klair shook her head. "Not okay."

Milton appeared with a water bottle. "It's open, but I just use it to fill Atticus' dish."

A twitch formed, despite herself, at the sight of Mrs. Klair swigging back the water as if a western outlaw chugging whiskey from a bottle. She even wiped her mouth with the back of her hand. Oooh, she'd be embarrassed if she remembered that later.

"The Stadtler's. House engulfed. No one knows where Sophie is."

Harper swayed. In a semi-out-of-body moment, she also delighted in realizing that the movement wasn't a literary device used to tell the reader something without using a whole lot of words. It really was a thing. Milton dragged the stool they kept behind the counter over to her and pushed her onto it. "Sophie?" The first tear fell.

One by one, Milton asked all the questions she wanted to and couldn't. Who had seen the child last? Did they get pets out? Did anyone know how it started? The urge—no, the *need*—to scream at him became impossible to stifle. "Wha—?" And then it disappeared. Of course, he asked. He could see that she couldn't. "Thank you." The words came out in a raspy whisper, but she managed to say it anyway.

Atticus said, "Beat it."

"Rude."

Milton laughed, and so did Mrs. Klair. "It's German," he explained. "For 'you're welcome.' Just easier for a bird to say. Atticus gets new words all the time. It's crazy."

Then it happened. She and the bird locked gazes, and Harper felt a moment of connection. "Give the bird a treat."

"Pretty, pretty."

The retort prompted a laugh that ended in a sob. Turning to Mrs. Klair, she asked, "Who do we know that can give us an update?"

Milton answered first. "Jake the cop."

Harper didn't hesitate. She zipped a text message, now grateful for the back and forth on her AC unit and secretary. How else would she have known how to get a hold of him? HAVE THEY FOUND SOPHIE STADTLER?

Never had time felt so indefinite as it did waiting the seven whole minutes they did for a reply. It came just as a gaggle of well-dressed women entered. They might be dressed in the latest fashions and have salon-perfect hair, but they still nattered and gossiped like old biddies in an English village—designer handbags notwithstanding.

Harper tore her gaze from the group as her phone buzzed. EMILY SAYS SHE'S AT A FRIEND'S HOUSE, BUT THEY CAN'T GET A HOLD OF THE FRIEND'S FAMILY. TAMMY IS ON HER WAY TO CHECK.

Relief dripped from her pores. All right, it was probably just good, old-fashioned sweat, but in Harper's mind, it was relief. "They think they know where she is."

Just a hint of color flooded Mrs. Klair's face. "That's good. I wonder if anything is salvageable."

Harper zipped back thanks and added, CAN THEY SAVE THEIR HOME?

This time the answer followed in less than a minute. NO. TOTAL LOSS. TRYING TO SAVE THE NEIGHBOR'S HOUSE

AT THIS POINT. EMILY THINKS IT'S HER FAULT. CAN'T TELL
WHY.

"Oh, no!" Four eyes locked on her—six if you
counted Atticus. Atticus demanded to be counted. Six,
then. "Emily's blaming herself. He says they 'can't tell why.'
I don't know if that's because he's not allowed to or if he
can't understand a freaked-out kid."

"Possibly both," Milton suggested.

That comment stopped her thumbs. Maybe she
shouldn't ask. Then a buzz startled her, and she dropped
her phone. It clattered to the floor, making two of the
women now clustered around the mystery section squeak.
Probably were already in find the murderer mode.

She swiped the screen and closed her eyes. Inhaled.
Exhaled. A sob shook her. "Candle. Emily thinks she left a
candle lit on her windowsill."

Mrs. Klair's voice trembled as much as her hand as
she pulled *The Hunchback of Notre Dame* from her bag.
"Here's this. I think I need Manderley today... and I need
to go home."

Milton took the book from her. "Did you enjoy
Esmerelda and Quasimodo?"

"I did—what little we get of them. I forgot how
much in love with architecture Hugo was. That's the real
romance of the book."

His laughter rankled. How could anyone laugh at a
time like this? The Stadtler's home! Their pets... their
memories... Harper gasped, tears refusing to be repressed
now. "Their books!"

A single tear slid down Mrs. Klair's cheek. "I know.
That was my first thought after I heard Sophie was
probably all right."

As if a cue, her phone buzzed and the words, SOPHIE
FOUND appeared. "They found her—Sophie, I mean. But
the books! They *love* their books."

The growing sense of helplessness began to dissipate.
Harper stood. "You wanted *Rebecca?*"

Mrs. Klair nodded. "And I might just need to hire

one of those Ubers. I don't think I can walk home. Not today."

"I'll take you, Mrs. Klair. Let me get your books recorded, and we'll go out the back way to save walking."

While Milton did that, Harper picked up Atticus—and the silly bird even let her—and put him in his cage. She dumped the bag of green peppers in his little food dish, half of it spilling all over the floor, and closed the door. Ignoring the ladies who now argued over whether *Fifty Shades of Grey* was art or smut, she unceremoniously dumped the books that occupied her little metal cart onto the floor and began filling it again. *Love, Mary Elisabeth* went on it first thing. *The Way Things Work Now* for Dalton for sure. *Ballet Shoes* for Sophie. Or maybe *Eloise at Christmastime*...No, she'd save that for close to Christmas. It would be an excuse to give them all more books. They'd have to start rebuilding their library somehow.

Just the expense of that choked her up. When you had no clothes or beds, books probably weren't most people's priority. One of the ladies commented that she'd prefer the mysteries to "trash like that," and that reminded her that Tammy had been reading Jacqueline Winspear. Back to mysteries and… she had book three. Hopefully, Tammy didn't binge mysteries as fast as she did. For Brian… oh, that was a tough one. He liked Michael Crichton, but he also loved his theology books.

That thought sent her spiraling into a whirlwind of despair. "Their *Bibles*!"

The gaggle of glamor grannies (not fair, but Harper didn't care) stared at her. She snatched up *The Andromeda Solution* on her way to the "Religion" shelves. There she grabbed *Haley's Bible Handbook,* a *Strong's Concordance*, a pink Bible for Sophie, teal for Emily, and the weird duct tape one for Dalton. Brown for Brian, purple for Tammy.

In the middle of it all, she thought she heard Milton call out saying they were going, but she ignored it. She had things to do. Like find something to encourage them. Something… important. Stirring without being preachy or just a literary platitude.

The answer came at the thought of what Noah would say to that. He considered most books just that—literary platitudes. He'd never said it, but she'd felt it. *Narnia*.

She only had one complete set—pricey, too. But what were dollars when the soul was starved for story? And it would be. Yes, they could go to the library. They could. But people, especially children, needed the confidence of a book that belonged to *them*.

She plucked the hardbound, slip-cased set of Narnias off the shelf, added it to the cart, and moved to the counter where two of the ladies stood with books in hand. Harper just managed to avoid a groan. Didn't they understand she had things to do? Then again, those sales might help defray the cost of this gift box.

And that thought gave her another idea. She'd wrap them pretty. Brown paper. String. Stickers from the journaling desk. Okay, maybe the ladies weren't awful. Or not *that* awful.

Stuck to a fifty-dollar bill, a note said, *From Mrs. Klair—to help pay for the books you're sending over. Great idea.*

"Aw…" New tears formed—nice ones this time.

"Everything all right?"

Harper shook her head, not even realizing she'd done it until one of the ladies asked what was wrong. "One of my regular families. Their house is on fire—they've lost everything, and Mrs. Klair—the lady who was in here when you came in…." Harper gulped in air. "She just donated to help start them a new library."

As if synchronized and rehearsed for months, every woman opened her purse, pulled out a wallet, and withdrew a bill. One by one, they laid them on the counter. The arguer for "art" over smut on the "Naughty Stories of Shady Fame" said, "We want to help, too."

It took every bit of her emotional and vocal strength to choke out, "Thank you."

Twenty-One

Parenting tip #149: When you fail, just say so. They knew it before you did, anyway.

Bennie sat in stony silence. After the third question, Noah gave up asking about his day and focused on the road home—and the pathetic chili dog supper he had planned. He really needed to learn to cook better. Throwing a can of vegetables on the stove to supplement a sub-par main "course" didn't really count as "healthy," and kids needed healthy.

They need to be safe too.

And therein lay the problem. Bennie had found out about his meeting with the Hansens, his teacher, and the school principal. He didn't know *how* Bennie knew, but it was the only thing that could account for the overt coldness. While his son had finally begun to warm to him, he'd never chosen to be cold—just wary. This... utter rejection.

He feels like I betrayed him. All right, Lord. Help me out here. How do I make him understand that sometimes doing the right thing makes us uncomfortable, but it's best for everyone in the long run? And how do I do that without making him feel like the sacrificial lamb?

That thought occurred as he turned onto East 7th Street and prompted a smile. *Harper would like it—it's kind of a literary illusion... or is it allusion? I don't remember which is*

158

which. Never cared before. A rebellious twist in his gut prompted him to add, *Still don't.*

As he pulled the car up to the house, Noah realized he'd have to drain the pool finally. He'd been putting it off, but they hadn't used it in over a month, and it would freeze soon enough. Time to put it away until next year. Saturday—after he worked the two hours he owed his boss for the meeting time at the school. Those were two hours he needed to find a new sitter. His mother couldn't be his backup every day.

Noah grabbed his jacket and reached for the door locks that kept Bennie trapped in the backseat. He met Bennie's gaze in the rearview mirror before the boy looked away. "I don't know why you're mad at me, *son...*" He emphasized the relationship automatically. "I can guess, though. We'll talk about it later. But right now, you need to know one thing."

For half a second, Bennie's gaze flicked back to the mirror.

"I love you. I'm gonna make a lot of mistakes."

The kid huffed.

"But every one I make is still going to be because I love you. Sometimes you're going to think what I do is a mistake or is wrong, and *you'll* be wrong about it. I'm still going to love you then too."

He'd lost the kid now. Too many words. How he remembered hating his mother's emotional pleas to know how loved he was. He'd hated his father's long, confusing lectures even more. And yet... here he was doing both combined into one and wishing he could have just one more lecture from Dad. *How to navigate fatherhood would be a good one right about now.*

With his son closed off to him even further, Noah clicked the lock and tried to stifle the ache the followed as Bennie raced away from him. Seeing his son's desperate need to get into the house prompted a ridiculous but desperate need to appease the kid. He kept his voice nonchalant as he unlocked the door and said, "Remind me to give you a spare key. No reason you shouldn't be able to get into your own house without having to wait for your old dad."

Old. He'd just called himself old. At thirty. But before he could ponder that thought, Bennie shot a look at him. "Really?"

Heart twisting at the thought that he might have broken through with something so simple, Noah managed a shrug before pushing open the door. "Sure. Don't you think a kid ought to have a key to his own house?"

Maybe it was his imagination, but he could've sworn he heard Bennie whisper, "My house," on the way upstairs. A bag of Doritos on the fridge caught his attention. Behind that bag was a little door, and behind that little cabinet door stood a thermos. He could do it—heat up the chili, take plastic bowls and chips and cheese… go eat up at Memorial Park. Maybe even play a little disk golf if they hurried.

That thought decided it. If Bennie had to take so much ballet, he'd at least expose the kid to things that other kids talked about. Football. He'd make a raving fan out of the kid if it killed him. *With my luck, he'll stand there in his bicycle shorts, ballet shoes, and Vikings jersey doing those spinny things with his arm over his head.* Right then and there, Noah laid down a law that only he knew at the moment. Bennie would *never* be allowed to wear a tutu. A guy had limits.

Bennie's rebellion hadn't stretched to refusal to do homework. He carried down a few worksheets, his pencil, and an eraser and set them on the table. The one on top was a story to read—from the remedial reading class. Poor kid.

Six hadn't seemed too young. After all, lots of kids didn't really read until first grade. But Bennie's six was soon to turn seven… and he'd been put in remedial reading. The other kids knew it, and Noah had wondered if that had been the trigger for the mess with Gage Hansen rather than the ballet.

"Got much homework tonight?"

"No."

160

Well, it was a word anyway. Two whole words tonight. One more and someone might consider it a sentence. Especially if the next one was like… "way" or something. "Really, no way!" worked. Didn't it?

"How about we take supper up to Memorial? Maybe play a bit of disc golf or wander around a bit."

"Okay."

Noah's lips twisted. Despite "Really, no okay" not being a sentence, Bennie had been forced to stifle his eagerness. Anything to avoid reading work. Poor kid. He came by it honestly. There was a reason Noah hadn't ever gotten into the *Harry Potter* books like his friends and cousins. He'd never read the Series of Unfortunate Events, either. His cousin Janelle had loved them, badgering him for weeks to try it. *"You'll love them. They're not all happily-ever-after. It's more like, 'survivally-ever-after.'"*

With hot chili in the thermos, cheese and pop in the cooler (hopefully his mom wouldn't find out), and bowls, spoons, and chips in a bag, they headed back out again. A little bonding was kind of essential right now.

Memorial Park overlooks the town of Red Wing on the site of what used to be a limestone quarry on "Sorin's Bluff." Now, it offers a lookout over the city, disc golf, hiking trails, and picnic spots—a perfect place for a bit of activity and a lot of retying of relationship strings.

Bennie still didn't speak all the way up the road, and Noah decided not to push it. The tension had lessened some, probably due to the lingering soothing scent of cheap canned chili. The stuff looked like dog food, even smelled a little like it, but once heated… something changed. Magical.

At the top of the hill, he parked, and Bennie took the cooler. Noah grabbed the bag and a couple of discs from the trunk, and they took off up and around the trails up by the sugar loaf. Apparently, families had had similar ideas. Several of the nearest tables were full of people with takeout bags, coolers, and even an actual picnic basket with a tablecloth over the picnic table.

He didn't have to ask where Bennie wanted to sit. The kid froze, stared at one of the concrete picnic tables, and made a beeline for it. While Noah filled their bowls with Doritos and poured chili over the top, Bennie sat and stared at the table, palms flat on it as if trying to feel something. His head went down, cheek pressed close.

What a weird kid. Maybe it wasn't nice to think that about your son, but weird kid or not, Bennie was his, and Noah wouldn't have him any other way. He started to tack on, *Even the ballet. He wouldn't be Bennie without it,* but Noah wasn't quite there yet.

As he nudged Bennie with the bowl, Noah said, "Eat up."

In slow motion, Bennie raised his head, hands still flat on the table, and looked around. "It's magical, isn't it?"

All the emotions tangled into a knot in his stomach. "What is?"

The kid's eyes shuttered, and he picked up a chip with chili and cheese dripping off it. "Nothing."

He had to salvage this and quick. Pretend there were so many magical things it was impossible to know or beg to share in magic? He hadn't finished forming the thought before knowing the answer. "Will you let me in on the secret?"

Chili smeared across the kid's cheek, and Noah realized he hadn't brought napkins or paper towels or anything. Once again, his fledgling parenting skills face planted. Bennie swiped his mouth across his shirt sleeve and grabbed another chip.

"I don't think it's magical if you have to be told." As an afterthought, he added, "Sorry."

Another crack in the wall. He'd take it. And maybe now was the time to talk about the marauding elephant destroying everything that had become so good. Noah ate a few chips loaded with chili first. Just in case. Sustenance never hurt.

"I know you're mad at me, Bennie."

The kid scowled and super-glued a rock into that

crack in the wall between them.

"I'm sorry. I made a mistake."

The kid's entire body language rose up and bellowed out, "Ya think?"

But Noah kept going. "I tried to handle things like I would have wanted to when I was a kid. You don't make a fuss. You let things go. You avoid the jerk, or it gets worse."

How could a kid relax and stiffen at the same time?

"Here's the thing, though. It's the wrong way to handle it and not just because I picked the wrong kid to help, either."

That earned him a scowl but one with a curious look behind it. Noah kept going.

"If Gage gets away with hurting you—inside or outside—he'll hurt someone else too. And if other kids see him get away with it, they might. People have to stand up to this stuff." His father would have pointed out people like Hitler, Stalin, and Nicolae Ceausescu. That last one he only remembered the name, but Dad had mentioned him a few times too. Instinct told him going into Dad 2.0 right now would ensure he lost Bennie for good.

Though Bennie wouldn't look at him, Noah noticed a change. All the anger disappeared and something else replaced it. Noah just couldn't identify what that "something else" was.

Only a sniffle hinted at tears he couldn't see. Noah jumped up and nearly vaulted the tabletop to get to his son. Scooping him up, he held the boy fast. "What is it? You're safe. You will always be safe. We'll find a way to pay for a private school if we have to, but you are *safe*."

The boy's head shook faster than a dog out of water. "No, no, no…"

For one ridiculous moment, Noah thought the boy *wanted* to be bullied or something. He even questioned if kids could become so used to abuse that they forced it to keep happening. But then he remembered Bennie's reaction to hearing Gage's name and knew that couldn't be it. *How stupid can I be? Want to be abused. Sure he does.*

Bennie's whisper was nearly inaudible even next to his ear. "I don't want to go back."

"To school? Okay. Like I said. We'll—"

"No!" That's when the sobs overtook the kid. Shaking, heaving, gasping. "*Back!*"

"Back where?" Then understanding smacked him upside the head. "You mean to foster care?"

Bennie nodded.

"Son, you're *never* going back. This is permanent. Your name change is official even. I should have new birth certificates any day now and they will say Benedict John Pedersen Lampe."

Any hope of reassuring the kid dissolved in Bennie's continuing tears. "Amy said so. She said," his voice twisted into a warped caricature of Amy Foley's voice. "'If there are any problems, we'll come get you and put you somewhere safe.' I don't want to go somewhere safe. I want to stay with you."

And if that wouldn't break any guy's heart, nothing would. "Well, kids don't always get what they want," Noah began, "but this time you definitely do, because you're stuck with me, kid."

With Bennie's face buried in his neck and arms squeezing what was left of it, Noah couldn't be sure he heard right, but he felt confident Bennie had said, "Good."

Twenty-Two

Milton had officially gone crazy. Between making unproductive phone calls, reviewing her accounts, chatting with customers, and carrying on bizarre conversations with Atticus, he'd call out to her every now and then. "If the word mystery didn't exist, what would *you* want to call that shelf?"

"Stop Blaming the Butler." One of these times she'd say something ridiculous like, "The Fairy's Godmother." That'd confuse him. For reasons she couldn't fathom, Milton had decided she amused him. Well, wasn't that just sweet.

"YA?"

It came so fast, she couldn't think of anything ridiculous. "Angsty Hormones on Steroids."

One of the customers in back near the YA section laughed—a deep, rich, sonorous laugh that filled most of the store.

Something in the questions triggered an idea. "What do you think of switching up the Romance section by trope. Friends-to-lovers, enemies-to-lovers, love triangle, secret baby—"

A man in his fifties stopped and stared at her. "That's a trope?"

"Yep. Popular one too."

As if he just couldn't believe it, he tried again. "As in, some guy's girlfriend gets pregnant and never tells him? Then what? They meet up again and…"

"Yep."

After shaking his head a couple of times and turning back to the shelf of epic fantasy, the guy smacked the book in his hand and said, "Not possible." He turned back to her. "That girl would have slapped a child-support petition on him so fast his bank account would still be spinning."

A quiet voice near the front said, "Not always."

Harper turned to see Noah and Bennie entering. Bennie grinned and ran to her. "I take ballet on Fridays now too. Miss Courtney says I can be a mouse in *The Nutcracker!* I fight the toy soldiers." He frowned at her. "But they're girls. I don't want to fight girls, but I have to."

Harper couldn't stand the little guy's sad face. "But Bennie… when you're on stage, something magical happens. You're not a boy, and they're not girls. You're a mouse and they're toy soldiers. Don't fight them when you get off stage, or that wouldn't be good, but while you're there…"

As if in a trance, he repeated, "I'm not a boy, I'm a mouse. Because magic." His eyes lit up. He pulled her closer and whispered, "I found the stone table."

"What?" He couldn't have said—

A little louder, Bennie said it again. "I found it. Up at the park. The stone table."

Comprehension flicked a switch in her mind. "Did you?" She dropped her voice to a whisper and asked, "Did you hear him?"

Bennie nodded. "Mmm-hmm… I put my ear to the table, and it came! I heard it!"

It began in her middle—a warming that spread through her, filling her so much Harper's heart ached. This little guy… he listened for Aslan and *heard* him. How beautiful was that?

He tugged her sleeve, glanced around, and stood on tiptoe to get even closer. "I think the roar is the real magic."

That was an interesting theory. "I like that idea. What made you think of it?" The sight of *Lord of the Flies* being in the gardening section between *Easy-to-Make Green Pesticides* and *Useful Garden Insects* didn't amuse her. She beckoned Bennie to follow as she moved over to the "classics" section and shoved it a few books to the right of its proper place and as far back as it would go. *Loathsome thing.*

This time, Bennie looked around as if hiding before he whispered, "Because of Dad." He threw his arms around her middle. "I don't ever have to go. He promised."

Where would he go? She squeezed him back, staring over at an obviously hurting Noah. Maybe he couldn't go tonight with Bennie so… weird. You couldn't say he was upset, but he wasn't himself. So if Noah needed to be home, well, Milton could just deal. *And I can read* The Last Bookshop in Paris… *finally. She hesitated. Or is it in London?*

"Well, I'm glad you get to stay here. So when is your performance? I want tickets."

"I don't know. But Dad says I need to get the book, so I know the whole story really well. Do you have it?"

She did—the best copy ever. "I do. Come see it." Some of the nicer copies of the book had old-fashioned typefaces that were difficult to read and made the book cluttered, but she'd found one with legible fonts and sweet illustrations published by Reverie the previous year and had bought several copies to keep on hand.

In a small section of the children's "room," as Milton had begun to call it, up on a shelf that would be swapped out with the autumn books later, she ran her fingers along the spines and snatched at a blue one without even reading the words. "Here you go."

"Gramma is going to read it to me while you guys are on your date."

Harper's throat closed. A choking sound behind her told Harper that Noah had followed them. "It's not a—"

"—date, Bennie. We're just doing some work for Mr. Milton."

"Gramma said it was a date. She said it's about time—"

"Never mind what she said. She misunderstood. And we don't even know if they still want us to go on this thing. I may stay home and read the book to you myself."

Before Harper could suggest that it was a great idea, Milton appeared and assured Noah that they definitely needed to go. He didn't even back down when Noah balked a bit and said he wasn't sure if he should leave Bennie right now.

Bennie needed lessons in picking up subtext. "Oh, Gramma and I will read it. We'll have fun. And you can tell me all about the ghosts, and I can show Gramma my pliés and relevés. She said she'd try them."

"What's a plea—yay?" Yes, Harper knew what a plié was, but she also knew he'd love telling her.

Bennie's giggle shot straight to her heart, wrapped itself in a cozy blanket, and made itself right at home there. "Like this." He stuck out his arm and rested his hand on the bookshelf. "You can't squeeze. Just barely touch. Then your heels kiss, but your toes are bashful." He frowned and whispered, "What's bashful? Miss Courtney never said."

If her heart hadn't been stolen, that would have done it. "It's shy. They don't want to get too close."

"Yes! See…" He pointed with his other fingers. "This one's looking at those books down there and that one's looking for something else." A bright smile followed. "Probably for the wardrobe!"

"Probably," she agreed.

"Then you keep your bottom straight under your shoulders and bend your knees." His heels started to come up, but he scowled as he pushed them into place again. "Heels down too. That's first position."

Harper clapped and moved to face him. She grabbed

where two bookshelves met and pretended to hold on for dear life. Sticking her feet out like a basset hound, she stuck her backside way out and squatted, heels tapping her rear. "Like that?"

He giggled. "No… but you know that."

With a wink, she pulled her toes in, rested her hand on the shelf like his, tried to stand tall, and bent her legs. They barely moved before her backside tried to pop out. "Ugh. I can't go straight down very far."

"You're not flexible. Miss Courtney says we do pliés and relevés to keep our bodies flexible when we're old."

And look at that. I just became old. She tried again, going on tiptoe like he did before dropping her heels back to the floor and bending her knees. "Can't I just let my buuuum stick out a little?"

A swift shake of the head told her his opinion on *that.* "Just do them every day. I got mine right by the end of camp."

Noah interrupted the impromptu lesson with a reminder that Gramma was waiting. "Unless you'd rather skip it," he added to Harper.

Harper hadn't been excited to go herself, but the way Noah kept trying to get out of it was becoming offensive. She vacillated between telling him she'd find someone else and wanting to make him suffer with her to teach him a lesson. The memory of Bennie's excitement to spend time with his grandmother did it. "Not at all. I'm looking forward to it."

For half a second, she thought she'd have to confess it was a lie, but then she realized… it wasn't. *Now* she did. She looked forward to making him as miserable as she could the whole time. He'd never agree again, and life could go on as usual.

"I'll come by at six forty-five? Milton said it starts at the depot?"

"Can't wait."

Okay, now that was a lie.

The crisp air combined with the nearly full moon between the skeletons of tree branches that rained leaves down on them at every puff of wind—a better night for a ghost walk, they couldn't have special ordered. Well, fog might have been a cool addition. Those leaves crunched beneath the feet of the ghost walkers as they made their way up and down the streets of downtown Red Wing.

As long as Harper didn't insist that he admit that the walk was pretty cool, perhaps the night would end up a decent memory. Yes, some of the "ghosts" were a stretch, but their guide did a great job of giving it all the spooky vibes people liked in October. If you wanted to go all out, closer to Halloween would have been good, but this was definitely a reconnaissance mission for the store, and with a week of October already gone, it had become a "now or never" situation.

As they passed Twice Sold Tales, random beams of a flashlight hinted at some sort of Morse code. It probably wasn't, of course. But the flashes as it moved between the shelves, in and out of the cozy spaces where people loved to read signaled an eerie message, even if no real pattern existed. Harper started to move toward the door, muttering about how someone had broken in, but Noah stopped her in time. "It's Milton," he whispered. "I bet he turned off the lights just when he thought we'd all get close. You know," he added when she shot him a disgusted look, "to add to the spooky illusion."

The spiel about Liberty's Restaurant prompted a snicker. "What my dad would say to find out his favorite restaurant might have been a brothel at one time…"

"You should bring him on the walk."

A fresh tear in his heart stole his ability to speak. Harper stopped short and stared at him. A sigh followed. "Your dad's dea—um, passed away—isn't he?"

What should've hurt more just made him smile.

Harper Brevig just didn't "do" those words… what were they called? Platitudes? Maybe. Maybe not. Whatever it was, she didn't do it well.

"Dad died three years ago. Heart attack. No one saw it coming." His voice broke on that last bit. Would it ever *not*?

"I'm sorry." Though simple and automatic, he heard something deep in the two brief words he rarely noticed in people's condolences. Sincerity.

"Thank you."

Almost as an afterthought, she fumbled for his hand, squeezed it, and let go so quickly you'd think she'd been burned. Still, it was sweet that she'd tried.

Every now and then, Harper took out her phone and tapped on it a bit. Messages to Milton? Notes about the books she'd thought of? He didn't look, but he was curious. She paid attention and even asked a few intelligent questions that he suspected meant she'd been a teacher favorite. Teachers loved kids who listened well enough to think of something meaningful to ask. He'd never been that kid.

Perhaps it was the darkness, the owl hooting in a nearby tree, or even just the creepy tone the guide's voice assumed, but when he began talking about the Lake Pepin Monster, the hairs on Noah's neck stood and tried to flee. Harper gasped and leaned close to whisper, "Did you know about that?"

Vaguely, he remembered some elementary school teacher assigning a project about Pepie, but that was about it. "There isn't much about it. Just that he exists… allegedly."

At the St. James Hotel, the stories ramped up. The ghosts of the victims of the Sea Wing disaster being the creepiest. Harrowing tales of crying children searching for parents as they wandered the halls and left water in their wake made more than one of the walkers shiver.

Harper's hand slid into his again and this time gripped him hard. Only when she whispered, "I don't remember any story about child ghosts at the St. James," did his own hackles rise. Harper had whispered into his other ear.

It probably said more about his manliness and bravery than he cared to examine, but Noah resisted looking down until his phone buzzed in his left pocket. Instinct sent him reaching for it, and there he saw Bennie, clutching his hand as if it were the only thing keeping the kid from being snatched up by ghosts and carried off to the St. James.

"Bennie!"

His phone buzzed again. Noah stopped and let the rest of the group move ahead. Harper looked ready to bust out laughing. "What are you doing here?"

"You didn't want to come, so I thought maybe you were scared." The boy's lip quivered. "I didn't think I'd be scared. I watched *Scooby Doo* with Mommy." Tears began slipping down Bennie's cheeks. "But I *am* scared. I don't want kid ghosts."

Ignoring the phone going crazy in his pocket, he scooped up the boy and held him close. Bennie wrapped his legs around Noah's waist. Burrowing his head in Noah's chest, he added, "I'm sorry."

Everything in him wanted to scold the kid for going out in the dark without permission, for wandering around town… for *all* the stupidity of what Bennie had done, but he couldn't. His son had tried to protect *him*, and something about that made his heart sing. "We'll talk about it later, but right now I'll say thank you for caring."

When his phone buzzed again, Noah's heart slammed against his chest. "Mom!" He set down Bennie and fumbled for the phone. Sure enough, Mom.

Her frantic jumble of words ended with four comprehensible ones. "—can't find Bennie anywhere." He'd just started to tell her all was well when she added, "I called the police, but—"

Now he broke in. "Call them back. I have him. He followed us here somehow. We'll be home soon."

Hearing his mother near tears ripped at him again.

He'd have to scold Bennie later. Mom couldn't be put through something like this again. But when he turned back to his son and Harper, that decision reversed.

"—dad would have killed me. I don't think my dad ever picked me up and hugged me like that—even when I did something good. So you need to make sure you get permission next time. Kids can't just go wandering around without letting people know where they are. It's one of the dumb things about being a kid."

"What's dumb about being a grown up?"

"You're responsible for whatever that kid does if he wanders around and gets hurt."

Oooh... good one.

"I'm sorry."

Harper turned the boy around to face Noah. "Don't tell me. Tell him."

Bennie looked back at her. "But I already did!"

"Do it again, kid. You can never be too nice when you've scared someone half to death." She grinned. "And look! You made sure you were right! Your dad *did* get scared on the walk."

Just for that, he'd probably find some practical joke to play on her. But he'd think about it some other day. Right now, he needed to get his son home to his overwrought mother. "Hey, Harper? Mind if we leave early? I'll drop off Bennie and then take you home?"

"I can walk—"

No way. This might not be a date, but she'd just comforted his kid *and* taught a great lesson. You didn't just abandon someone after that. "Just give me ten minutes at home and then we'll go back—maybe stop at the local brothel for dessert."

Harper laughed.

He froze. *No way. I did not just say that.* "Um..."

Bennie asked what a brothel was. Harper laughed harder. *Can this get any worse?* Noah stopped that thought before it could grow. *I don't even want to know.*

173

Twenty-Three

I closed my book to be here.

She'd wanted to say no. Despite the humor of his unfortunate invitation, she just wanted to go home and read a book—any book. Even *Mill on the Floss* or *How Green Was My Valley* sounded bearable about now. But something about Noah's invitation screamed desperation, and she just couldn't refuse. *This is why you don't engage with people. You start to care what they think or what is polite or... anything.*

On the way to Noah's house, Bennie explained how he'd made it sound like he'd gone upstairs and instead, had sneaked out of the house and onto the floorboard in the backseat of the car. As much as she admired the kid's ingenuity, she inwardly cheered as Noah gave his opinion on that.

"Did you not think—not even once— 'If I have to hide from my dad, then maybe this isn't a good thing to do?'"

But Bennie protested, "You have to hide surprises and presents. That's what makes them surprises and presents."

Harper could feel Noah stiffen beside her as they pulled into a narrow driveway. She peered up at the small, two-story house, and something settled itself in her spirit. This was exactly the kind of house Bennie should grow up in—cozy and traditional. He was just the sort of kid who would like that and feel secure in it.

A woman flew around the corner of the house, and Noah groaned. "Hey, keep him here until I signal, will you? Mom needs some calming."

"Sure."

The sigh from the backseat prodded her out of her musings of what a house like that might cost and into "help Noah" mode. "Can I let you in on a secret?"

"Yeah." The word had as much life and enthusiasm to it as roadkill.

How to say this without piling on top of what would likely be coming? After a couple of false starts, she landed on close to what she wanted him to feel. "Your dad and grandma are both going to scold you. They'll tell you how dangerous it is to go out like that. They'll tell you it was deceitful and all kinds of things."

"Yeah…" Now Bennie just sounded defeated.

"But what they might forget to tell you, or even if they do, you might not hear, is that they are upset because they're scared. They're scared because they love you. Just remember that when what they say hurts. They love you."

"Yeah?"

Apparently, the ordeal had reduced the kid's vocabulary to a monosyllabic word that had to be run through an emotion detector to translate. Still, she understood him perfectly. "Yeah."

Noah beckoned, and Harper turned back to give him a reassuring smile. "Okay, kid. Time to go say you're sorry and mean it."

Instead of bolting out of the car or even dragging himself through the back passenger door, Bennie squeezed himself between the front seats, hugged her, and whispered, "I love you, Harper," before scrambling out Noah's door.

This time the strange warmth in her chest introduced itself. It had a name. Love. *I love you too, little guy.*

Noah went inside for several minutes before

appearing again, shoulders slumped and head down. When he slid behind the wheel, he gripped it hard. "I'm failing at this."

Laughing probably wasn't the most sensitive reaction, but she couldn't help it. Noah shot her a nasty look which only made her laugh harder. "You're such an idiot."

If the steering wheel had been a neck, he'd be up on strangulation charges by morning. "Thanks."

"I'm serious," she choked out between gasps and guffaws. "That kid loves you so much that he'd risk everything to keep you safe. Where do you think he learned that?"

"His mother, I suppose."

Okay, the guy really was an idiot. He actually thought there was any question. "You, Noah. He learned it from you. When you took him to class and watched over him. When you tried to find a way to protect him from the bullies. *You* taught him to take care of people you love."

Noah shot her a sidelong glance but said nothing. He backed out, drove toward the highway and back into town. As he turned onto Plum, something changed. "Thanks." It might have just been the weird shadows from the streetlights, but it looked like he relaxed. "Really… thanks."

That's when it hit her. "You really don't have a clue, do you?"

At 3rd, he pulled onto the street and parked across from Liberty's. "A clue about what?"

Silly guy. Harper stopped him from climbing out of the car. "You're doing a great job. I don't know what it's like to have a great kid like him, and I know he has to miss his mom something awful, but he's secure in you. He loves you so much."

After a quick look at her, Noah flung open his door and escaped. Harper sighed and followed, but he'd almost made it in time to open her door. When she stepped aside and shut it, he gave her a quick hug he choked out, "Thank you."

Almost as quickly, he moved away and as he led her

across the road, asked, "So what's your favorite dessert here?"

"The bread pudding."

He stared at her. "Are you kidding? They have turtle cheesecake, Ho-Ho cake, sundaes, Mississippi mud pie, choco—"

"You asked. I told you," she groused. "My mom's is mushy and nasty. Theirs tastes like what going home should taste like—if it had a taste."

From the looks of things, several others from the ghost walk had decided to head on over once it was finished. People smiled and waved, and Harper hoped they remembered her and the bookstore when they thought about the Sea Wing disaster or Pepie. And she'd have to make sure she had books on them. "Children's books!"

Noah paused by the booth they'd been offered and stared. "What?"

"There should be picture books of Pepie! I don't know of any. I wonder if Red Wing or Lake City has a good illustrator who knows how to rhyme. Rhyming ones are the best—well… if they have good rhymes."

"And how," Noah said as he slid into his seat, "is a lake *monster* supposed to be a good role model for kids. I mean, Pepie's probably guilty of causing the Sea Wing disaster."

He wasn't wrong, and she could have beat him over the head with her Webster's 1828 dictionary for it. But the moment she'd given her order, and before Noah could say, "Turtle cheesecake," the answer came to her. "But that's the story! And the moral. People blamed Pepie for it for years. And he's innocent. One kid kayaking with his dad finds out and decides to set the record straight." She propped her elbows on the table and plopped her head in her hands. "I wish I could rhyme… and paint or draw or make tissue paper art like Eric Carle."

Only after she'd delivered that genius idea did Harper realize she'd interrupted their server. But the girl was gone, and Noah sat there grinning at her. "Excited much?"

"I talked over you guys, didn't I?"

He nodded. "We understood, though." After another moment, he asked, "So… gonna do a kid's picture book about ghost kids searching for their parents at the St. James?"

Now she really did want that dictionary. A new idea hit her. "Oh, the kid could be Bennie. It's just the kind of thing he'd do. Can't you see it?"

In what looked like slow motion, Noah wilted. "I can't see him kayaking, no. But if he did, and if he met Pepie, he'd totally want to set the record straight."

Bennie was afraid of water? She didn't believe it. He'd told her about swimming in their pool. "Why not kayaking?"

"He likes *dance*."

"So?"

"So he's not going to want something like kayaking." At her attempt at an "are you nuts" look, he kept explaining. "I tried to talk him into soccer or hockey or even swim team. He wasn't interested."

This really bothered him. The ballet? Apparently, although she couldn't comprehend why. Then again, did it matter? She didn't think so. "Look. Those are *team* sports. He's probably not ready to be the littlest kid on a team. He's so *small*. But in ballet, that's probably an advantage— at least for adults. It doesn't mean he might not want to kick a soccer ball around with you."

"Hit the ice?"

She nodded. "I bet he'd love it if he wasn't worried about some kid twice his size barreling at him with a stick."

If his expression meant what she thought it did, he'd never considered that. "Oh, man… Maybe in a few years when he hits a growth spurt. I mean, Tara wasn't tiny like him."

Their server arrived with steaming mugs of hot chocolate for him and tea for her even as panic sent a flurry of warnings to her lips. A rare moment of prudence made her bite them back. Why she needed to be careful, Harper didn't know. *That* she did, she had no doubt. Then a parallel laid itself out in neat lines before her. Harper scooped it up and ran with it.

"It's kind of like the books. You weren't a big reader. You didn't really care about books. But you discovered you liked reading *with* him, right?"

Though Noah nodded, she almost had the feeling he actually didn't like the reading time with Bennie. That poor kid. He thought reading time with Daddy was the best thing ever.

"Well, it might not be your favorite thing to do, but you'd miss doing it with him, right?"

The nod felt a little more certain now. Harper breathed easier. "At the very least, I bet anything you do with Bennie will be like that for him too. At the *least*, he'll enjoy himself because he's with you. But I also bet he'll enjoy a lot of things for their own merit."

"But not ghost walks."

Nearly dropping their plates, the server backed up for half a second before setting them down. "The things you hear when you approach a table?" Noah said with a grin.

She nodded and dashed away.

"Ghost *kids*," Harper muttered before filling her face with the first enormous bite of bread pudding. "Mmmm….aaaah!"

Noah burst out laughing. "Hot?"

"Oooooh…" she sucked in cooling air. "'Youbetcha,' as my Aunt Trudy would say."

"A bit stereotypical, don't you think?"

Maybe she'd get her head bitten off, but with the deliciousness before her, Harper didn't think she cared. "They exist for a reason. Might not be valid anymore, but at one time…"

"So your aunt is a relic?"

"If the stereotype fits…" she retorted as she stuffed in another bite, tossing mouth-preservation to the wind.

Despite a growing dread that he'd try to get her to talk through eating her favorite dessert, it never happened.

The moment Noah tasted his own, all his attention focused on the slow, deliberate consumption of it until not even a single graham crumb was left on his plate.

They didn't even talk on the way back to the store for her tote bag or as he drove her up East Avenue to her apartment. But when she gestured to the correct house, he gave a low whistle. "Nice place."

"I live in the never-used mother-in-law suite. Small and still too expensive for me. I'll have to move if Milton can't fix my tax issues."

Noah let the engine idle and stared at her. "Tax issues?"

"It's breaking me. Milton's driving down to Cedar Rapids to talk with my accountant. He's afraid the guy is cooking the books." Harper couldn't help wrinkling her nose. "I sound like a modern-day penny dreadful."

"Does that make sense to you?"

She laughed. "I called Milton a lit, woke Gen-somethinger. I guess this makes me an out-of-date bluestocking or something."

After gazing at her long enough to become uncomfortable, Noah turned off the ignition and climbed out. Harper followed and met him on the sidewalk. "Well, thanks for the ride and for being a good sport about going."

Noah stuck his hands in his pockets and didn't *quite* meet her gaze. "I'll admit I wasn't happy about it." He gave her an abashed smile. "I'll also admit I was wrong. This was really good for me. And…" He rubbed the back of his neck before shoving his hand back in his pocket. "It was fun."

"Yeah. It was. Just go easy on Bennie. He meant well."

The guy was obviously not ready to think about that fiasco, so he ignored it, nudged her toward her door, and said, "If you ever need a reconnaissance buddy again, just call. I hereby volunteer as tribute."

A smile formed before Harper could stop it. "See… you've read a book."

"Huh?"

"*The Hunger Games.*"

Noah shook his head. "I saw the movie."

Could they be more opposite? "I didn't. I was sure they'd ruin it."

His chuckles told her she hadn't offended him. "Well… it's Jennifer Lawrence. You either love her or hate her." He followed her up the step just like in some movie. So help her, if he tried to kiss her on a coerced non-date, she'd kick him even if she weren't in fourth grade anymore.

"I've never seen anything with her in it. I don't watch that many movies."

"Watch it with me. Come over Sunday night and watch it."

Maybe it was rude of her to laugh at him, but Noah looked so startled she couldn't help it. "I'm sorry…" She reached for the door handle. "I didn't hear that."

But he repeated himself even louder. A second glance at him told her he meant it. "Bennie's too little for it."

"We can watch something for him first… I'll make chili dogs. I make great chili dogs." Noah winced and shook his head. "That's a lie. They're ordinary at best, but *Bennie* thinks they're the best."

Maybe the guy was lonely. A kid was great, but maybe… She shot him a quick look, trying to guess if this was some kind of backhanded pickup line. "I could invite Milton. He probably doesn't get many invitations."

"Great!"

The guy's evident relief reassured her. Maybe it wouldn't be too bad. "Okay, I'll do it."

Noah grinned. "Awesome. I need a veggie with dinner. What do you like?"

"The ones that I can't taste." When he started to argue, she shook her head. "I don't do veggies. You're not going to make me. Give the kid a night off for Pete's sake!" When she saw he'd agree, she threw one more thing at him. "But I'll come on one condition."

"What's that?"

"You read the first chapter of *The Hunger Games*."

At first, she thought he'd say no, then he shrugged. "I would, but I don't own it and can't afford to buy it."

That's all it took. Harper let herself in, ignored the sharp intake of breath behind her, and dove for the bottom of a stack beside the end table next to the couch. With a shout of triumph, she passed it to him and said, "See you on Sunday."

Twenty-Four

Book recommendation: No Less Days *by Amanda G. Stevens is perfect for combining a bit of fantasy in a contemporary setting and all wrapped up in a book that couldn't be a cozier autumnal read if you custom ordered it.*

Instead of enjoying the lovely riot of colors along the route from Red Wing to Cedar Rapids, Milton spent the entire trip letting Atticus know what he thought of Harper backing out of their movie night. Bennie had been crushed, and Noah minded far more than he realized, which amused Milton more than it should.

Atticus, however, couldn't read Milton's emotions well and flip-flopped his comments from "Sucker!" to "Freedom!" (it really was "freedom," Milton decided) to "Milty."

The bird lived, a true testimony to the grace of God.

By the time he turned off Edgewood Road NW, Atticus had gone to sleep, and Milton just wished he could. A glance at the clock told him he still had twenty minutes before his appointment. With the window cracked for fresh air, he took off on a brisk walk around the adjoining shopping center. He could get "Happy Nails" if he wanted them, buy trophies, get a new gaming system, or even buy what looked like a lot of books. Milton resisted the temptation. Barely.

Despite the interior temperature of the Land Rover

remaining pleasant, Milton coaxed the bird into his carrier and hefted it (because Atticus' mango and pepper addiction made him a hefty thirty-one grams these days) and the messenger bag out of the Rover and headed into the office building.

He'd expected a receptionist of some kind. There wasn't one. Instead, a voice from down a very short hall called out, "Milton Coleridge?"

"Yes."

A chair creaked and a thump followed before a man stepped into the hall and moved forward. It wasn't often that Milton met someone shorter than he was, but this man couldn't even be five and a half feet. Shocking red hair, more freckles than anyone he'd ever seen, and teeth so brilliant white they looked photoshopped, "Tom the Tax Tallier" (as Harper called him) greeted him.

"Glad you found me all right. I'd about decided to make a trip to Red Wing whether Harper wanted me to or not."

The first alarm bell rang. "Harper said not to come up? When?"

The guy was astute. Instead of answering, he nodded. "I'll come. I just thought it was grief talking—not ready to deal with things yet." Tom gestured into an office that looked surprisingly cozy—not at all like the dental office rejects he'd expected.

Milton's surprise must have showed, because Tom laughed and said, "I figured if I have to work in this place, I should be comfortable. So, I let my last girlfriend decorate it for me as one of her school projects. She got an A. Her instructor loved that it wasn't another generic CPA office that looked like an eighties dental office."

"I can neither confirm nor deny that I had a similar thought—except that this was lacking that aesthetic, not that it had it."

Tom offered coffee, and when Milton said yes, discovered that the little "mini bar" cabinet opened to an espresso machine, mini fridge, and snack haven. "Sugar?"

So, with one of the best coffees he'd ever had in hand, the name of the bean company in his phone, and all the documents he'd brought with him spread out over a gate-leg desk, Milton and Tom began comparing records. Line by line, month by month, everything seemed reasonable.

Then Tom tapped a line on the printout. "Wait. Wait. Why is she paying the property taxes and the insurance out of the bookstore account?"

"Is there another account she should use?"

The way Tom stared at him sent tingles up and down Milton's spine. And when Tom answered with, "The property account?" his whole body went cold. He'd found it. He might not know what "it" was, but this was it.

"There's a whole account for the building and the property taxes? Separate?"

"Lorene didn't like the rentals and everything mixed up with the bookstore. She said they were two different businesses."

If Spidey senses were a thing, his would be zinging. "Rentals?"

Leaning back in his chair, head slung in his hands, Tom closed his eyes. "I should have pushed."

There was a story there. Milton could almost guess it, but he waited.

"When we had the first meeting after the transfer, Harper decided she wanted me to do her taxes, but she didn't need me for 'all that other stuff.'"

Milton couldn't help but snicker. "That sounds like her. Anders Brevig called me for help when he ran the store for a couple of months last fall. When she returned, she said her mom wasn't dead and that I could go. Almost without a breath between them. Let me call and ask about the property accounts."

While he did that, Tom said he'd pull out what info he had about those bank accounts while he was at it. "I need to get her approval to show you those, however."

"I'll keep her on the phone when we're done so you

can talk to her."

But Tom refused. Insisting he had to call her himself and get her to e-sign authorization again, he smiled an apology and began printing out other documents.

Milton left Atticus in the office and stepped outside. Harper answered on the first ring, excitement bubbling over.

"It's better than I could have imagined!"

"What is?"

"Remember how those ladies left money for the Stadtlers? Well, other people heard about it."

He remembered. "And you told them that what would be more meaningful was if they donated a favorite book or bought it and donated it."

"Right!" Harper's response sounded more like a compliment to him than anything. "Well, people are doing it! I have two *boxes* of books here for them. Everyone's leaving notes in them saying why they donated it. Mrs. Klair brought *and* bought several picture books because she said no one would. Sophie's too big for them. But she said that someday those kids would want books that they'd had when they were little, so she brought her favorites and asked me to find out the kids' favorites too."

"That woman is a gem." And not for the first time, he wished she were a few decades younger.

"Right???"

Apparently, Harper's vocabulary had been reduced to one, monosyllabic word that had to be translated through the lens of inflection.

"Guess what book she brought them?" Harper may not have screamed, "Eeep!" but he heard it, nonetheless. "*Drummer Hoff!*"

It killed him to do it, but Milton had to admit that he didn't know it. "What's it about? Who's the author?"

"'Corporal Farrell brought the barrel, but Drummer Hoff fired it off?'"

Vowing to buy his own copy that very day, Milton admitted he was not familiar with the book. "Who's the

186

author again?"

"Barbara Emberley. It's one of those delightful building rhymes where you repeat the previous ones."

"Order me one. I need it. Now, how much money is in the property accounts?"

When she asked, "What property accounts?" Milton could have screamed, "Bingo!"

Instead, he said, "Can you make an appointment with your lawyer and call Tom? I think we've found your problem. I fear it might be a big one, but I think it also means you're golden." He'd almost disconnected when he decided what the book he wanted to donate was. "Oh, and order whatever series they liked the most for me."

"Great! Awesome. Thanks!" Did she have any idea how contagious her enthusiasm was? Milton doubted it. But before he could tell her, Harper added, "It won't be the same, but all the notes inside and the community support will make them being new worth the loss of looseleft."

He'd done that thing he hated to see people do—listened with an ear to knowing when he could reply rather than *hearing* and attuning to what she'd said—and now he fumbled. "I—wait. Looseleft?"

"It's from *The Dictionary of Obscure Sorrows*. Remember? I showed you, and you ordered one? It's here, by the way."

This girl. Did she have any idea how her enthusiasm alone could sell books if she'd just treat all customers as if they loved books as much as she did? Doubtful, but she would by the time he left. When she called his name, Milton jerked from his thoughts. "Sorry, so what does looseleft mean?"

"That feeling you get when a book ends and the characters are locked away between the covers of the book."

"So… like looseleaf, but you're left feeling… loosed from them. Yes…" Milton had to admit it was a good one. "I need that book."

No response. Not a word. No mumble to a customer, no "just a minute" or any other commonly spoken phrase to show her mind had been distracted. Then Harper whispered, "Do you really think you can save the store?"

"Yes. And it won't be as hard as we thought."

"Then I'll do it."

His heart kicked in, thrumming to what he suspected was the first crack in the glass bubble Harper moved in whenever near people. "What?"

"Learn how to people." A sigh escaped. "If more people were like *these* people—the ones who came in today and wanted to help build this library…"

It might need repeating. Oh, who was he kidding? He'd have to repeat it often—possibly daily. But Milton said it anyway. "Harper, most people *are* interesting and even more multi-layered than the best-crafted character. Some you just have to get a little further into the pages of their stories before they show it."

What else he said, Milton knew she didn't hear. She'd need to chew on that for a bit. So he disconnected and sent a follow-up text. DON'T FORGET TO CALL THE LAWYER. WE NEED A MEETING ASAP.

Milton's words swirled through her mind with the grace of a desultory leaf in an autumn breeze. Could people really be that interesting? And if they weren't, was it because she hadn't opened the covers of their personalities to discover the stories within?

"People as books…"

Another thought tried to pry open another cover, but the shop doors opened, and Mr. Laffey sauntered in, slamming that thought tightly shut again. "The gaggle is out in fine force today. I decided on an early escape."

"Great idea!" She sounded freaky even to her own ears.

The old guy gave her an odd look and then stared at the boxes, interest lighting his eyes. "Sale?"

"Donations—for the Stadtlers. We're rebuilding their

library, remember?" She pulled out *Drummer Hoff.* "Look at this one from Mrs. Klair! See the inscription?" Thrusting the book at him, Harper stood back and waited for his reaction.

"'My daughter loved this book so much that we felt compelled to replace the library's copy when she wore it out. You may not have loved it as small children, but as C. S. Lewis suggests, the day will come when you will be old enough to love it as you might have when you were young enough.'" The sheen that covered his eyes was quickly followed by tears that he couldn't hold back. "I think I'll go settle into the children's room. I think I should be ready for it by now, and if not, what better place to do some growing up?"

Heart swelling, Harper dashed around the counter and hugged him. "I love you, Mr. Laffey." Then she realized what she'd done and jumped back. The man's ears were red, but he swiped at the corners of his eye with one hand and patted her arm with the other.

"Thank you, Harper. I love you too." As he made his way to the back, she heard him add as if only to himself, "You are why this store is so important."

Heart swelling from that thought, Harper remembered Milton's admonition and hurried to the front of the store. While 3rd Street wasn't deserted, she didn't see any regulars wandering up and down the sidewalks and tourists were noticeably absent. Then again, it was early. Confident she could get the appointment set up before anyone came in, and knowing Mr. Laffey wouldn't let the secret book thieves of Red Wing come in and clear her out while she was in her office, Harper dashed upstairs.

Steve Carron's receptionist promised that she could have a Wednesday appointment at a quarter to five. Harper's heart dropped at the time. She'd miss Noah. She owed him an apology. Remembering the woman waiting on the other end, she said, "Thanks. We'll be there," and disconnected.

Now what? She'd have to close the store early. She

really needed an employee. Having Milton around had proven that. She hadn't had to close the store to go to the bank or the dentist or anything since he'd come, and he'd been there less than three weeks!

"That's the first thing I'm doing if he saves my business. I'm hiring help—maybe *my* book thief. Maybe if he has a job here, he'll bring the books back when he's done so I don't have to go hunting around all the little library boxes to find them again."

Mr. Laffey's voice called from downstairs, "Did you need something, Harper?"

And talking to myself is only allowed in my head! Dumb, dumb...

"Harper?"

"I'm fine. Just working out some problems." She saw a copy of *The Mysterious Affair at Styles* and frowned. When had she bought that? A glance inside showed a price of five hundred. A glance at the copyright date, the publisher... "It's a *first* edition—English, anyway! It's worth heaps more than five hundred bucks!"

A creak on the stairs told her she'd freaked out Mr. Laffey. "What's that?"

Turning the pages, she couldn't believe the tightness. No one had ever read this book. What idiot would buy a mystery and then *never read it?* "This book. It's a first UK edition of *The Mysterious Affair at Styles.* Published by The Bodley Head in 1921. It's pristine! Totally worth more than the five hundred bucks someone wrote inside. And it wasn't me or Milton. Not our writing."

Without a word, the man took the book and gently thumbed its pages. "Nice copy. I was thirteen when I read this. *Loved* it. Became a Poirot fan instantly. That's when I became too 'mature' for something as silly as the Hardy boys books." After examining it closer, Mr. Laffey shook his head. "It is a beautiful book. If I could afford it, I'd buy it myself, but it has to be worth many times more than the five hundred I don't have to spare on a single book."

"My thought exactly." As he handed it over, Harper

curled it to her chest and hugged it there. "I think I'll put it in the office and ask Milton about it."

But in the office, she couldn't help but thumb through it, looking for some hint of whose it might be. There wasn't even a book plate from the original owner. No penciled in name at the top of an end leaf. Nothing to hint of who had purchased it or left it behind.

"This is a nice space you've created up here. I hadn't come up to see it yet—my knees, you know." Mr. Laffey rambled on about the displays, the careful way Milton had arranged to protect covers from the light of the windows, the naturalist collection in one corner... "Oh, what a nice little note someone left on your jour—oh, and another. These must encourage you..." But what else he said came out in a mumble she couldn't hear.

Harper locked the book away and hurried out to see if she'd missed a message and found him at the back of the journal reading a two-page spread. "Hmm... I haven't seen those."

"Someone thinks well of you." Again, he patted her arm and went off to his corner in the children's room.

The words on the page swam in jumbled nonsense as she pulled out the chair, plopped her backside down, and propped her head in her hands, elbows resting on the desk. Then the words ordered themselves into reasonably straight, block-letter lines.

You're doing a good thing here.

The world needs more Harpers in it.

You know how they say dogs are a good judge of character? Kids are too. Kids like you. Think about it.

The Lord outdid Himself when He made you.

You're a fighter. Keep fighting for your store.

I just admitted it to myself. I like coming in the store to see you as much as anything else.

"Wow..."

It was probably just Milton, but wow. She had a

friend... a *real* friend. And maybe he wouldn't be here for all that much longer, but they could be pen pals or something. Maybe swap books... be *book* pals. And that would be almost as good.

Twenty-Five

Parenting tip #158: Encouraging good habits always counts—even if your own motives aren't pristine.

Noah parked the Cherokee in the "pick up" space, another ignition recall on the books. A text message came through as he headed back to the bay for his next job. Harper. Interesting. She'd bailed on the movie with no explanation other than, "I just can't tonight." Milton hadn't had a clue either, but they'd turned the movie night into a "teach Bennie how to play Sequence" night. Bennie had stomped them both.

The text message read simply, CAN YOU CALL?

Taking a detour around the side of the building to grab a soda, he hit the call button. Harper answered on the first ring. "Hey! That was fast."

"Just happened to be between cars. What's up?"

"First an apology. Had a hard day at church on Sunday and couldn't people. I didn't know how to explain it. Sorry."

It shouldn't have made sense that she hadn't just told him that on Sunday, but unexpected understanding flooded him. *She couldn't. She was overwhelmed.* With that in mind, Noah worked to calm her. "It's fine. I mean, you still owe me a movie night, or I'm not reading that chapter."

Her "Deal!" and subsequent laughter broke off. "Except you're really going to hate me now."

193

"Not going to happen over a missed movie."

"What about a closed store while your son is in class?" Before he could process that question, Harper rattled on. "I have an appointment and have to close. I'm really sorry."

He fed coins into the machine as she explained about the meeting at the lawyer's office and something about accounts. It was all a jumbled mess, but he had to sort out why her calling to tell him the store would be closed made him... happy. When she apologized again, he snapped out of it. "It's all right. I just hate that you have to close when people are getting off work. Want me to see if my boss'll let me off early? I could hold the fort until after Bennie's class." He sighed. "Wait... that won't work. I have to go get Bennie first. Well, I could close long enough to walk—"

"If you want to open the store and watch while you're in there, I can bring you the key. Just come when you can? You can lock it behind you, too. I should have thought of the key."

Again, she started rambling, and this time he stopped her. "Harper?"

"Hmmm?"

Noah popped the top of his can and took a swig before saying, "Just drop off the key at the front desk and tell them it's for me. And thanks for thinking of me. It means a lot."

The call lingered in his thoughts all through a diagnostic, a radiator flush, and lunch. By four o'clock, he'd finally decided that he was just glad she'd come clean. That was all. Nothing too earth-shattering there. And if he repeated it enough, he'd believe it. Someday.

At four-fifteen, with his hands full of grease, he ordered his phone to play back a voicemail asking where he worked. *"I forgot to ask. Stupid me. If I don't get an answer before I have to leave, you can find the keys in the dead plant next to my door at my house."*

"Call Twice Sold Tales in Red Wing."

The phone confirmed the request as if he'd made a

ridiculous decision and dialed. "Hey, Harper. I'm at R & W Auto Works. Do you know where that is? I'd say leave them at your house, but you probably shouldn't."

"I know where it is, and it's not really out of our way. See you in fifteen. Thanks for opening. If it gets to be too much, just close up."

"I'll keep it open. We need all the revenue we can bring in." That sentence brought him up short. *We?*

What else she said, he didn't hear. She disconnected, and he stared at the phone. Julio called to him on the way to the pop machine. "What's wrong with you?"

And for reasons he'd probably never uncover, Noah said, "I have to man a bookstore instead of watching out for Bennie today."

"You can't do that. Those girls will eat him alive if no one watches."

He met the small, wiry man's gaze. "But Harper is giving me the keys so that I can at least watch some, so I have to make that a priority."

Julio eyed him, his features inscrutable. Then he turned and said, "Come on. I have the thing."

"The thing" turned out to be his drone. They'd all taken turns manning the drone at the Memorial Day picnic. "You take it. You can fly it anywhere and watch the camera. Is perfect."

Noah tried to repress a smile. Julio had near perfect English skills, but when the man became excited, he sometimes swapped out words. But the idea... Sense screamed at him to think. "I can't do this, Julio. If I broke it."

"I have th—" He broke off and tried again, catching his near verbal fumble. "I have insurance. Is fine. You remember how to attach the phone?" Without waiting for an answer, Julio took Noah's phone and had him unlock it. "You just download the app..."

They were still playing with when Milton's Land Rover pulled in. Harper jumped out and strode over, a smile on her face. "Hey!" She stopped. "What's that?"

"Drone… to watch Bennie from downstairs." As much as he tried to make it sound nonchalant, Noah heard a hint of a question at the end of his words.

The wind wisped around them and sent her hair swirling and his senses spinning. Harper grinned. "You have to show me how it works! That's so cool!" Pressing the keys into his hand, she dashed off. "See you later!"

Later. He'd deal with his heart's ridiculous reaction to her touch later. Much, *much* later.

The red brick wall behind Steve Carron's sleek, glass-topped desk kept Harper riveted while she waited for him to enter. It felt much like waiting for a doctor at a checkup. Had she been shown into an empty room when he told her about her inheritance? She didn't remember. If she were honest with herself, she didn't remember much more than, "Lorene left you the bookstore." The rest had presumably gone in one ear, and it had either gotten lost on the way out and was still wandering around the corridors of her mind, or it had dashed out right away.

Milton reached over and squeezed her hand. "It's not the principal's office. You're not in trouble. Breathe."

"I have to pay for this." Harper turned to him, and even as she said, "I didn't think of that," her gaze landed on a painting of *The Sea Wing* on the wall to her right.

The door opened, and the lawyer entered. "Sorry for making you wait. We had an emergency earlier, and I got dirty, and…" The man ran his hand over still-damp hair. "Thank you for your patience."

Steve Carron shook their hands before moving to his side of the desk and dropping into the chair. "Now… Hilary said you wanted information about the will? Did I not give you a copy? I thought—"

He broke off as Harper and Milton exchanged glances. Harper shrugged. "Maybe? It would be in the filing cabinet somewhere." She stood. "Maybe we should go and see?"

Milton tugged her back into the chair. That's when Harper noticed that the high-backed chair with narrow little wings was actually quite comfortable. The cheery mustard color felt incongruous with a dreary lawyer's office, but the office wasn't dreary. And maybe that was the problem. It didn't fit any book she'd ever read.

"If you could explain to her what the actual inheritance entails and any responsibilities she has, I think it would help. I'll take notes." As if to reinforce his words, Milton pulled out his phone and opened an app.

"And you are…?"

Introductions and explanations as to who Milton was and why the bookstore needed a "doctor" followed. Mr. Carron—no, she couldn't think of him as "mister." He couldn't be more than ten years older than she was.

Steve Carron looked confused. "What happened to the bookstore? I thought it seemed as busy as ever—maybe more so."

Harper, in an unexpected and miserable moment of emotional turmoil choked up and gave Milton a "please explain" look.

"Revenue is up, and expenses related to merchandise and overhead are down. However taxes are excessive as is insurance."

"Did Mandy's close? What about the apartment above it? Did the tenant move?"

Harper shrugged. "I don't think so…"

"Then why aren't the rents covering the costs of insurance and taxes? There's been no increase that I know of."

Her heart pounded hard enough to jump into her throat. Milton squeezed her hand again and asked, "And what rents would those be?"

The lawyer gave them both an odd look and after a moment, pulled a few folders from a tray to his left and laid it open on his desk. "There's the property currently occupied by Mandy's Cafe…" He flipped through a few papers before finding the one he wanted and flipping it upside down onto a copier behind him. A moment later, he highlighted a few lines. "And the apartment above. Also at 427 and 429." He passed the documents over. "Taxes and insurance should only be about twenty percent of the total drain on the income. What's happening with the rest of your rents?"

At first, Harper's stomach churned, and she felt the blood drain from her body. Then a flush followed as she realized she didn't *owe* those rents—someone owed her. "So… I *own* these buildings? Not just 415?"

"Yes. We went over this at our meeting back—"

Harper cut him off. "I wasn't really paying attention. Once you told me that the aunt I thought hated me had left me her store, I was kind of dazed." She was kind of dazed right now too—no, no kind of about it. Her mind refused to work anymore.

"And your accountant? Why—?"

Here Milton took over with an explanation while she processed things. Her mind tried to make a mental note to have an advocate with her on all business meetings, but even as she did, she realized she probably wouldn't remember.

And whatever else they discussed, she couldn't have said. Only one thing stuck firm in her mind. *I'm not going to lose the store.*

When Bennie heard that Noah would be taking care of Harper's store, he begged to miss ballet class. Of all days for his kid to want to skip class, it would be the *one* day that he wanted Bennie in there. Convincing himself that the reason was "because we need to stick with our commitments" was harder than convincing Bennie. The boy remembered that he'd been given a role to play and that was a privilege. Bless Miss Courtney for drilling that into the kids' heads.

198

He'd only been behind the register for five minutes when a kid came in and sauntered downstairs to "the dregs" room. Should he leave the front and check on things down there, or…? Before he could decide, two jabbering, middle-aged ladies came in, followed by harassed-looking men. Husbands, of course.

"Welcome to Twice Sold Tales. If you need help, just ask. I'll probably be useless—just filling in for a friend—but please ask. I'll do my best."

One of the men stared at him and then gave a slow clap. In Noah's world, that was often sarcastic, but this guy nodded as he did and said, "Finally. Someone admits they don't know everything. Refreshing."

"When it comes to books, I really don't know about anything but the first few Narnia books. My son's a fan."

The men went upstairs to the new "collectors'" room and the women headed over to romances and rom coms. Noah pulled out his drone and pulled up the app to pair them. While everyone seemed busy, he stepped outside and put it on the ground. Getting the hang of things again took more effort than he would have expected, but eventually it rose, flew across the street, and hovered by the window.

Elbowing his way inside again, Noah kept his gaze trained on the screen as he tried to get the best view of his son. It wasn't working. He tried again, his mind going through every instruction Julio had ever given them, every conversation about the stupid thing. Why hadn't he paid better attention? Why had he gotten all worked up about this? It was just a stupid toy!

Panic set in, and he ran up the stairs as fast as he could. He'd watch it with one eye on the actual drone and one on the screen until he got the thing safely across the street again. No more silly tech solutions for what his eyeballs could do just fine on their own. At the windows, he struggled again. The men came alongside, watching and offering "helpful" suggestions.

After several commands that did nothing, the drone finally reversed. Midway across the street, it dipped a bit, but Noah managed to convince it to steady out to eye level with him. That's when he realized radio interference had to be at work. If he could only avoid the "loss link" message. Then it came. One minute, he'd finally had the thing zipping along the street at a nice, slow pace and the next, it shot forward and smashed into the top of the window above Noah's head.

A couple of pieces of glass fell and smashed onto the floor. Both men cheered for reasons Noah couldn't fathom. A voice at his shoulder said, "Let me have it. I'll get it down."

He turned to find the kid who had gone downstairs standing there, hand outstretched. Like an idiot, he passed over the controls and watched as the kid angled, adjusted, and without looking where he was going, went downstairs to retrieve the thing. He hoped.

That's when Noah realized the drone could be damaged. *I can't afford to replace this. And insurance or no, I can't expect Julio to cover it. That's just wrong.*

It all happened at once. The kid returned with an undamaged (as far as Noah could tell) drone while the women asked about *Finley Donovan Is Killing It.* Harper walked in just as the kid handed over the drone and informed the women that the book was great, and he had high hopes for the second and third ones in the series.

"Harper hasn't gotten them yet."

Harper broke in. "Well, Harper thinks she can afford to now. And I'd like to talk to you upstairs in my office, please."

The please sounded tacked on to his ears, and something in the kid's stance unnerved him, so Noah stepped to the left to block the exit. The bulge of at least two books jutted out from the kid's back. Great. Now he'd have to chew out the kid for stealing even if he didn't bolt, which Noah suspected would happen any moment now.

After staring at Harper for a moment, though, the kid shrugged and took off upstairs. Noah moved to ring up the book, but Milton was there. Harper pulled him aside and bounced on her toes. "It's not so bad—I mean, it is. Money—lots of it—has gone missing, but we can find it. And even if we don't, I can get the future rent money and I'll be okay!"

Everything around them faded away from his consciousness, and only Harper's gray-blue eyes sparkling up at him mattered. "You found the problem then."

She nodded. "I didn't listen to the will thing very well. My inheritance is way big. I don't think even my cousins know what it involves. And I'm *not* running the store into the ground." Harper bounced up on her toes, hugging herself. "Milton says I'm actually doing a really good job. I can order more books!" Before he could congratulate her, she gave him a shove toward the stairs. "Get up there and watch for Bennie. We can talk later. I want to watch that movie. Okay?"

"Pizza after class? I'll buy. Celebration for all of us."

She followed him up the stairs. "Get enough for one more. I'll pay for it. I'm going to hire me some help. I just hope he says yes."

Noah's heart sank. "You can't do that. He's got two books hidden in his jacket. The kid's stealing from you."

Half a minute later, he stood there at the top of the stairs, staring at the semi-closed office door, her "I know!" still ringing in his ears.

Twenty-Six

Reader (noun) def: explorer of alternate realities

Just as Harper began to shut the door to her office, The Kid shook his head and stood. "You shut the door and I leave. No one's gonna accuse me of some kind of assault."

He had a point... the same could go the other way, and with Noah out there listening, she'd have a witness. She left it at halfway and moved a stack of books from the stool next to her desk. The Kid offered the swivel chair he'd already claimed, but Harper shook her head. "I'm good." She nodded at his jacket. "So what are you reading today?"

All bravado drained, and he reached into his jacket to remove the books. He passed *World Without End* by Ken Follett and *Salted with Fire* by George MacDonald over to her without a word. After comparing them for a moment, she shrugged and handed them back. "You're an eclectic reader, aren't you? I thought you preferred classics, but first Finlay Donovan and now Follett?"

"Just call the cops and get it over with."

Flicking on her tea kettle with one hand, Harper reached for her box of teas with another, ignoring the comment. "Okay... going for Lyons. Jennifer Deibel swears by it according to a podcast I heard, and so I tried it. So good. Want some?"

The Kid just shrugged.

"I'll take that as a yes," she said and pulled down another mug. "Sugar? Half & half?"

"Both."

Wow. He speaks again. While she readied their mugs, she laid out her plan. "So… I wondered how you felt about a job."

Silence.

"You read a lot. You know books. I mean, you're like George in *You've Got Mail.* You know everything. I need you."

This time, The Kid looked up and stared at her. "I steal books from you, and you give me a job? What's that about?"

Even Harper admitted that her argument was illogical at best, but she plunged forward, anyway. She needed the help, and a kid who loved books, knew about them, and didn't talk all the time was the perfect employee as far as she was concerned. "I figure you can't afford the books, and you don't have a library card for reasons I don't understand." He would have spoken, but she shushed him. "I don't even care. So a job here means you can read whatever books we have, take home and bring back whatever books you want, *and* I don't have to go all over town trying to find the books you've left everywhere."

"If you figured out the system, you would've known where to go every night."

So she was right. He did read a book every day. "How do you get schoolwork and homework and all that reading done?"

"Simple." He accepted the mug when she passed it his way. "I don't do my stupid homework."

"You should."

The Kid just shrugged, and that annoyed her.

"Okay, I need a name. I can't keep thinking of you as 'The Kid.' What's your name?"

After a tentative sip, The Kid set down the mug and said, "Devon."

"Romantic name."

He snorted. "Dorschmitt."

"You should change that when you become an author."

That earned her a sharp look. "How'd you know I want to be an author?"

She shrugged and pulled out her phone. "Let me ask Milton how to hire someone."

"I didn't say I'd work here."

"But you will. I'll pay a dollar over minimum wage and a twenty percent off employee discount. Afternoons and evenings from three to seven. Any hours you want on Saturdays or holidays." Harper tapped the screen before grabbing a pen and a pad of sticky notes. "So… what hours do you want?"

Milton answered with, "All the ones you can give me" at the same time Devon said, "All of them."

"Great. A couple of wise guys. Whatever. Milton, I need your help hiring Devon. I don't know how to do this."

He promised that he was already on his way up and would send Noah back down, so she disconnected and sipped at her tea. "Mind telling me why you don't just go to the library?"

"Can't get a card."

Behind those four short words lay a novel's worth of subtext. She could just feel it. "Misspent youth?"

"My mom's husband." The adjective he used before "husband" filled in half that subtext.

"Look, I don't want to start things off on a bossy note, but the swearing stays outside or between the covers of books that idiot publishers didn't let me edit."

Devon rolled his eyes. "You like a sanitized world? Or do you just think that the use of four-letter words is evidence of a limited vocabulary or whatever?"

"Neither. I just like to see authors be creative enough to show the meaning of the language or what prompted it rather than take the easy route." She gave him a grin. "But as far as the store, I just want this to be a place where parents don't have to worry about what their kids'll hear." Before Devon could take it off into an argument, she added, "So, you have to have parental consent to get a library card?" She didn't remember that.

The anger that flashed in the kid's eyes told of deep-seated resentment and who knew what else. "I had one. But after the third time he destroyed a book while having a tantrum over whatever rule he made up *after* I broke it, they took the card away."

"Destroyed a *book*?" She slammed down her tea mug and then scrambled for tissues to mop up the splotches of tea that spattered everywhere. "What kind of monster destroys books?"

When Devon didn't answer, she glanced up to see Milton leaning against the doorjamb sharing amused expressions with him. "What?"

"I think what Devon isn't saying is that you answered your own question," Milton said. After a moment he turned his attention on the boy. "I have to ask. Are you safe at home?"

"Basically. Nothing I care about is, so I have to care about nothing—or at least be perceived as not caring."

Something in the words sent a shiver through her heart. "Is your mom…?"

"Oh, I hate her. Didn't you know? Can't speak a civil word, always steal from her purse, never sneak off campus at weird times to see her at work. Because I'm a bad son who…" He lifted his hands with a hint of an upturn to one side of his lips.

Cold fury combined with incredulity tumbled together until Harper's self-control fled in its wake. "That—"

"Is not pleasant to hear," Milton broke in. "Let me get Devon squared away, and I'll explain the process later. Right now, you're needed downstairs. Several people have books for the Stadtlers, Mrs. Klair is back and in a heated discussion with Mr. Laffey over the merits and demerits of the anti-federalists, and the T-shirt order arrived. You'll find the cut-outs in the closet downstairs."

Harper might not have passed "Reading Social Cues 101," but she knew a "get out" when she heard it. "Fine." To Devon she added, "Get my address from him. If you ever need a safe place, it's there."

"No." Harper and Devon looked Milton's way. "That's just the kind of thing a man like that would exploit to get at him. Give him a key to the store and keep an air mattress or something in a closet, find a *family*—not just a man—for him to go to, but not your place or Noah's."

Noah's? Why would he go to Noah's?

She'd have argued, but Devon nodded. "He's right. Sid would totally ruin someone else's life to get to me."

Fine. She'd just talk to Jake about it, then. Meanwhile, she hurried downstairs. The moment played out like a trailer for a movie or something. Harper breezed past the bickering older couple with a "Take your spat outside. You're irritating the owner." At the counter, she gratefully accepted an armful of books that filled the next box, told a reporter where he could take his article about the Stadtler box collection and threatened to sue if he gave away the surprise by trying to interview them, and dove for the large box blocking the path to the right of the counter.

"Oh, look. It's a fire hazard. I'll have to open it right away. So sad."

A chuckle behind her nearly made her drop the box cutter she'd grabbed. "You're a lousy actress, but fabulous at sarcasm," Noah informed her. He took the cutter from her. "And you'll ruin T-shirts if you wield that like I've seen you do before."

Ruin? How would—? "Ohhh…"

They'd chosen five T-shirt options to start with and had promptly ordered five more which would probably arrive in a day or two. Of course, *Reading is lit* and *Book boyfriends don't cheat* had made the cut, what with the cutouts they'd ordered. They'd argued for ages and finally decided on: *Read me alone* and *It's read o'clock* for two more. Harper wanted the last one Milton had suggested—wanted it desperately—but she'd been convinced it was too much. Only when Mr. Laffey had insisted he'd buy one if she got it in his size had she agreed to *Books: your best defense against unwanted conversation.* Old advice doesn't just die hard, it resurrects like that stupid fern she'd buried under the lilac bush.

One by one, she pulled the shirts from the box—two of each size in both men's and women's. They'd even ordered kid sizes for *It's read o'clock.* Now she wished she had more. "I need to order a set of these T-shirts for the Stadtlers."

"I want one for Bennie. He wears fives and sixes."

Harper dug through the box until she found a Youth S. "Look at that one. I have an extra small too, but it's probably too small."

A middle-aged woman on the other side of the counter asked for a book boyfriends shirt, and Harper felt compelled to give Jake's opinion on it. "I mean, he's not wrong," she said as a final admission, "but I still wear mine when no one will see me."

"He *is* wrong. It's not cheating if everyone consents, and books by nature are meant to be shared."

Though she agreed in theory, Harper couldn't help but feel like she'd just turned reading into risqué behavior. *Can we talk about that one later, Lord? I'm all confused now.*

Behind that woman, another voice called out, "I'd like a 'read me alone' in a unisex medium if you have it." The girl... no, she was definitely a woman, peered around book boyfriend lady and smiled. "I want them all, but let's start here. I just spent way too much on a purse as it is and..." she held up a stack of books. "I kind of blew my book budget just walking in the door."

That "movie trailer" feeling reappeared. Harper turned, almost hearing the voiceover playing in her head. *Harper Brevig: book lover, plant killer, and soon-to-be successful bookstore owner. In a small Minnesota town, one little bookstore proves that books bring people together in unexpected ways.*

And it was true. A group had clustered around the counter, necks craning to see what she'd pull out next. Two men near the back held out tote bags that obviously held books. "For the people whose house burned down. We heard about it at Liberty's and came right over," one said. The other added, "You should get some of those T-shirt graphics put on tote bags."

Harper turned to Noah. "Can you grab a sticky note pad and go around and take orders? The next shirts, mugs, and tote bags coming are…" She fought to remember their final selections. "*Crazy book lady (cats optional), Booktrovert: A person who prefers the company of fictional characters to real people, Books > People, I don't hoard books. I rescue them from bookstores,* and one about the definition of readers being explorers of alternate realities—but it looks like a dictionary entry."

"No." When she sighed and reached for the notepad, he added, "What's the store's email? I'll tell them what's coming, and they can email an order. That way if something isn't clear, you have contact information that I didn't get written down wrong or something."

"Even better. Do that." She stood on her toes, kissed his cheek, and went back to stacking T-shirts. Right up to the second she realized what she'd done. Then she fled.

Twenty-Seven

Book recommendation: If you're looking for mystery with a dash of almost slow-burn romance, you can't go wrong with Rosemary for Remembrance *by Audrey Stallsmith.*

I f he and Devon hadn't come downstairs at the precise moment they had, he'd have missed it. The crowd, the mess, the "kiss." Then again, could you really call such a brief peck an actual kiss? Considering how Harper bolted less than three minutes later, clearly, *she* had. And now with her first hire on the books and a significant dent in her new T-shirt line, Milton arranged Mr. Darcy and Anne Shirley on either side of the T-shirt display and went over everything they'd learned with Atticus.

"It all ties back to the management company. The question being, are they ignorant of her ignorance and just socking away rents into the account, unaware that she isn't collecting them, *or* are they siphoning off some? That's what we have to find out."

"Sucker!"

But despite the little guy's taunting cry, Atticus flew up to Milton's shoulder and nuzzled his neck. Milton crooked his finger and stroked his buddy's head. "I hope it's just a miscommunication, but something feels off."

The parrotlet purred as if desperate to comfort. As much as Milton liked to joke about his bird's antagonism, Atticus couldn't have been a more affectionate friend. He still had nightmares about the accident that should have cost the ornery bird's life. "I think we should send Mercedes a box of steaks soon—maybe while we watch a movie tonight."

"Popcorn."

Atticus' new word. Once the little guy had begun talking, he'd come up with a new one every two or three months, and most of the time used them with surprising accuracy. "Definitely popcorn."

What he wanted to do was clear away the mess of rearranging the front room, go over to Noah's, and watch everything play out there. A little romance was just what his heart ordered, but the situation wouldn't solve itself, and he had gotten an email from a woman in the Florida Keys asking if he would help her figure out how to stir up the locals and get them interested in reading. The store itself did great with the tourist trade, but she'd bought it as a way to get to know her new community and now…

"First up, where are Harper's bank records? Checkbooks? All the things that should've been red flags. Where are they?"

Upstairs, of course. In the office. But despite the extremely neat and tidy place, nothing was actually organized. *"Aunt Lorene had a system but beats me what it is,"* Harper had muttered when asked.

"Let's go, fellow. We'll find the stuff and see what it all means."

Atticus hated Harper's office for reasons Milton hadn't decided on yet. So, he set down the mini baking sheet with a few sheets of newsprint in the bottom for Atticus to do his business and opened the office door. It wasn't a tiny room, but fitting more than two people would definitely make it a bit crowded. The back wall had been fitted with one of those cube shelves from Ikea. The left wall held a desk with more shelving above it. The right wall had only some shelving and a file cabinet in the corner.

"I'll start with the files, Atticus."

"Sucker!"

210

"No cucumber for you."

"Pretty, pretty."

He'd created a flattering monster. But at least the little guy was cute. And fun. *And the best friend I have.*

The file cabinet turned out to be a bust. Instead of hanging folders of invoices and paid bills, it held packaging in one drawer, a one-cup coffee pot, filters, and coffee in another, a first aid kit in the third, and the bottom drawer held… a blanket? Milton didn't want to know why.

By the third cube on the shelving system, Milton couldn't take it anymore. All wrapping and packaging supplies went into one stack. The tax files—did she even know she had those just sitting on a shelf?—went in another. Two dozen books (all rare) had been tucked away among the different shelves and drawers in the room. They now sat nestled in a box he'd found downstairs. A ledger recording all the rare book sales—well, up until Harper took over, he suspected—had kept company with misprinted paper bags. It now sat in the rare book box. She'd have to help him update it.

Then he found it. A cash box—fireproof and locked. Where to find that key…? Or was it one of the ones on the ring in the register drawer? Milton hurried out and smiled at Atticus sitting on the journal and contemplating the corner. "Don't you dare chew on that."

"Pretty, pretty."

"And we'll keep it that way," Milton agreed. He stepped close and held out his hand. Atticus hopped on and gazed at him. People could say what they liked, but his bird knew how to look adoring when the moment called for it.

Three weeks. He'd been in Red Wing three weeks. How had it been so long? Though he tried to reset the clock to just over two, the truth was… three. In another couple of weeks, Halloween would be here. Then Thanksgiving. Then off to Noel, Missouri for a Christmas wedding.

"Where should we spend Thanksgiving this year? We

211

don't have any corporate work until that thing in Houston at the end of January."

The answer was Florida, and he knew it. He'd go, help out, stick around, and have shrimp stuffing or some other revolting idea for his Thanksgiving dinner. Probably in a little restaurant manned by people resenting not being at home.

Just as he turned away from the journal, Milton caught sight not just of the words on the page it was open to but of ghosting from the other side of the paper. He paused to read. *What you're doing for this community is better than your rarest book.*

He flipped the page to read what had shadowed through and found a thick set of block letters. BOOKS DARED ME TO DREAM AGAIN. THANKS.

Beside it, another message read, *Why are real life guys never like the ones in books?*

Though Harper hadn't noticed it yet, one of the things he'd bought at IKEA was a semi-Windsor-looking chair in black to sit at the journaling desk. He'd also bought replacement knobs. Milton suspected she'd notice those first—if she ever quit avoiding looking at that "awful desk."

Seated on the new chair, Atticus resting on the neck of his T-shirt, Milton flipped back to the first page. It just had a date penciled in. Page by page, he flipped but he'd gone ten or fifteen before the first note appeared. *I read a book once where a couple met in a bookstore, fell in love, and eventually ran it together. I want that to be my story someday.* Had the writing not been so overtly feminine, he might have wondered if it had been meant as a not-so-subtle pick-up line.

The next entry was almost near the middle. It had been embellished, unlike most of the others, with a viny border, little flowers, and a banner. Inside, in beautiful hand lettering, the caption read, *Some say books are like drugs, which would make bookstores dealers. I say books are like therapy and bookstores are mental-health facilities.*

He snapped a picture of that one. It described his

own personal relationships with books and bookstores perfectly. "I'll share it on Instagram, but I want it for when I'm struggling myself," he whispered to Atticus. The bird purred and nuzzled his neck.

The next entry couldn't have been more opposite. *Books are stupid and so are the people who read them.*

"I think someone got his gaming system taken away and was told to pick out a book."

"Stupid."

"You said it, Atticus."

"Read it!"

Milton stroked the little guy's head and turned to the next page. *Is there a book that tells me what to do with my life? Not a "there will be a nurse shortage in ten years, so go into the medical field" kind of do but something that gives me purpose outside of making a buck?*

That the writer would ever return to see if anyone had left an answer—probably not likely. But Milton pulled out a dark green pen and wrote, *John 1:1 "In the beginning was the Word, and the Word was with God, and the Word was God." If you are looking for answers that have stood the test of time, you won't find a better book than God's. There's one waiting for you at the counter. Just ask for it. No charge.*

Three pages of differing versions of "I like books" written in childish print prompted a grin. Another few blank pages followed until he found one with one word in tiny print. BROKEN.

It ripped out his heart. "How do people make it through the day, much less a week or a year or a *life,* without Jesus?"

Atticus probably *didn't* say "Jesus," but it sure sounded like it.

"Might not want to pick up that one. People might think you're being flippant with the use of one of God's names."

A crude poem followed a few pages later. Milton covered it in sticky notes and set an alarm to remind himself to warn Harper about that. Several more pages over, another group of messages were clustered across a two-page spread. They'd obviously been left by a group of friends shopping their way across Minnesota bookstores. His favorite? *When they start allowing people to identify as bookstores, can I marry Twice Sold Tales?*

He passed comments about how stupid or great this or that book was, comments about how old books are better than new and new are better than old, and even comments sharing how excited the person was about an upcoming release. One page held a small square with the words, "I read because the moms in books understand me." Below it, right at the bottom of the page and in tiny script was, *Moms read in hopes that they will learn how to show their kids how much they love them.*

When he finally got to the block list, Milton grinned and pulled out his phone again. "I was right. It is him. Time for Harper to read and see herself through a good man's eyes."

The phone buzzed just as he went to take the picture and blurred it. "Hey, Noah. How goes the movie and pizza?"

"Sure you don't want to come help me eat all this. Bennie and I will be eating pizza for days. Even Devon didn't eat enough to make a dent."

"What about Harper?"

"Didn't show. Again."

The man sounded as discouraged as a guy could be. Milton covered Atticus with his hand and rose. "Give her a few minutes. She'll be there."

"Maybe it's best. I probably—"

He couldn't let Noah give up on something so important. They needed each other. Even if they couldn't see it, he could. So Milton broke in. "Will you trust me when I say it's important—to both of you?"

"I don't know… and it's a school night."

A year ago, I bet you'd have laughed at the idea of "school nights" meaning anything to you anymore.

But before he could argue, Noah sighed. "Well, if you

can get her to come, maybe we can salvage things. As it is, I think she's going to run and keep running… indefinitely."

"Make popcorn. She'll be there in fifteen."

If only he felt as confident as he sounded. After taking a *good* picture of the journal, he hurried downstairs, put Atticus in the carrier, and locked doors behind him. It was only a two-minute drive to Harper's house, and she answered at first knock.

"I saw you drive up. What's wrong? Did you find something?"

"I think I found what we need, but in the meantime, I also found what *you* need—to *read*."

Relief had never looked so stiff and uncomfortable, but relief it was. It masked feelings and uncertainties, and who knew what else. "Give over. I need an escape."

Milton passed the phone to her.

"I guessed that you wrote those. You're an—" She broke off and whispered, "'*Why do I feel like a middle-school girl who doesn't want to wash her face again?*'" As if in denial, she reread it again… and then again, louder each time. Lifting her head, she met his gaze and whispered, "I thought it was you. I thought we'd be *book* pals, writing back and forth about what we were reading."

"Well," Milton couldn't help it. "As Wodehouse said once, 'There is no surer foundation for a beautiful friendship than a mutual taste in literature.' I definitely want to be your 'book pal,' but I didn't write those."

Harper stared at the screen again. "I guess not. Looks like I'll have to go into the book merch business after all. I can never go back to that store now."

Did she have any idea how like a melodramatic middle-schooler *she* sounded? It was too delicious. "Yes, you can. But first you're going to put on a clean shirt and comfy jeans. You're going over to Noah's house, and you're going to watch that movie."

"But—"

But nothing. Milton wasn't having any more of the middle-school girlishness. Noah had pegged that right, but he'd pegged it on the wrong person. "But nothing. You'll apologize for overreacting to a simple thank you and sit through a few miserable minutes until you both relax again. Then you'll thank me tomorrow. Now go."

Leaves rained down from the trees around them, some swirling at his feet. Harper stared at him for a moment, and he expected to have to argue the point. When the door closed, he debated between opening it again and walking on in or pounding. Instead, he prayed. Truthfully, it felt a little silly standing on a girl's porch on a half-moonlit night and praying that she'd open the door and go make up with a guy who was nearly as unsure about her as she was about him.

Milton zipped up his coat against the ever-chilling night air, leaned against the porch railing, and gazed out over the lawn, up, down, and across the street, and to each house on either side of him. Many had been decorated in some form for fall or Halloween. One had an enormous skeleton—six feet or more—and bats "flying" all about it. In reality, they'd been put on stiff, narrow springs that bounced in the breeze. Several had jack-o-lanterns. Others just a bit of hay or a few gourds.

Was it his imagination, or had people gone all out for the season this year? She'd want to keep note of that for next year if it became a trend. *And you're avoiding prayer. If you can't talk to your Best Friend when you have a problem, what can you do?*

He really didn't know the answer to that, but Milton made it as far as, *Give me wisdom, Lord,* when the door opened, and Harper stepped out.

"I'm going, but I don't have to like it."

A girl like Harper wouldn't be much into hugs or other physical contact, but Milton couldn't help but think she needed it. Oh, well. Maybe Noah could handle that for her. After all, *she'd* been the one to kiss *him*.

"Just remember, Harper. He's a good man. He obviously admires you, and he's in a tough spot. He might need encouragement."

216

She'd started down the steps, but that stopped her. "Encouragement for what?"

"To explore how he feels. It'll take him time. You'll need to be patient—"

"But I don't *want* to do the feels and the—"

This time Milton broke in. "Yes, you do. Think about it. You *do*. So give him the space he needs but also encouragement. And he'll do the same for you. Trust me."

With a huff, she took off down the steps, but at the sidewalk she turned back. "You're supposed to be my business advisor. When did you become my relationship coach?"

The silly girl... she thought she had a choice. He jogged down to meet her and draped an arm around her shoulder, ignoring the way she stiffened at first. "That's easy. When I became your friend."

Twenty-Eight

*Parenting tip #172: Make no promises that depend on others. It
won't save you from your own mistakes but...*

Noah sat on the couch, still gripping his phone. Not
for the first time (that minute), he checked the
clock. Ten minutes down, five to go. Maybe he'd
relax when fifteen came and went without any
sign of Harper. That she'd refuse, he had no doubt.

At eleven minutes, the room came into focus. Open
pizza boxes, paper plates, pop cans. Cleaning it up for
Harper's benefit—total waste of time. However, he couldn't
leave it forever, and once cleared away, he'd feel less...
um... *reminded* of getting stood up. Again.

This time it hit harder too. He'd ignored the
disappointment the first time. After all, he hadn't admitted
to himself then that he *was* interested. But now that he
couldn't deny it, her excitement about coming ending in
another no-show had sucker-punched him. *Not gonna lie,
God. This one hurt.*

With pizza stuffed in Ziploc baggies in the fridge, the
boxes stashed in the recycle cans, and the few dishes left
from breakfast stowed in the dishwasher, he decided that
grabbing the laundry and starting a load might be smart
too. Halfway up the stairs, his phone buzzed with a
message. SHE'S COMING.

Noah froze. Was she, though? Really? And even if

she did, would she the next time she said she would? Bennie had been crushed when she hadn't arrived. He couldn't do that to his son—couldn't let anyone else do it either. And yet, to his disgust, he turned around and went to flip on the porch light. Just in case.

After all, people can be funny when they're embarrassed. His neck burned at the memory of that page in the journal. *Like admit they're acting like a silly teen girl.*

Noah stopped his hand from going to his cheek just in time. Good grief! It was bad enough that he'd felt the half-second touch of her lips on his cheek for far longer than he'd ever admit, but did he *have* to tell her about it? And even now, did he *have* to wonder what it would be like knowing she'd *chosen* to…

"Enough." His voice echoed as he hit the top of the stairs. A quick peek in at Bennie showed the kid out cold. Considering the blankets were half off, that might not be an exaggeration, either. Noah took a moment to pull them up over the boy's shoulders and tuck his foot back onto the bed.

At the door, he glanced back, remembering how hard Bennie had worked to hide tears. No, he couldn't let this happen again. He'd learn to fly a drone and sit in Mandy's every Wednesday and Friday and all during rehearsal week and watch from there. They'd order their books from Amazon, save money in the process, and just let her fade out of their lives.

Despite this resolve, Noah kept one ear trained for the doorbell as he dumped the armload of clothes from the hamper into the washing machine, dropped a Tide pod into the mess, and cranked the old dial. Say what you would about those old washers—they sure kept chugging away while newer ones went on strike on a regular basis.

Ten minutes later, he gave up and went to turn out the light. A shadow flickered across the door window. *No way…*

When he opened the door, he noted a rustling of leaves rather than the drone of cicadas and chirping of crickets. The cold air—it must be down into the thirties—sent a shiver through him. Harper had turned, walking away when the creak of the door reached her. She turned. "Hi."

A suspicion prompted him to ask, "How long have you been out here?"

"Um…" She shoved her hands in her pockets. "I—"

Regardless of what he thought of her (or, rather, wanted to), the thermometer to her left read thirty. He couldn't leave her in the cold. "Maybe you should come in."

That earned him a cocked head and the furnace kicking on at the same time. "You're not mad at me?"

"Frankly, I am. But I'm going to be madder if you get me arrested for global warming or climate change, or whatever it is this week. Either come in—"

Harper squeezed past him, her gaze lingering on his cheek for just a moment. *Interesting…*

"Sorry I didn't come." She stood in his tiny entryway, hands stuffed in her coat pockets, trying *not* to look at him and failing. "I…" She gave up on that and shrugged.

Noah managed to squelch the groan he *felt* into a sigh. Leaning against the arched doorway to his living room, he gazed at her. Something was different, but he couldn't figure out what. Hair? No. Makeup? He stared closer and stopped himself from shaking his head just in time. He needed to say something before she bolted. He'd figure out what it was later. "I didn't take it to mean anything, Harper. I saw it as you just being thankful for the help."

That little round face flamed. *Glasses!* Though he tried to repress a smile, it crept up on him before he could stop it.

Harper glared. "What's so funny?"

"Not funny… I just like your glasses."

This time the irritation didn't come. Instead, hurt flashed in her eyes, and she moved to the door. "Fine. Whatever."

She'd managed to twist the knob and wrench it open

before he caught on. "Where are you going?"

"Anywhere they're not going to make fun of me. Ugh, this really is like middle school."

"I'm not." He moved to half-block the door. "Seriously, Harper. I've always thought you'd look adorable with big round glasses… and you do." The glasses were such a bright blue that they turned her usually gray-green eyes nearly aqua, which made him wonder why she ever went without them.

After hesitating a moment, she turned and stomped into his living room and plopped down on the couch. "I don't understand you."

That makes two of us, sweetheart. The thought came in a Humphrey Bogart accent, and Noah couldn't help but wonder how he knew that. "What don't you understand?"

"You're mad at me."

No matter how hard he tried to deny it, he couldn't. "Yeah."

"But you compliment my glasses."

There he shook his head. She scowled, and Noah rushed to explain. "You, Harper. I'm complimenting how *you* look wearing them. Couldn't care less about the glasses. They just bring out your eyes." And with the skeptical look she threw him, he went for broke. "They really are beautiful eyes."

"Stop flirting."

This time he laughed and sank into his usual chair— the one he never got to sit in anymore, because Bennie had taken to wanting to snuggle up next to him whenever they sat in the living room. What dad would miss out on that? "I wasn't flirting."

"Were too."

He might annoy her more than ever, but two things made him continue to argue. First, *he* was still annoyed with *her*. But even more than that… it was fun. "Trust me, Harper. When you're ready for me to flirt with you, and I do, it won't look anything like me mentioning your eyes in some offhand comment. You'll *know* I'm flirting."

And he was good at it. Out of practice? Definitely. Three years as a Christian had been three years of no dating—partly out of his own sense of self-preservation and partly because rumors had gotten around about his "BC" behavior. The "nice girls" at church wanted proof he'd really changed. The rest of the singles group—ones with more… *experience* like he had—knew that like alcoholics avoided booze traps, they needed to avoid their own temptations.

Never had the absence of conversation screamed so loudly at him. Noah fumbled for *something* to say, and if the way Harper picked at her jeans and squirmed meant anything, she felt it too. Just as he remembered to offer her a drink and started to ask, her head popped up. "So, are you going to start the movie?"

She's really here to watch it? Noah didn't think so. He pulled out his phone and sighed. "It's almost nine. We won't get done until eleven, we'll talk about it. It'll be midnight, and I have to be up at six. That means I'll spend the whole time *not* enjoying it."

"I'll go." Harper jumped up and rezipped a coat he hadn't noticed her unzip in the first place. Had she gone out with it open? "I really came to say sorry—and to keep my word this time. So… again, sorry. Tell Bennie—"

"No." His mom would kill him for not walking a guest to the door, but his ire had flared again, and he didn't know if he could be civil if he got up. And if he were honest with himself, which he definitely would not be, he'd be tempted to show her what a kiss really looked like— what it really felt like. And he could do it with just a couple of seconds of his lips on *her* cheek. Not a good idea.

"No?" Harper shrugged and moved toward the door. "Fine. Whatever."

"You tell him yourself. He cried, Harper. He's convinced that he did something to make you not like him." She would have protested, but he kept going, throwing the words at her with the speed and accuracy of a professional dart thrower. He'd deal with how good it felt later. The twisting of his gut hinted that it wasn't right. "He said, and I quote, 'She's not mad at *you*. She kissed *you*. So it *has* to be me,' when I tried to convince him you were upset with me."

"But I wasn't! I was upset at me. I was embarrassed and—" The words broke off in what might have been a sob. Noah refused to look and see. "Did he really cry?"

Noah sighed and dropped his head in his hands. "Yeah."

It felt like a clock should be ticking. Stupid as it was, maybe he'd ask for one for Christmas. No... he needed practical things. Like that area rug he still hadn't bought. Then he felt it—a hand on his shoulder. "I'm sorry. Can you bring him tomorrow? I'll apologize. Explain that it was my fault. That I broke your trust."

That's when he remembered something. "Like I broke your window." He raised his head and stared at her. "I forgot. I broke it. I'll pay for it—or replace it myself if I can. I'm sorry."

"What window?"

"Upstairs."

A slow smile formed. "Leaning against it?"

Noah rose and shoved his hands in his pockets and shook his head. "Drone attack. Pilot error. No worries. He's been grounded." Of course, Noah realized if that were true, he couldn't buy a drone and use it at Mandy's. "Think the owner of that bookstore would let me keep watching with her binoculars instead?"

"Maybe if you let me have a piece of cold pizza since her dinner is now shriveled and cold in the microwave?"

He retrieved the baggie of pepperoni pizza and carried it to her car for her. Instinct said to flirt, but uncertainty won out. An apology didn't negate the fact that she'd hurt his kid. There was no rush. If things were supposed to go that way... they would. Someday. But that day didn't have to be today.

So instead, he stood on the sidewalk and watched her drive away. The taillights went up the road, turned around, and shot past him. Had she waved? Why did it matter if she did?

"Gah! I don't know what I'm doing here! I could use some help, God!"

But the Lord didn't boom out answers from heaven, so Noah went inside, shut and locked the door, and pulled out his phone. The Bible app began playing the moment he tapped the button, but when the narrator got to the part where the Levite sent out his concubine to protect himself from the men of the city, he shut it off.

"Not sure what kind of help that's supposed to be, but it's not the mental picture I want to have before I go to bed. Sorry, Lord."

He kicked back in his chair, pulled out his phone, and ten minutes into playing *The Walking Dead*, realized the hypocrisy of his complaint. Before he could stop himself, he uninstalled the game. *I shouldn't have this where Bennie can see it anyway. It would freak the kid out.* And if it would freak out his kid and was as gruesome as a Bible story he'd considered too much to listen to at bedtime, maybe...

Well, he didn't have to decide if games like that were right or wrong right now. He did have to protect his son from them, though. So that's what he'd do.

I'll just figure out what You think of it all later, okay? As an afterthought, he added, *And I'd love to know what You think of the whole Harper thing?*

Twenty-Nine

Give me books over "real life."
(Real life makes a Dickens plot look simplistic).

T he cash box yielded a treasure trove of information. Checks, past registers, a small, handmade notebook of passwords and important information, and a key to a safe-deposit box at Associated Bank. Her name was on paperwork as the beneficiary. According to the notebook, it also held the deed to all properties managed by Rivertown Management. *See Paul Kinford,* it read below the information.

While Harper gathered everything together, Milton called Tom the Tax Tallier—she really needed to stop thinking of him that way. She listened with one ear out for anything telling, but all she could be certain of was that Tom would be going over all accounts and books—in her store. He was coming to Red Wing.

I never wanted all that fuss. I just wanted to be with the books.

Sandy the mail gal came in with the day's haul—no bills, thank goodness—and it included a modest-sized but heavy box. The handwritten name on the return address *felt* familiar, but she couldn't place it. A slash with the counter scissors opened it in a jiffy, and Harper unfolded the flaps to find several well-loved but good condition Agatha Christie paperbacks, a few yellow-backed Nancy Drews, two Hardy Boys, several Gladys Mitchells, and a collection of Sherlock Holmes stories. An envelope at the bottom had the flap tucked in, so while Harper felt confident they were meant for the Stadtlers, since her name was on the box and no name on the envelope, she opened it and pulled out a small note card with a few small sheets of paper enclosed. She read.

Harper and her friends,
Lorene and I were friends from the first day we discovered the Bobbsey Twins at the library. We were only allowed three books back then, so we each took three and walked the mile between our houses every other day to swap books. We did that for the rest of Lorene's life. This box contains some of our favorites, and I hope you enjoy them and share our love of mystery. I didn't have any Bobbsey Twins to include. Perhaps Harper would grab a couple and invoice me?
I was devastated to hear of your loss, and while these can't make up for it, I hope they may offer a little distraction.
Cordially,
Tess (Ivers) McCall

Book swap… an idea sparked, but the cover of *The Murder at the Vicarage* caught Harper's attention. She'd never seen this one with its clerical garb and a tennis racket for a face and neck instead of a person. Clever… She ran a thumb over the cover. Maybe this had been one of the books they'd swapped. Aunt Lorene might have read it. She peeked inside to find the penciled words, *Beware of dying parishioners* on the flyleaf.

Laughter bubbled over. One by one, she opened them all to see tiny hints of what they'd find inside without actually giving away any spoilers. Genius!

"Milton! Check this out."

The man jogged down the stairs and came to her side. "Funny you should say that. Tom's coming to check out the accounts. He'll be here tomorrow, but he wants you to sign onto the bank's website and print out copies of the statements for the last eighteen months. He also wants you to go down there and see what all is in the safe deposit box.

Deeds, obviously, but he wants to be sure there isn't anything else."

Before she could respond, he looked at the box, the book in her hands, and the letter. "More donations?"

"Yes. This one's the *best*. I don't know how she found out about it, but it's wonderful."

The door opened again, and Mrs. Klair pushed through. "Morning, Harper." She set *Britt-Marie Was Here* on the counter and thumped the cover. "Better than a lot of garbage published today, but not up to his usual standard." She stared at the box. "Mysteries? Nice... Eclectic..." She thumbed open *The Murder at the Vicarage* and saw the name inside. "Whew! Tess Ivers. I haven't seen that name in a decade or three. She was a frie—" A smile formed. "Nice inscription. She sent it for the Stadtlers, didn't she?"

"She did," Harper said. But she watched Mrs. Klair, uncertain. Something about her seemed... off. "Are you feeling all right?"

"Just a bit winded. I've been all over town this morning."

Was it her imagination, or did the woman sway? "Why don't you have a seat, and I'll get you some tea and a book?" Though she tried to make it sound like a suggestion rather than an order, Harper suspected that escorting the woman to the nearest chair and thrusting the first book she could grab at her might be a bit on the demanding side.

Mrs. Klair set down her handbag and stared at the cover. "*The Extraordinary Deaths of Mrs. Kip.*" A smirk played around the corner of her lips. "Is this a hint, Harper dear? Should we grab a sharpie and turn Kip into Klair?"

"No!" And before she could be even more awkward, Harper bolted for the stairs. If the chuckles that followed meant anything, her attempt failed. Oh, well. As long as she rested and was fine. Harper *needed* her to be fine.

You're just being ridiculous after getting that note from Aunt Lorene's friend. Face it, Brevig. You didn't think of Aunt Lorene as having friends. You used it as an excuse to avoid them. Now what?

That was just the trouble, she thought as she filled the tea kettle with water and flicked the lever. She'd nearly convinced herself that when Noah decided friendship was out of the question, it wouldn't matter. She didn't *need* friends. "But I need *them*," Harper whispered to herself.

Her favorite tea only half filled the infuser, so she pulled out another similar one and compared. Both had black tea and cornflower. One had safflower and jasmine while the other had green tea and mallow petals. Close enough. She nearly filled the infuser with the second blend and stopped. Didn't she have some German breakfast somewhere? It would have some more caffeine to boost her a bit.

So, with a blend that may or may not be delicious, Harper ignored her identity crisis and focused on Mrs. Klair's tea. She added sugar for a boost but no half & half. With so little of the breakfast tea, it wouldn't need the smoothing effects of cream—even if Mrs. Klair turned out to be a heavy creamer.

She arrived, tea in hand, to hear Mrs. Klair telling Milton about the Stadtler's new house. "Apparently, the kitchen is 'abysmal,' according to Tammy, but they'll refurbish it next spring. For now, since it's unoccupied, they're renting it—moving in today in fact. They don't have much to move, so it's not going to take long, but Sammon's is delivering mattresses, and they've got a few people dropping off donations."

Harper whirled to face Milton. "Can you go to Ikea again? Get a few matching bookshelves? I like those." She pointed to the shelves that ran along the left wall. "Just found out they're Ikea. Lia-something. The assembly instructions are in the office. We'll drop them and the books off on their porch tonight and do a ding-dong-ditch."

"You and Noah will. If I lift those into my Rover, you guys will have to get them out."

It seemed flimsy to her, but Harper was too excited to care. Then again… "Or I can see if Devon is available."

228

The guy's expression shifted to a combination of panic, and she could see the wheels turning—proof. Milton Coleridge was playing matchmaker. She'd suspected a time or two, but this couldn't have been more obvious if he'd slapped it on a T-shirt and tied it to their Ebenezer Scrooge cutout in the "dregs room." Well… they'd see about that.

But before she could begin implementing the diabolical plan to thwart him (the one she hadn't thought up yet), Milton turned her toward the door. "Go to the bank. I'll call to have the upstairs window repaired, and then I'll hit up Ikea when you get back."

Window? Oh… the one Noah broke. Bank? Right. Bank. "Be right back. It's just a block over."

She'd made it to the door and adjusted a stack of manga offerings near the window when Milton called out. "Can you start printing out the statements before you go? I can start looking into those while you're gone."

Back upstairs, into the computer, get the security code, dig it out of the store's email, back into the website… and for what? She'd return before it all finished printing. Still, ten minutes later, she sat in the little room at the bank, staring at the contents of the safe deposit box. The letter explaining Aunt Lorene's decision to leave her the store— the one that Harper had just *known* would be in there— wasn't. There wasn't even one for Anders explaining why he, the favorite nephew, hadn't inherited anything but an equal portion of her personal bank account, stocks, and life insurance. A share that Harper hadn't gotten, of course.

Instead, the box held the deeds to the Twice Sold Tales building, Mandy's, 427, and 429. That was it. She held back the last two deeds and put back hers and the coffee shop's. An idea had been growing ever since Steve had informed her that she *owned* them. It was only right, after all. Giving her the store was one thing. Harper loved books. The building only made sense. But those other two…

By the time she returned to the shop, she'd settled it. Unless Milton saw a reason she was being totally ridiculous, she'd do it. She'd give Anders those other buildings. *It's not like they've done anything but bleed me dry anyway…*

The air in the bookstore sizzled with something Noah couldn't put his finger on. Beside him, Bennie clung to his hand, still uncertain that this was a good idea. Only after seeing how unsettled the kid was had he realized how right Harper had been. She *did* need to apologize. And after a night of tossing and turning over everything, he needed to kindly but firmly friend zone her. Not that it would bother her any. The kindness and firmness were all for him.

A customer at the counter asked Milton something, and the guy lit up. "Harper! Get down here!" The poor woman looked terrified until Milton murmured something to her. Holding her phone to her ear, Harper jogged down the stairs, stopped in the middle, disconnected, and raced the rest of the way to Bennie's side. She dropped to her knees before him and, oh help, tears. Now what would he do?

"I was a bad friend last night. I didn't come when I said I would. Again. I'm sorry."

Turmoil radiated from Bennie—the desire to forgive and be restored, the fear that it wasn't real. Noah felt every emotion rippling off his son, and it tore at him. Who had taught him that apologies weren't to be trusted? Tara? He hoped not. One of her (apparently) many boyfriends? That would be almost as bad. Foster care? Would the day ever come when he didn't want to blame something else on something that should never have been a part of his child's life in the first place?

"I trusted you."

Whoa… of all the things to say after an apology. Part of him felt like he should scold Bennie. Another part wondered if it would only teach the kid to hide his feelings. He'd have an ulcer by the time he was ten if he kept it up.

"I know. I broke that trust." Harper's gray-green eyes

never left Bennie's. "I hope you'll give me another chance. I'm still learning how to be a friend. I haven't had very many."

"Me either." Bennie's hand relaxed in Noah's. "I—" After a couple of false starts, Bennie released Noah and flung his arms around Harper. "I love you, Harper."

Heart constricting, Noah stared helpless as she hugged his son and shot him silent pleas for assistance. He shrugged. She glared. "I love you too, Bennie."

Though the words sounded wrung from her under protest, no one would have doubted her sincerity. Bennie moved first, his feet shuffling and pink spots on his cheeks. "Are you coming to watch a movie tonight?"

She shook her head. "Can't tonight. But any Friday, Saturday, or Sunday your dad says is okay, I'll come." Though Noah expected her to add, "I promise," she didn't. If anything, it added a ring of sincerity those words couldn't have.

"Harper?" Milton gave them an apologetic look. "Sorry to interrupt, but I thought you'd like to see the first coupon redeemed."

Bennie went to look at books, but Noah inched closer, wondering what the coupon was and why it mattered. Then he remembered. The bookshelves they'd put in Mandy's. The woman using it even agreed to a photo for Instagram, which was perfect as far as he was concerned.

Milton scooted his way and watched with him as Harper discussed the woman's book. It sounded like some minimalist thing that everyone was talking about these days. "She has no idea how good she is at this," Milton murmured.

It was true. Then again, did Milton know how good he was at finding problems, fixing problems, and bringing out the best in people? "Well, if you ever decide you want to take up some kind of childcare matchmaking service, I'd be your first customer."

"One of the biggest woes of modern times," Milton

agreed.

"I can't afford what it's worth. It's more than I make. I mean, how do you put a price on someone taking care of your kid. But if I don't put a price on it, *I* can't afford to take care of him."

"Have you asked at church?" When Noah admitted he had, Milton shrugged. "Had to ask. Sometimes people don't start with the obvious. What about other churches? Cornerstone? Harper's church? Did you ask the ballet teacher?"

He hadn't asked Harper or Miss Courtney. "Those are good places to try next. Thanks."

"You could ask Harper about it tonight if you're willing to help with the book delivery. It's all in my Rover and ready to go, but Harper needs help, and I already loaded stuff. I'd appreciate if someone else unloaded."

"Is there room for Bennie in the car? Mom's busy through Monday—out of town with some of her friends."

"No... I have the seats down." Before Noah could apologize and back out, Milton said, "But Bennie and I can hang out here with Atticus." The man glanced around before lowering his voice and whispering, "We got in a copy of *Teach Your Child to Read in 100 Easy Lessons* today. I've been wondering if a different approach might not be just what Bennie needs. I could let him see me try to decide where to put it, and maybe it would spark a conversation. If I could get him to ask..."

"Please. The remedial classes aren't doing a thing. If anything, he's regressed. Can you even *do* that?"

Milton's shrug was not reassuring.

Thirty

Parenting tip #197: Don't be afraid or too proud to accept help from others.

Anyone who said hefting long bookcase boxes from Ikea was easy lied. Then again, had anyone actually *said* that? Moving them across a lawn littered with crunchy leaves and propped up next to the stoop without alerting the inhabitants of a house? Equally difficult. Actually, Noah decided it was harder. Stacking heavy boxes of books so that opening the door was still possible… frankly, the whole job had turned out to be a near nightmare.

Twice the front light had come on and the front door had opened. No one stepped out onto the screened in porch, however. He just had to hope that the neighbors assumed they were the Stadtlers moving in more of their stuff. Anyone really thinking about it (and knew who had moved in) would know better, though.

With everything in place, Harper hissed for him to move Milton's Land Rover. "I'll ring the bell and then run across the street and hide behind that bush—whatever kind it is." Though she didn't ask, an implied question hung between them.

Noah shrugged. "No clue." And before he had to defend his lack of horticultural knowledge, he dashed off to move the Rover.

233

Harper waited for him to get into place before pounding on the storm door and racing to his side. They hid behind the bush and peered through and around it as an irritated Tammy Stadtler stormed out, ready to do battle, and froze at the sight of the boxes. Then she saw the Ikea boxes leaning next to the door. "Brian! Get out here!" A second later, she added, "And bring the kids!"

Tammy scanned the area but didn't see them, or if she did, she pretended not to. "She'll know it's you," he whispered.

Harper seemed to deflate. "I know... I just hoped maybe they'd be so excited, they wouldn't think about it."

Across the street, Dalton called out, "Mom! It's *The Hobbit!*"

Sophie squealed and dove into a box. Tammy's head swung from the kids digging into boxes to her husband wrestling with the bookshelves. Then she burst into tears. A hand slipped into Noah's, and this time he had no doubt it was Harper's.

"Let's go," she whispered.

Noah kept hold of that hand until they reached the Land Rover. Once behind the wheel, he started the engine and leaned back in his seat. "Thanks for letting me be a part of that," he whispered.

"Thanks for coming." Her whisper was nearly inaudible. Then she added just a bit louder. "Why are we whispering?"

Though Noah tried to move away from a whisper, he wasn't much louder. "I don't know." That prompted a few nervous chuckles.

Twisted in her seat, Harper watched as the family wrestled everything inside before saying, "Maybe we should've just helped."

Again, he watched her, looking deep into each flicker of interest in her eyes, each tug of amusement on her lips, each spark of interest in the world around her. "You know, you like to keep to yourself a lot, but you're also pretty generous with your time and resources."

"Their *books!* They lost all their books!" she protested.

But Noah shook his head and cranked up the heater a bit. "I don't buy it. You like to help."

Harper countered that with, "I like to *have* helped. I don't actually like doing it most of the time. I'm just glad I did when it's over."

"Remind me never to ask you to babysit." He'd meant to joke, but it came out harsher than intended. "Sorry. That—"

"Anytime." In the distant glow of a streetlight, he could see she meant it. "I love Bennie. He's such a neat kid. If you have some work thing or a date or whatever… just call."

Did she know that Milton would have him on that date with *her?* He suspected she did. Harper might be a bit socially awkward, but she wasn't stupid. "Too bad you have a store to run and bills to pay. I'd hire you to watch him after school. At least he'd feel safe with you." There, that was a good lead in to asking for childcare recommendations.

"Can he walk from school?" Before he could answer, Harper added, "Or… would you care if Devon walked him to the store from school? He could hang out with us for a couple of hours every day. It would be fun."

Any other person saying, "It would be fun," in a near monotone wouldn't have been remotely believable, but Noah felt it. Sincerity. "I—"

But Harper fumbled overhead until she found the dome light and broke in on his reply. "I'm not usually unreliable, Noah. If I say I'll be waiting for him, I will." She shot him an awkward smile. "Even if I embarrass myself."

"I wasn't angling for an offer," he protested.

As if she didn't hear him, Harper made another one. "Or we could try it out a few times—see how it works."

Noah turned off the light, put the car in gear, and pulled away from the curb. "Why does it matt—?" He shifted his thoughts as the answer came to him. "You don't have to try to make up for not showing. It's over. Done."

235

"I wasn't."

As he rolled through leaf-strewn streets back to the store, Noah realized it was true. She wasn't. She just liked Bennie and wanted to help. He'd have to figure out what it meant long-term, but he also needed her to know that he didn't take advantage of friendships that way. And that was the moment he realized that the friendship would stay. It had to. Whatever else it did or didn't become didn't matter right now.

He pulled over in front of a house he'd wanted during his house hunt. It had everything—a big yard that would be easy to mow, three large bedrooms, an upstairs *and* a downstairs bathroom, great kitchen that maybe, just maybe, he'd someday learn to use well. It was bigger than the house on Wilkinson Street, but not so big it would be a burden to keep up. And the payments… very top of his affordability quotient.

His mother had advised against it, and his realtor had agreed. Kids were expensive. What if Bennie needed braces or turned out to be a piano virtuoso? Could you be a virtuoso on anything but a violin? It didn't sound like it, but what did he know? The point had been, they'd been right, and he'd settled for a good, solid house where he and Bennie could make memories.

Now he pointed it out to Harper. "I almost bought that place."

"Too bad you didn't. Bennie could've gone home after school, and I'd be just a minute away if he needed anything."

"No." At her sharp look, he sighed. "I don't want him alone that much. He's too little now, and even in five years, it's not healthy. Most of the kids who got into stupid stuff when I was in school were kids who had no one home when they got there."

"That doesn't mean…" Harper went on, trying to reassure him.

But she didn't understand. She didn't feel the weight of knowing that if he messed this up, he'd have to live with it for the rest of his life. He *needed* Bennie to have every advantage, every confidence, all the security the kid could ever dream of. Because he knew what it was like to lose a dad as an adult. Losing a mom as a little guy? Unthinkable, even if Tara hadn't settled down. He still didn't know if he wanted to know the truth on that score.

"—but he's your son. You know what he needs. If you want him safe with an adult somewhere, then the shop is perfect. He has lots of help for homework, a place to work puzzles or build something with Legos, and I can even send him to drop off packages at the Post Office when you think he's old enough so he can get some exercise. Oh!" She grabbed his arm. "We can get him a scooter. He can scoot up and down the back walk too. It'll be great."

He couldn't let himself laugh, but the way she practically squealed while hardly changing her inflection sounded a bit like the robotic tones of an artificial intelligence reader, and it was funny. "We'll try it—at least until I can find someone I can afford."

Harper sank back looking pensive. "And if Bennie loves it and doesn't want to go somewhere else, will you think about letting him stay?"

Noah put the car in park and turned to her. The girl was too cute for his own good. Her expression shifted from pensive to hopeful. Much to his disgust, Noah realized he was sunk. "Think, Harper. I'll *think* about it." And he'd have to think hard too. Because in that moment, he realized that if Bennie got too attached and things didn't work out with Harper on even a friendly level, his son would be hurt all over again.

At six o'clock on the dot, Milton locked the doors and turned out all but the back lights. He left the window lights on, though, and moved to the counter to close out the cash drawer and put the day's take in the bank bag.

He'd lock it in the safe for Harper to deal with later, but for now, it had to go. A glance back at Bennie showed the boy almost buried in the huge bean bag chairs, book in hand, face scrunched up, lips moving.

It had been a good day. Most of the days at Twice Sold Tales kept enough sales going to keep the store in business and still provide a profit, but ever since Harper had started the book drive for the Stadtlers (and her 25% off "Stadtler Special" hadn't hurt), it had bumped up enough to even create a decent living. But was it just the sale, or had their Instagram campaign already begun to draw in new customers? He could only hope.

"Hey, Bennie?" The boy looked up. "I'm going to take this upstairs. I'll be right back."

The office was still a mess, but he had managed to put files in the top drawer of the filing cabinet. Baby steps. The bank bag went into the fire safe and got locked in there before he hurried back downstairs. Behind the counter, he pulled out a box of books he'd been squirreling away the whole time Noah and Harper had been gone. Kids' books mostly. Atticus squeaked at him.

"Sorry, pal. Let me just set out your poop tray…" That done, he opened Atticus' cage and offered his hand. Atticus hopped on, but the moment he was free, the bird flew to the pan and left a deposit. Milton offered a piece of bell pepper and hefted the book. "Teaching you to use that was the smartest move I've made yet."

"Read it!"

Bennie looked up as he moved into the back room. "It's taking them a long time. Do you think they got caught?"

With a shrug, Milton pulled out the first book, a semi-battered but beautiful mass market paperback of *The Little White Horse*. The enchanted forest background set off the little unicorn nicely, and the silhouette of Maria looked… ethereal. That was the word for it.

He held it up. "Have you and your father read this one?"

"What is it?" Bennie didn't even look up from the book he struggled so hard to read.

While Milton described the story of the London orphan, her uncle Sir Benjamin, and life at Moonacre Manor, an idea he wanted to explore presented itself. "Feel like helping me find homes for these books?"

The bean bag rustled as Bennie extracted himself from it. "I guess."

Well, if nothing else, the boy would get a break from the reading struggle. "It's a classic," he explained as he showed Bennie the book. "But it's also fantasy. Where do you think I should put it?"

"By Narnia. It looks like it belongs with Narnia." Bennie took the book and slid it on the shelf next to the motley collection of Narnia editions. "There."

"How about this one?" *Ramona the Pest.* Beverly Cleary was always a good idea.

If anyone had doubted Bennie's attachment to the little room at the back of the store, they'd have squashed them at the sight of Bennie heading straight for the other Beverly Cleary books. "It goes here. See? There's another one with that word right there." And so there was. *Beezus and Ramona.*

"Good catch." He pulled out a few more, two they set aside for the YA section out front, and finally he reached in and pulled out *100 Easy Lessons.* "Hmm… I wonder if this should be back here or up with the educational stuff."

"What is it?" Bennie stood on tiptoe to see. "Looks like for grownups."

The copy was an older one—with the yellow border and a sketch of an adult working with a child. But Bennie had said exactly what he'd hoped. "Well, yes and no. It's for parents to help their kids learn to read—to make it easy for them. So maybe it goes where kids are looking, or maybe it goes where parents might search for help."

"Does it work?" Bennie's expression took on a comical, skeptical look. "Reading isn't easy."

239

"It's not at first, no. But the *lessons* are easy."

"Oh." Bennie then scowled at the book. "Can you show me? If they're really easy, it should be here—where kids need easy. If it's not, you don't want to make kids sad when they can't do it."

Bennie marched over to the little table set out for kids, but Milton lowered himself into one of the beanbag chairs. "You don't have to sit *with* me, but I need comfy if I'm going to learn." Pull up a chair or a beanbag, or I can scooch over and make room."

To his relief, Bennie came and leaned close next to the chair but didn't climb up with him. It hinted that the boy wasn't starved for connection. Noah might need to know that.

"This will probably be really basic for you. After all, you're almost reading, but it's good to go through all of it in case you missed some of it after your mom passed away."

Though Milton heard the boy swallow hard, Bennie didn't cry. Was that good? He wasn't confident it was or wasn't. It just seemed like he'd heard children needed loss acknowledged, and so he did it.

A soft, "Mommy didn't help me with reading. She said it was teacher's job."

"I'm sure your mom had a good reason for saying that, but I don't agree with her. She probably just had been taught that, though."

"Whose job is it, then?"

Wishing Noah were there to stop him if he overstepped, Milton tried to sound nonchalant as he said, "I think anyone who cares about a child should help him read. Parents, teachers, grandparents, friends... even silly birds if they know how," he added when Atticus flew to sit on Bennie's knee.

That seemed to relieve the boy. "Yeah. If Atticus could teach me, I know I could learn."

"I know you can learn period. When is always the key. But look how simple this is." Milton opened the book and began with mmmm as he moved his finger along the line.

By the time they finished the lesson, which only took about five minutes, Bennie had decided. "You should have that book on both shelves. That way kids and grownups can see it. But I want it. I can do this. I know I can."

He passed over the book. "Then take it home. It's yours."

"I don't have any money."

As much as Milton wanted to say it didn't matter, a basic marketing principle stopped him. "Well, then you'll have to do a little work for it." Some kids might have insisted that their parents would pay for it, but Bennie hopped up. "I can do work. I'm good at my jobs. What do I do?"

The dust-free shelves got a sound dusting, the books got straightened, and the floor Swiffered before Noah and Harper walked in. Bennie dashed over to Harper to show the book, and Milton pulled Noah aside. "I think the blockage comes from trying too hard compounded by him just getting the hang of things when his mother died. Try cuddling up on the couch and making it a game. Let him lead. I bet he'll want more than one lesson a day at first. Just let him do it."

Noah looked ready to break down. "What do I owe you?"

"Nothing. Your son just worked his little heart out to earn it." At Noah's quick look, Milton smiled. "If you had even the hint of an idea that he didn't *want* to learn, you were dead wrong."

Thirty-One

Your nose in a book keeps it out of other people's business.

"*The days passed on, the weeks passed on, and the track of the golden autumn wound its bright way visibly through the green summer of the trees.*"

Could there be a more autumnal, late-October read than Wilkie Collins' *The Woman in White?* Harper didn't think so.

Curled up in her favorite, over-sized chair, she shifted the throw to cover her toes, took a sip of still-hot tea (Those mug warmer things were amazing. She'd have to get them for the store.) and resumed her read. The convoluted wills of the English never ceased to confuse Harper. Twenty thousand pounds for this, ten for that, income for this, goes to the husband for that, but if she doesn't marry, then nothing for this or for that. If she does, her son (if she had one) received the other.

It was enough for her to send a heartfelt, "Thank Aunt Lorene for me," skyward and hope the Lord passed on the message. Of course, she'd botched Aunt Lorene's set up. If only she'd kept things the way the "old thing" (embracing her inner British now) had them set up, she wouldn't be in the mess she was now.

But it wasn't the time to think of that. Harper adjusted her throw pillow, draped her lower legs over the arm of the chair, and scooted sideways and settled back in.

Oh, how she hated both Fosco and Sir Percival. A delightful shiver ran through her. And that was one of the best things about fiction—hating whoever she wanted guilt-free.

An hour later, the brilliant Fosco line tripped her up. *"The fool's crime is the crime that is found out, and the wise man's crime is the crime that is not found out."*

Harper set the book on the floor, pulled her knees up to her chest, and considered this. Maybe she should call Jake the Cop and see what he thought. But was it a case for the police when she hadn't even *asked* about the accounts yet? Then again, if there was any hanky-panky going on with those accounts... Harper giggled. She shot a look at the fern doing its best to desiccate itself and said, "I really have turned into Aunt Lorene. Hanky-panky. What next? Referring to intimate relations as "houghmagandy"?

She snorted. "Probably. The price you pay for reading Victorian literature during Vic-tober."

But the deliberation continued in earnest. Tipping off embezzlers... probably not smart. Accusing people of embezzling with zero proof.... Definitely wrong. So what was a stupid bookseller to do?

Harper rolled herself out of the chair and dashed up to her room. Off went the fuzzy sleep pants and on went her fleece-lined leggings. Remembering how cold it had been earlier, she pulled the sleep pants back on. Over her long-sleeved tee, she pulled her MY BOOK OPEN= YOUR MOUTH CLOSED, sweatshirt. Too bad Jake wouldn't see it under her down-filled coat. Oh, yeah. She was going all out since she might be out until all hours. A glance at her clock showing nearly midnight amended that. "It is already 'all hours.'"

Backpack slung over her shoulder, Harper headed out the door, stopped, backtracked to grab the fern and her trowel, and took off out the back door instead. Might as well hide evidence now. Unlike the last time she'd apparently buried a plant prematurely, this was cold weather, and the thing wouldn't survive. Could you euthanize plants? Well, whatever you called it, she was doing it. Now.

Half an hour later, she'd emptied half her backpack already. At this rate, she'd be stuck going back to the store and refilling it. Especially since she'd added three books *into* it. A compilation of romcoms, *Book Nerds and Boyfriends?* A no-brainer. The exact edition of *The Outsiders* that she'd finally had to toss when she'd dropped it and the pages had scattered to the four winds… That hadn't been a good day, although the old guy who had made a joke about the "leaves" blowing in the street had been fun. Oh, and a copy of *A Place to Hang the Moon* for the Stadtlers. She'd leave it on their porch if they didn't lock the storm door.

Just as she pulled the final three books from her backpack—three miles from home, no less—the light appeared. Usually, that blinding spotlight was enough to infuriate her, but Harper sagged in relief. Then it moved past, and a window rolled down.

"Oh hey, Harper. Just making sure everything's okay. You're out late."

Lauren Ehrlich again. Ask her or just wait to see if she called out Jake? Harper chose the latter. "Thanks for keeping Red Wing safe."

"It's easier to do if innocent people don't wander around in the dark, but hey…" With that, the spotlight went off, and the cruiser did what its moniker claimed— cruised on down the road.

At every turn, she expected Jake's spotlight to accost her, but it didn't happen. When she crossed 3rd Street, Harper hesitated. Grab more books and head over by Noah's place or give up and go to bed? A glance at her phone answered. It was too late to do any more. Besides, her toes were turning into Popsicles. She trudged up East Avenue and slipped her hand back into her pocket as a truck pulled up in front of her and stopped.

Harper sighed. If she had to call for help after that last interaction with Ehrlich…

But Jake stepped out. No police-issued coat, no gun

belt. Just jeans, a heavy jacket and a lightweight knit cap on his head. "Heard you were making the rounds. Lauren's convinced you're going to get yourself killed."

They met at his tailgate. Harper dug her toe into the asphalt and sighed. "I was hoping you'd be out."

"Oh yeah?" He must have seen her shiver because he jerked a thumb at the cab. "Get in. I'll drive you back. It's warmer in there than out here for sure."

She wanted to protest—to say she was just fine. But her traitorous teeth chattered, so she conceded defeat and walked around to the passenger door. Once inside, the blasting heat began the defrosting process. As he climbed in beside her, Harper remembered to thank him, another testament to God's goodness.

"Okay… so… here's the deal."

"If you're asking me out, the answer is yes." Jake shot her a grin. "Does that help?"

"Nope." Grateful he couldn't see her burning cheeks, Harper plowed on. "I need professional advice."

"Oh."

Until that soft, deflated "oh," she'd thought the asking out thing was an ice breaker. Now she wasn't so sure. Uncertain how to process that, she plowed on. "So… I have properties. More than just the store, even. And I've been paying a ton in taxes and insurance. But here's the deal. I didn't know about the others. Mandy's building? Own it. And she pays rent to a management company. I've never heard from them. And…" Her heart sank. "Oh no! Did I pay income taxes on rent I didn't know they paid?"

He backed her up. Got her to start over. And then did it again when she (a habit of hers it seemed) got off the rails again. Then he summarized. "Basically, you inherited properties, didn't read the will or look at the accounts, didn't realize you should be receiving rent, and haven't looked at the bank statements since you inherited?"

"Yes."

"And you want to know if you should just go in with an auditor, tell the police that something feels off, or just ask outright?"

At least he was smarter than he looked. "Yes. I don't even know if there *is* any fraud here. But wouldn't they have sent *something* in the last eighteen months? Get approval for replacing a water heater or send an end-of-the-year statement or… something?"

"Seems like, but that kind of forensic accounting isn't my forte."

"I want to just go in and apologize for not being up on things and ask for an overview—to see what they say and everything—but I don't want to tip them off so they can hide stuff from me if they are doing something shady."

"Could be wrong…" Jake began. Lost in thought, he didn't continue for a moment, but then he plowed on. "But I doubt it's that easy to hide stuff that quickly these days. There are leases, bank accounts, and presumably records of expenditures. I'll ask around and get you an answer on whether to go in or not, but my guess is that you'll want to ask for an audit. I like you blaming your lack of attention to the business as a lead-in. It makes sense to have someone independent tell you where things are. If all's on the up-and-up, no one will object. If not, we'll be ready to jump in."

As if perfect punctuation to his assertions, Jake pulled up to her house just as he finished. They sat there, truck idling, both staring out the windshield. Harper found her voice first. "Well, thanks. I didn't know if I should call or not, so I just went out hoping you'd be working."

He gripped the steering wheel but didn't look her way. "Never hesitate to call or text. If I can't answer, I'll get back to you as soon as I can."

Harper pulled the door handle, but Jake's next words stopped her. "And I was kind of serious about going out. If you wanted to, I mean."

She couldn't stifle a half-laugh. "Was that an invitation?"

"I guess." He shot her a look. "If you want."

This time she pushed the door open and jumped

down. Turning back to him she said, "Here's a hint. If you want to ask, ask. Don't leave it up to the other person to have to figure out if you mean it or not."

She would have closed the door, but Jake stopped her again. "Harper? Want to go get pizza and see a movie next weekend?"

Telling him "yes, but not with him" would be cruel. Especially since she hadn't known it until that minute. Instead, she smiled. "Much better. Next time you ask someone, do it like that, but I'm not interested—not in a *date* anyway. If you mean it as just friends, then sure. Text me."

And feeling like a grown up for the first time in her life, Harper sauntered up the walk, up her steps, and into her apartment. She leaned against the door and sighed. "And I just killed that 'grown up' feeling by calling it being 'grown up.' How pathetic is that?"

Thirty-Two

Book Recommendation: If you're ready for the catharsis of a good cry as well as a justice triumphs over evil, Holes *by Louis Sachar is a great choice.*

Atticus greeted Mrs. Klair with a "Pretty, pretty" and by settling onto her shoulder the moment the woman dropped into the chair nearest the counter. "This little fellow would brighten even *Ove's* day." She dropped *Anxious People* onto the table beside her and smiled up at Milton. "Can you mark this returned? I'm winded and have nearly fallen flat on my face twice today."

"Are you all right?"

She waved away his concern. "Right as rain, as some say. Where's our girl?"

"Squaring away some of her accounts, I believe." He didn't want to give away too much of Harper's personal business, but Milton had never seen her hold back from Mrs. Klair.

"Well, that's good to hear. Lorene would approve. She was a little afraid that Harper would let things go, but I think the girl's done well for something so unexpected. She'd *wanted* to be a research librarian, but there aren't job openings for those in every city." Then as if prescient, Mrs. Klair peered at him. "What brought on this account reckoning desire?"

Remembering the story she'd told, Milton decided to

leave out the previous issues and stick to that. "It seems she was reading *The Woman in White* last night and something Fosco said sent her down that rabbit hole."

"Aaah... *The Woman in White*. One of those rare books when its quotes fit is content."

"Oh?" He could guess what she meant, but hearing others delight in favorite book quotes was a favorite pastime of his.

The old girl nodded and—was it his imagination, or had she winked at him? "Let's see... I think it goes, 'I have always held the old-fashioned opinion that the primary object of works of fiction should be to tell a story.' Well, Wilkie Collins most definitely told a story—a good one too." She paused, blinking. "Or..."

She realizes it wasn't part of the story.

"Was that in the preface, perhaps?"

"I believe so," Milton agreed.

The door opened and Harper stormed in. She tossed her bag under the counter and whirled to face him. "They're fired. I don't care if they're innocent... they're *insolent*, and I'm not paying for the privilege of being treated like that. Where do I find a new management company?"

"Good morning, Harper."

Watching the change come over her as Harper turned to greet Mrs. Klair solidified opinions Milton had formed of her. She genuinely loved the older woman. He'd only seen that look a few times. Mrs. Klair, Mr. Laffey, Bennie, Noah, and himself, but only once on a personal score. That morning in fact.

"Did you enjoy *Anxious People?*" This time Milton translated the question into something more personal. *"How are you feeling, Mrs. Klair?"* And if the look on the older woman's face meant what he thought it did, she heard the subtext.

"I did. I still love Ove best. I think..." She gave a little shrug and a small smile. "Perhaps it can be forgiven me if I prefer my first introduction into an author over his other works, even if they are technically better."

Harper dropped to the floor beside her chair and leaned against it, her knees drawn up to her chest. "A woman from my church brought *A Man Called Ove* back the other day. She was offended that there was a gay guy in it—and that Ove was nice to him."

"What did you tell her?"

Milton turned away before his grin gave away the answer. That had been a brilliant moment.

"I said I don't give refunds for general market books reflecting the opinions and preferences of the general market but that I'd buy it at the usual price for a paperback in good condition."

"Good for you." Slyness entered the old gal's tone as she asked, "And what did you think of that storyline?"

Atticus must have gotten bored on Mrs. Klair's shoulder, because he came to say hello to Milton. Usually, Milton would have chattered with the bird, but he didn't want to miss Harper's answer. Instead, he popped out three sunflower seeds and laid them on the counter. For good measure, he moved the "potty tray" closer.

"Well…" Harper didn't seem to know how to respond. "Well, I don't know if I'm right to think it, but I thought Ove managed to keep his own opinion of things while still treating others with his own version of respect. And it taught me how to live out my own convictions with grace toward those who don't know the One who gave them to me."

Mrs. Klair's snort came out of the blue. "Because Ove would have been gracious?"

Instead of answering that question, Harper answered the one behind it. "It's what his reaction in the book taught me. Maybe the Lord used the book and that situation to teach me what I couldn't figure out some other way. I don't know."

The shop door opened, and chattering children appeared. Even without looking up, Milton knew it had to be the Stadtlers. After the delivery the night before, and it being school hours, who else would it be. He turned in time to see Tammy Stadtler reach Harper's side, pull the girl up, and hug her. Harper stood there with one arm dangling and the other making awkward patting motions like men often did when they didn't know how to comfort.

Was it his imagination, or did Tammy whisper, "Thank you. You just don't know." No, she must have, because when the woman stepped back, she laughed and said, "But actually, I bet you do, don't you?"

She flipped through a thick planner and pulled out a list. "My order for November. It's a bit bigger this time, but we have to replace so many schoolbooks. I found ISBNs online." She glanced around and leaned close. "And do you have any recommendations for something for Emily? She's wracked with guilt and is now in the 'pretend it didn't happen and all is great' stage. We're trying, but…"

If Harper didn't know, he did. After thinking for a moment, Harper said, and without any hint of amusement in her tone, "I'll have to think about it, but I'm going to suggest you not put *Rebecca* on her high school lit list."

Tammy barked out a laugh. Milton's lips twitched, and even Mrs. Klair tittered. Harper clearly didn't see what had amused them all. "If Harper doesn't have any suggestions, I do." He pulled out his phone and tapped the screen. "Found it in a little free library this summer. I think it might be perfect, but there is some crude language. Mostly stuff you'd hear in a G-rated movie, but there might have been a couple of Biblical donkeys as well. Bet you could find out online."

He passed over his phone and Tammy read the synopsis. "*Lost in the Sun*… Lisa Graff…" After reading it, she nodded. "Grab that too. I'll see how it goes."

"The library probably has it," Harper offered. "You might not want it around forever."

As intelligent as Harper was, she could be pretty dense sometimes.

"I can always keep it in my room—just in case I think she needs a reread. If it opens conversations, I'll consider it a win."

In the middle of the conversation, Mrs. Klair started to rise and sat back down. Hard. She stared at Harper. "Lorene? What are you doing here?"

"Mrs. Klair?"

Milton stepped forward, watching as the confused woman tried to touch her head and closed her eyes. The hand fell. Her face slackened. He reached back, snatched his phone out of Tammy's hands, and hit the emergency call button. The dispatcher asked his emergency, and when he heard Mrs. Klair repeat, "Lllrreeennn," all doubt fled.

"We need an ambulance. Probable stroke in a…" Milton barked out, "How old is she?"

Harper stared first at him, then at Mrs. Klair. Tammy shrugged. "I don't know."

"Mrs. Klair? How old are you?"

The woman shook her head in slow, awkward sweeps. "Her purse." To the man on the call he said, "I'm going to guess over seventy. Maybe over eighty."

Was it his imagination, or did he already hear sirens? The Stadtler kids crowded around until Tammy ordered them back. Emily shook as sirens grew closer. Milton pulled Tammy closer and whispered, "Emily. She's reacting."

By now, the left side of Mrs. Klair's face had gone completely slack. Milton prayed—ordered God, if truth were told—to hurry up those paramedics.

No one greeted Noah as he rushed into the bookstore. By this time, he knew he didn't *need* to watch Bennie anymore. He'd known that since the day Harper had gone to save the day and Miss Courtney had proven herself more capable of handling kids than the schools were. Then again, those kids *wanted* to be there. Maybe that was the real solution to bullying. Create an environment that kids *wanted* to be in, and maybe they wouldn't tear each other apart. One could dream, anyway.

He'd made it halfway up the stairs before he caught sight of Atticus alone in the cage. "Where is everyone?"

"Read it!"

In the back, a toilet flushed. Well, duh. Booksellers needed occasional breaks too. He turned to greet Harper and found a haggard looking Milton headed his way. "Hey…" Noah had to ask. "You all right?"

Milton shook his head. "Not really. Hard afternoon. Mrs. Klair—" A lump the size of a walnut bobbed in Milton's neck. "She didn't make it. I sent Harper home."

Didn't make it? Make what? Then the words translated themselves from polite euphemisms. She'd had some kind of accident and had died. No wait… "Passed." People didn't even say "passed away" anymore—as if the "away" were too harsh as well. Odd… that sounded like something Harper would say.

"What happened?"

Milton scrubbed his hand over his face and sighed. "Stroke. She was gone before they got her out of the store."

Six months ago, he'd never met Mrs. Klair. Even now, he'd only seen her a few times, but the lady had always had a kind word for Benny and a twinkle in her eye. And Harper had loved her something fierce.

"If you're a pray-er, then pray for those Stadtler kids too. They were here."

"Oh, no…" That was just the thing. He *did* pray, but he didn't consider himself much of a prayer warrior. His prayers came out like sulky teen asides as he passed his Father in the kitchen. *Can you help me with my homework? Can I get that new video game? Haven't I been grounded long enough?* Except now they came out like, *Can I get a couple of hours of overtime to pay the sitter? Can You help me figure out what to do about Harper? How do I teach my kid to pray when I'm so lousy at it myself?*

He'd planned to try to talk Harper into that movie, but now… Promising to pray, and doing it as he went out the door so he wouldn't forget and make a liar of himself,

Noah took off on foot to Harper's place. At the corner, he hesitated and dashed for Family Fare instead of up East Avenue. But minutes later, he half walked, half jogged up the street and to her door.

Someone once told Noah that there was nothing more terrifying than a woman crying. The Harper who opened the door to him, her breath coming in ragged gasps, her eyes strained and flooded with unshed tears, her nose running in anticipation of an imminent sob fest all conspired against both of them. He held out the box of Little Debbie Swiss Rolls. "It was these or pink Hostess snowballs, but I didn't know if you like coconut."

The first tear made a bold move and slid down her cheek. Harper hugged the box to herself, shook trying to control emotions she clearly wanted to ignore, and flung herself at him. "She's gone!"

Thirty-Three

I like books and maybe three people. Maybe.

On the morning of Emmeline Klair's funeral, Harper sat in the pew at Christ Episcopal Church and glowered at the entire congregation. Someone had called it a "celebration of life" while others spoke of a "memorial service." Brooding in her heart (and in every other way to be honest), Harper refused to call it anything but what it was. A funeral. Mrs. Klair didn't care what they called it. She was probably dancing with Jesus or arguing with the apostle Paul over his ridiculous run-on sentences. She'd always threatened to.

Funerals (yes, *funerals*) were for those left behind, and she didn't have to rejoice for herself. She could mourn. The Bible said so.

Next to her, Milton sat in quiet contemplation, and on his other side were the Stadtlers. At the other end of the old-fashioned pew with its trefoils on the high-sided end pieces, Noah had wedged himself into the last little bit left, and the discomfort he showed may have been more from that than the service itself. But that wasn't really fair of her.

Platitudes abounded in the sweet (or so she assumed it was supposed to be) homily and the eulogy until Harper wanted to scream. While someone droned on about Mrs. Klair's "civic spirit" and "unfailing generosity," she mentally composed a real one—one Mrs. Klair would have

255

liked.

Emme Klair, a lifetime resident of Red Wing (and that she didn't leave is a testament to her *amazingness rather than Red Wing's), died last week, leaving friends bereft and any enemies she might have had (the idiots) cheering. Any toilet papering of those houses should not be attributed to Harper Brevig under any circumstances.*

Mrs. Klair lived as a widow for fifty years, having been a "war bride" during the Vietnam War. Her husband never came home. Though a woman with a wide range of interests, she was best known for her second love—books. Stingy with her star ratings, a book that received five stars from Emme was sure to become a classic (or had already achieved that status).

Everyone around her rose. The minister apologized for the closing hymn, insisting that Emme had chosen it herself and he felt compelled to honor that. The opening notes on the organ gave it away. "Onward Christian Soldiers." That sounded like Mrs. Klair. *Finally.*

She slipped out the moment the minister's "aaah…" from amen began. Though she should've gone back to the store, she walked up 4th Street to East Avenue and turned left toward home. There, she pulled out her coziest pajama bottoms and baggiest sweatshirt, grabbed a Kleenex box (the ones with lotion, duh), and curled up under the covers for a long, guilt-ridden cry.

After all, by comparison, she'd hardly noticed when Aunt Lorene died. She'd been sorry, of course. Her father loved the old gal who had been nearly twenty years older than him. She was sorry for *him.* But Aunt Lorene hadn't liked her, and she hadn't liked the old gal either. So her greatest sorrow had been losing an aunt she didn't really know—the loss of a relationship that could never form rather than one being taken away.

But Mrs. Klair had been everything Aunt Lorene hadn't—the companion, the book buddy, the mentor. And her death had hinted at something worse, something she'd never contemplated before. Harper's preference for older people and young children had a serious drawback. Older people died. Well, anyone could, but the older you got, the more certain it was that your time would soon be up. Younger children were a problem because they had to go through all those middle years before they got interesting again.

"I'll have to learn to like adults, I suppose. I don't want to, but if everyone dies around me, I'll die too."

Her voice echoed in her room—an acoustical impossibility with the many blankets, books, and thick area rug. And yet it did. Maybe only Harper would understand how, but then she was the only one who needed to.

Could there be a Halloween Eve? Didn't that make it "All Hallows Eve *Eve?*" And wouldn't it then just be Halloween Adam like Milton had said about Christmas Eve Eve being Christmas Adam? After nearly two weeks locked in her house, moping, grieving, and moping some more, Harper didn't know if she cared.

Instead, she sat at home, reading, crying, and rewatching *You've Got Mail,* and commiserating as if some jerk face Joe Fox had just put her out of business. If anyone put her out of business, it would be herself. Or Mrs. Klair. She'd died, after all. A sob broke through her thoughts, but Harper stuffed it down again.

"That's just great," she growled on her way to grab another pint of Ben & Jerry's. She'd found a "break up" list on a website that picked out the best flavor depending on the kind of breakup you'd had. Harper had flip-flopped between the "age difference" one (she and Mrs. Klair *were* about fifty years apart after all) and the "no reason" which really fit too. So, since she'd eaten "Cake My Day" to mourn the "no reason" last time, she grabbed "Everything but the…" and a spoon. Who knew breakups had such a science to them? One more reason to avoid relationships at all costs. Even platonic ones it seemed.

She'd made it halfway through the pint and got to the

singing hot dog in the movie theater when her doorbell rang. Nobody but nobody used the doorbell, which probably meant a package. Only she hadn't ordered anything. Maybe she'd been served papers by the property management company. That would serve her right. Because the one thing she *had* done since watching them wheel Mrs. Klair out of her bookstore on a gurney had been to fire that management company and give Milton permission to find someone else. And to pay himself too.

The bell rang again. With "Everything but the…" in one hand, she extricated herself from the serious butt dent she'd put in the couch (thanks to Angela Ruth Strong and *Husband Auditions* for that delightful and totally accurate description) and dragged herself to the door. But instead of some smarmy-looking loser standing there with legal-looking documents in a manilla envelope, she found Noah. Hands in pockets, apology written all over him and for what? He hadn't done anything wrong. *He* hadn't died and left her without a daily morning book borrower.

In her best Kathleen Kelly imitation (and without actually meaning to do it), she left him in the doorway and walked back to the couch, her butt dent, and her pint of "Everything but the…."

At least he closed the door before coming into the room. Too bad he didn't have daisies in hand. After all, he was being friendly, and they're the friendliest flower. Kathleen Kelly said so. With that thought burning a hole in her heart (and apparently in her wallet as well), Harper ignored Noah, pulled out her phone, found an online florist, and ordered a hundred bucks worth of daisies to be delivered the next day. That done, she jabbed her spoon in the now-soft ice cream and pulled out a mound of it. Looking up at Noah she asked, "What do you want?" *Now* that *was totally Kathleen Kelly. Ten points to Gryffindor.*

The tears flowed then. Mrs. Kline had been in the "Harry Potter is evil" camp, and she'd just sullied the lovely woman's grief fest with a book reference. What kind of monster was she? "Voldemort. Just call me Voldy."

Noah sat next to her and stared at his hands. "Everyone's worried about you."

"I'm fine" made it as far as her tongue and skittered back into the broken recesses of her heart. She wasn't fine. Not a bit. So, in what would probably be an awkward and miserable moment of raw honesty, she said, "They should be."

He squirmed without even the slightest twitch of a muscle. That took talent. "I volunteered to come and check on you," he said after several awkward moments. "I even came up with an honest reason."

Harper just jabbed her spoon into the ice cream and then decided she didn't want any more. Without a word, she carried it to the kitchen, rooted around for the lid, and finally found it on top of *Something Wicked This Way Comes* by Ray Bradbury. *It's wicked to risk ruining a book like that,* she scolded herself. But the feeling of guilt withered and died before she made it back to the couch.

She stood before him, wondering if she should resume her previous seat or drop into the armchair. Too weary to move the books piled on the chair, she sank back onto the couch next to Noah, hesitated, and dropped her head to his shoulder. "She won't bring back another book again."

"No."

Again they sat. Leaves pattered against her side window as the wind blew them from the neighbor's tree. She pulled up the blanket and tucked it in around her, making herself comfortable. If he didn't like it, he should have sat on the other end instead of the middle. It might have been the first time in her life that having someone else close—that *touching* someone—was preferable to solitude and a wide personal bubble. She'd examine why later. Or not. Probably not.

"What was your honest excuse?"

Noah startled at the direct question. "Halloween. I forgot."

She huffed. "How? The whole town is Halloween

259

mad this year. There are ten times the number of people decorating than previous years."

The couch groaned as Noah shifted to put an arm around her shoulder. Harper had an illogical desire to light a candle—something pumpkiny. Instead, she tried not to stiffen (total failure) and listened as he explained the difference between Halloween as an adult and as a parent. "I even bought candy to hand out," he admitted. "We probably don't get lots of kids over by us. I always went over to South Oaks Drive up by the high school—some of the people up there gave full-sized candy bars."

Throat tight, heart pounding, Harper whispered, "Mrs. Klair did. She said it didn't do to do things by halves." Her voice caught. "I read a quote by Coleridge yesterday. He said…" She fumbled for her phone and found it. "'There are three classes into which all the women past seventy that ever I knew were to be divided: one, that dear old soul; two, that old woman; three, that old witch.'" With the back of her hand, she wiped away a fresh tear.

"Mrs. Klair was definitely 'that dear old soul.' Did you go see Milton yesterday?"

"No."

"Call him then? He didn't say."

Harper shook her head just once and sighed. "I should call him. Tell him to lock the doors, write himself a check, and move along. I don't know—"

"Wait. No. That's not—" Then Noah stopped himself. "Wait. Wait. How'd Milton tell you about the old women if you didn't talk to him."

"Milton? No. Coler…" Harper smiled up at him before relaxing a bit and closing her eyes. "Not Milton, *Samuel Taylor* Coleridge. Poet from the early nineteenth century—or late eighteenth. Don't remember which." When he didn't seem to react, she added, "Water, water everywhere…"

"Sounds familiar."

Desperate to change the subject before her mind refocused on Mrs. Klair, Harper asked him what was wrong with Halloween. "What's Bennie going as?"

"That's my problem. I forgot about costumes, and he was afraid to ask. I only figured it out when Mom asked what he was going to be, and he couldn't answer."

The poor kid. She'd only pieced together bits of the story. Although usually Harper felt certain Bennie's mom was dead, other times she suspected abandonment. And Noah had not been a part of Bennie's life until recently. That much had been made clear. But how recently? A year? Two? More? Less? The worst of it was, he might have told her everything, and she hadn't listened. It wouldn't be the first time. Or maybe she just couldn't remember with her mind befuddled by despair.

"Does he have any idea what he wants to be? I mean it's tomorrow night."

"That's the thing. I'm afraid to ask him." Noah moved his arm and dropped his head into both hands. "What if he wants to go as a ballerina?" A groan followed. "Harper, I *can't* let him do that. I just can't."

The mental image of Noah's face when Bennie showed up in toe shoes and a tutu nearly did her in. Though she tried to stuff it down, she choked. Chortled. And with Noah staring at her horrified, it all turned to laughter.

"Are you all right?" At her nod, Noah shrugged. "I'm not so sure about that."

Why she noticed the disaster that was her living room at that moment, Harper didn't know. She just knew she couldn't stand it a minute longer. Hopping up, she began to collect the spoons attached to folded Kleenex, wadded up tissues, paper plates, and two pizza boxes. "What else does he like? Ballet isn't the *only* thing he likes."

"He likes you."

That stopped her in the middle of stacking up read books that needed to be put away somewhere. She smiled. "He could wear one of my snarky T-shirts, jeans, and blue sunglasses with the lenses popped out... but I doubt he'd want to."

Noah shook his head. "Probably not, but jeans are better than tutus and tights."

"What about a nutcracker? He likes that ballet, so…" Just seeing the wince on Noah's face nixed that. "What else?"

"He likes Narnia… but Lucy's his favorite."

What else Noah said she didn't hear. Harper's mind swirled until it probably resembled snow in a storm. The first question surprised even her. "Does he have a black, long-sleeved T-shirt?"

"Yeah…"

"Black pants for ballet?"

Though Noah winced, he nodded.

A smile formed. "Okay… I've got it. You're going to need those things and two of those little plastic pumpkin candy buckets. Oh, and a small flashlight, some cardboard or posterboard and either black paint or a few Sharpies."

Thirty-Four

I have no shelf control.

Though she would never have admitted it to anyone but the Lord (it's not like *He* didn't know anyway), getting up and down every few minutes to hand out the full-sized candy bars she'd had to leave her house to purchase was good for her. Two weeks of sheer, isolated, bliss... and misery... broken because none of the delivery services would deliver boxes of full-sized candy bars *that day*. But if she had to do this Halloween thing, she was going to honor Mrs. Klair in the process. Even if it killed her. It probably would.

But despite it all, tiny little ghosts, adorable pumpkins with orange sweatpants under them instead of tights like the costume packaging had probably shown, a plethora of Disney and Marvel characters, a couple of cheerleaders... it all lifted her spirits.

But best of all was Bennie Lampe standing on her stoop, grinning with a top tooth missing (she'd deal with the heartbreak of missing *that* later), and lisping out, "Trick or Treat!" while holding his arms out wide with those buckets hanging from each hand. In a stage whisper, and behind the paned mask strapped over his face, he said, "I'm the lamppost—because I'm Bennie *Lampe* now."

Out on the walk, Noah stood, a half-formed smile hovering about his lips. *I've never seen a dad love his kid more.*

Feeling his little arms squeeze her waist jerked her out of her thoughts. "I missed you. We were going to watch a movie, but Dad says we can't ask yet. Because Mrs. Klair died." His face shone up at her, despite the troubled expression in his eyes. The flashlight, of course. "I'm sorry she died. She was nice." After a moment, he added in a whisper, "Do you think she's in heaven?"

Harper nodded. "She knew Jesus. She was His. So she's with Him now." Oh, why didn't that comfort her like it should?

"Do you think my mommy knew Jesus?"

She stopped herself before the words, *"If you have to ask, probably not,"* flew out of her mouth. How was she supposed to know? It was all well and good to throw out things about knowing people by their fruit, but *she* didn't know anything about "Tara." That was the woman's name. Wasn't it?

"I don't know. I didn't know your mom. I wish I did." A swift glance at Noah told her this wasn't the first time the kid had asked. "Know what I do know?"

"Hmmm?" Though he asked, Bennie stared at his toes.

She dropped to her knees, ignored the heat escaping from her house and the shivers that threatened to overtake her, and met the boy's gaze. "I know Jesus knows. And isn't that what matters? Jesus knows *His* sheep. And He's the *Good* Shepherd. So we can trust Him with it since we don't know."

"Okay…"

Harper gave him a hug and whispered, "Go get lots of candy. And if you get any Sweet Tarts, save one for me, okay?"

"Okay!"

As Bennie scrambled down the steps, Noah met her gaze and held it. *"Thank you,"* he mouthed before taking Bennie's hand and leading him up the walk to Myrna's door.

Back inside, Harper turned out the porch light, turned

off the living room lights, and went upstairs. Just inside her door, *The Haunted Bookshop* caught her gaze, and she snatched it up. So what if she'd just read it a couple of months ago. Roger Mifflin and his bookshop were exactly the sort of therapy she needed.

Near the end of the first chapter, she sent her first text to Noah. LOOK AT THIS QUOTE. It took longer to type out, "There is indeed a heaven on this earth, a heaven which we inhabit when we read a good book," than she might have liked, but Harper did it. Then she added, MRS. KLAIR JUST SWAPPED HEAVENS, I GUESS.

One by one as she read through the first chapters, she dinged him with enough quotes that she probably should've just taken pictures of the pages. But what if he read the wrong lines and missed the genius? She couldn't have that, so she read on, shared on, and had only the vaguest sense of everything seeming a bit better.

Something Mr. Gilbert said reminded her of an earlier quote and put it in new light. Harper zipped it to Noah too, asking if, "There is no one so grateful as the man to whom you have given just the book his soul needed, and he never knew it. No advertisement on earth is as potent as a grateful customer," might not be enough reason for the world to need more bookstores.

Noah shot back a swift, DEFINITELY.

That brought a smile—one of the first real smiles she'd felt deep in her soul since "that day," and she thanked him for it in her heart. She wouldn't bother thanking him directly. He wouldn't understand.

Early in chapter six, she found another one that she just *had* to share. Maybe the book was responsible, or it might have been the quotes and commentaries and his replies. Regardless, something had shifted. He sent pictures of Bennie and even a video where Bennie explained to an old man what his costume was. Her heart squeezed. I WISH I WAS THERE. Though she typed out the words, she deleted them and sent that quote instead. "THE BEAUTY OF BEING A BOOKSELLER IS THAT YOU DON'T HAVE TO BE A LITERARY

CRITIC: ALL YOU HAVE TO DO TO BOOKS IS ENJOY THEM."

His reply of, THAT'S YOU ALL OVER. DID I TELL YOU HOW MUCH BENNIE LOVES TELLING PEOPLE HIS LAST NAME?

He didn't have to. The kid's pride had shone through every word, but Harper didn't tell Noah that. She just pointed out that any kid would be proud to be a Lampe, and if he got to be a lampe-post, well... all the better.

As with every reading of *The Haunted Bookshop*, chapter six proved the richest, most emotionally satisfying of all. She didn't send, "It's in books that most of us learn how splendidly worth-while life is," but she wanted to. However, when she reached one of her favorite passages, her breath caught. Harper read... reread... stared... smiled.

She punched Noah's contact and waited for him to answer. His concerned tone touched her heart as he said, "Everything okay?" even without a hello.

"Yeah. I just wanted you to hear this one. It's Mrs. Klair all over. Listen."

"Okay..."

"'Words can't describe the cunning of some books. You'll think you've shaken them off your trail, and then one day some innocent-looking customer will pop in and begin to talk, and you'll know he's an unconscious agent of book-destiny.' That was her, Noah. She was definitely an 'unconscious agent of book destiny.' I want to be that. I want to embrace book*selling,* not just bookstore *owning.* I just don't know how to do it."

A knock on his trailer door startled Milton out of his mystery and required him to order his heart to remove itself from his throat. Surely, kids weren't trick-or-treating in an RV park! Still, he grabbed a couple of clementines and prayed his trailer wouldn't get egged for it.

But when he opened the door, Bennie stood there, arms outstretched with pumpkin buckets dangling from them. "You look like the streetlights downtown—like… *lampposts* downtown. Are you *the* lamppost?"

The boy nodded and grinned as Milton dropped a clementine in each bucket. Behind him, Noah asked if they could talk for a minute. "Sure! Come in. Sorry." He started to say that he'd assumed they'd want to get to the next house but realized how that might sound just in time.

They sat at his dining booth, and Bennie began sorting his loot. "Can I eat one?"

Noah nodded. "One big one or three little ones—that's all."

"Okay." The boy removed the odd cardboard mask and turned off the little flashlight that made it glow before digging around and pulling out all the Sweet Tarts. "These are for Harper."

"She only asked for one."

Bennie shrugged and said, "But I have lots of candy, and she's sad. I want her to have them."

As if that settled everything (and it probably did), Noah pulled out his phone and scrolled up quite a way. "Will you read through this? I don't know what to make of it. Total radio and personal silence and then this tonight."

Milton read. With each text, his heart lightened. With each quote, he wished he had his copy of the book. *Oh, well… there's always Kindle.*

"What do you think?"

Handing the phone back, Milton leaned back on the bench and smiled. "I think she'll be at work tomorrow. She's still grieving, but she's found *purpose* in the store—beyond just doing what her aunt expected. And the timing couldn't be more perfect."

"Why's that?"

For just a moment, Milton wondered if it was right to say something when Harper didn't even know yet. Then again, she'd told him to do whatever he thought best… After a glance at Bennie and seeing the boy engrossed in counting mini-Snickers bars, he turned back to Noah.

"Tomorrow, they arrest Paul Kinford for fraud. The

tax guy and the independent auditor found the evidence right away. Kinford is an idiot. He didn't even try to create fake invoices, repairs, or anything. He just moved money into his own account on a regular basis and called it a 'service fee' without reporting it as income on his end. So the IRS is going to have a field day."

Without looking up from arranging single Reese's cups into a line, Bennie said, "I hope he has to work hard and give back all her money. He's a creep, and he made her worry," before starting in on little packets of Skittles.

Thirty-Five

Booktrovert: A person who prefers the company of fictional characters to real people.

Harper didn't go to the bookstore on November first. Instead, she cleaned her apartment, gave her statement to the police, did some grocery shopping, and in a fit of a need for change, got her hair cut in a messy bob that made her look like a nineteenth-century damsel who had recovered from a terrible fever in which they'd had to cut her hair. Even she could see it wasn't a good look for her.

On November second, she and Milton interviewed two other management companies. One had an excellent reputation but did not offer the total hands-off approach she wanted. Milton suggested that since it hadn't been an overwhelming success the first time, perhaps that was a good thing. Harper disagreed. Aunt Lorene had chosen that path, so it had to be right. Didn't it? In the end, she'd driven to the second company, began signing paperwork, and froze mid signature. "But I'm not Aunt Lorene. And this is the way that got me in trouble in the first place," she'd said and promptly walked out. Milton said the poor woman behind the counter was so confused she'd called to ask if Harper needed medical attention.

On the second, she'd also begun returning phone calls and made an appointment to speak with a lawyer on

November third. It would be a half day for her—and since the appointment was at one o'clock, she'd miss the time that Mrs. Klair would have *usually* been in. Perfection. Except when she left the lawyer's office in a daze at one-thirty, she'd gone home to read the letter left for her and arrange transport of a few boxes of books to her home.

It wasn't a long letter, but after reading it, Harper had tucked it away in the back of her neglected commonplace book and promptly took it out and read it again.

> *My dearest Harper,*
> *Yes, I am being a sentimental old thing, and you can't stop me. You are very dear to me, girl.*
> *I'd never known what I would do with my book collection. It seemed wrong to donate it to some indifferent society for them to sell off without any idea of its value. I've headed up too many of these things to believe they'd do their homework before donating the lot to a Friends of the Library sale for a tax receipt of a hundred dollars.*
> *Then Lorene left you her store, and I got to meet you. You will value my books for their literary merit <u>and</u> will understand their true worth. Keep the ones you particularly love, sell the others to save your store or buy a home or whatever you like.*
> *I'll leave you with one piece of advice that I pray you will take. Don't isolate yourself too much, dear Harper. While our book friends feed our minds, the Lord uses His people to feed our hearts and souls. Don't let any of your person starve. Thank you for being my friend and for indulging a silly old woman in her eccentricities.*
> *All my love,*
> *Emme Klair*

All through the rest of the day, Harper reread the letter a dozen times. Then, just before she climbed into bed, she'd sent Noah a text message. CAN WE DO THE

MOVIE NIGHT TOMORROW NIGHT?

His reply had come before she could get the case off her phone and onto the wireless charger. CAN'T WAIT. BENNIE WILL BE THRILLED. WE'VE MISSED YOU. AND HE HAS NEWS FOR YOU. PRAY FOR ME!

Harper had gone to sleep with visions of Bennie as Clara in *The Nutcracker* dancing in her head.

Friday, November fifth dawned cold and rainy. Harper pulled on her fleece-lined leggings and her over-sized sweatshirt that read: *Ink and paper are the best perfume.* She brushed the hair that used to be just wavy and stared at the fuzzball it had become. Not owning a flatiron, curling iron, *nor* a hairdryer, she had to content herself with throwing on a knit cap that featured adorable woodland creatures. And her contact lens went down the sink. Her *last* set of lenses. She'd forgotten to order refills. Glasses for her. On a rainy day. Great.

Dumping her tote bag into the night-rambles backpack, she pulled on her waterproof coat and set off for Hanisch's. Her spirit settled a little. There was something wonderful about resuming a beloved and familiar routine. She ordered two bacon and egg breakfast sandwiches—both on bagels—and enjoyed watching Jamie blink. Fridays were English muffin bread days, and she knew it.

She stepped into the store, rain dripping off her umbrella, dumped the whole thing in the old metal bucket left for that purpose, and closed and locked the door behind her. Standing there, she closed her eyes and inhaled, sniffing the wonderful aroma of ink and paper like her sweatshirt said. *Biblichor… it's the best.*

The backpack bouncing with each step, she hurried upstairs to her office and pushed open the door. This had changed, and she liked it. Everything made sense now—the packaging and supplies in the cubbyholes, the filing cabinet holding *all* the files, and a clear desk for her to spread out her breakfast.

The tea kettle flicked on with a touch of the lever. Lyons Gold today—a perfect tea for a rainy morning.

271

Harper pulled out her phone, tapped her Bible app, and picked up where she'd left off the last day she'd stepped into her shop. Second Timothy chapter two.

With Paul's charge to be a good soldier, a good competitor, and a faithful servant ringing in her ears, Harper finished her food and went to wash up. She pulled off the hat, stared at her wild hair, and jammed it back down on her head. The words on her shirt danced with each movement, and Harper remembered that moment she always enjoyed as she stepped into the store. Uncertainty warred within her until determination took it in hand.

She snatched up her phone and dashed down the stairs with a clatter that sounded like thunder had come to join the rain. Flicking on the lights to ensure a better picture, Harper Brevig took her first ever selfie. Okay, it took about fifty to get one with her eyes closed, her shirt in view, and her not looking like she was high on some wacky mushrooms or something. But one finally captured how she felt—mostly.

Opening the store's Instagram account, she hit the + button and began typing out the description. *My favorite moment of every day is when I step into the store, lock the doors behind me, close my eyes, and inhale. Biblichor is a beautiful thing. Come in and see why. I'd love to meet you.* Her hand shook a little as she hit the post button. She was forgetting something. Who knew what, but she'd done it. She'd posted her first social media post and had lived to tell about it.

Like a silly woman in some British period drama, Noah fussed with the daisies he'd bought. Stupid, stupid thing to do, but now that Bennie knew about them, he couldn't toss them in the trash before Harper arrived. He'd seen her phone after she'd ordered them and before the screen went dark, and he'd seen them from the open door when Bennie had knocked on her door in his lamppost costume. She liked daisies. So he got her some.

272

And now he felt like an idiot.

At the table, Bennie squatted and rose on tiptoe, squatted and rose, one hand always resting on the tabletop. Tiny little steps on his toes… and down… Noah stifled a sigh and prayed Harper would have some encouraging words for him.

Then he prayed she'd actually show. This time he'd understand if she didn't, but Bennie probably wouldn't. As if the boy read his thoughts, he shot a glance at the old kitchen clock that hung over the doorway. The previous owners had left it, and Noah hadn't bothered to take it down. Bennie's face scrunched up. "Does that say seven o'clock?"

"Five minutes after."

The kid swallowed so hard Noah could see it. "Will she really come?"

"She's still hurting, so she might forget or—" The doorbell broke off his words. Bennie dashed for the front door, his ballet shoes making soft slaps on the kitchen floor and growing silent when he hit the carpet.

Casting one last look at the mortifying daisies, Noah followed. Bennie chattered as Harper entered—all about how the girl who had been cast as Clara's sister had sprained her ankle in cheerleading, so she had to back out of the performance. "I get to be Fitz—like the *real* nutcracker story. I get to break the nutcracker *and* be a mouse too!"

"Wow!" Harper shrugged out of her coat and hung it on one of the empty hooks by the door. "You're going to be a *star!*" She cocked her head and asked, "When little girls are in a performance, people give them flowers. What do they give little boys?"

Bennie's, "Hugs!" earned him a couple of chuckles, but Noah added to his ever-growing list of things to do and buy, *One nutcracker doll.* He sighed. *Great. I'm buying my son a doll now.*

Meeting Noah's gaze, Harper said, "I'll be sure to remember that. Hugs. Great, big, bear hugs."

"Lion hugs," Bennie corrected. "*Aslan* hugs."

That seemed to stop Harper in her tracks. "That's strange," she whispered. "But Aslan's roar *is* like a hug—to *his* people. To his enemies, it's a battle cry."

"That's why Aslan's the best." Bennie grinned over at Noah before adding, "Dad got you something. Come see. Then I'll show you how I have to fight over the doll and break it."

As they spoke, Noah took in Harper. She still wore her stocking cap. Had she walked over? Surely, not. And she wore those glasses that made her eyes turn almost aqua. Never had he been so observant about a woman's eyes, but the change was so startling, no one could have helped it.

She passed him with a smile, and Noah reached out and plucked the hat from her head. He stared when her hair puffed out like a dandelion head. "What'd you do to your hair?"

Bennie giggled. "It's all messy!"

Her pink cheeks *could've* been from the cold and rain, but they weren't. She rolled her eyes and huffed, "I got reckless and let them cut it into a more 'modern' style." The air quotes didn't fit her either. "Stupid move. And my hair grows slowly too." She reached for the hat. "At least it's cold weather so I can cover it up."

Harper shoved the cap back down on her head, and a few curls ended up plastered to her forehead and cheeks. She did look pretty cute. Especially with those glasses. His son (the traitor) dragged Harper away before Noah could find a way to compliment her.

"Look!"

The look she gave him told Noah that if he'd planned to keep things platonic (and he didn't, despite all the best efforts to convince himself he would), it would probably fail. "Daisies are my favorite," she told Bennie without taking her eyes off him.

Definitely would fail.

Then Bennie invited her to his birthday party. "It's on Vet-er-an's Day. At Godfather's Pizza. Can you come?"

Noah held his breath much like he expected Bennie did. Harper bounced on her toes. "Yes!" She leaned close and whispered, "Can I tell you a secret?"

Bennie's solemn nod would've won over the heart of the crustiest old codger.

"I haven't been invited to a birthday party in *years*. You'll have to tell me what to bring, and when to sing, and how to play the games, okay?"

She fingered the petals of one of the daisies as Bennie showed her how he battled the toy soldiers and then how he had to fight over the nutcracker doll. "Then I get really mad when I get the doll away from Clara, and I throw it to the ground!" He made a great, sweeping motion before pretending to smash the thing. "They make it so it'll break in two pieces and then stick back together. It's magnets, so I have to make sure I hit it hard, so the pieces don't snap back together by themselves!"

"That is going to be fantastic. What does your costume look like?"

Bennie wrinkled his nose, which did wonders for Noah's heart. At least the kid didn't like the velvet suit with lace collar and cuffs that Miss Courtney had showed them. "It's all lacy and silly. It's *December*, and I have to wear shorts!" As if that weren't insult enough, he added, "And *pink* tights!"

Thank You, Lord. I needed that.

As if he'd just realized what he said, Bennie shot Noah a look. "I'm really happy, though. Miss Courtney says that new dancers *never* get a role like this. And costumes are supposed to be stupid—um, fancy."

Noah decided his son needed a bit of support. "Stupid's right, kid. I'm with you. But you'd look pretty silly up there in jeans and your *It's read o'clock* shirt next to the girls with their frilly dresses and big hair bows."

It must have been the right thing to say because Bennie giggled. "That's true." Another one of Bennie's spontaneous hugs accompanied the agreement, which was just what Noah needed. The kid shifted topics so fast Noah had to chase it down to catch up. "Do you want popcorn? We're going to watch a *Phineas and Ferb*. Then Dad's going to read our next chapters and our devotional. Then you get to have your date."

It was Noah's turn for a red face, but Harper beat him to it. Then she looked at him, back at Bennie, and at him again. "Did your dad call this a date, Bennie?"

Bennie sighed. "No. Gramma did. She said it would take an act of God or, at least Congress, to get dad to 'knowledge a date." Bennie's forehead furrowed, and he whispered, "What's Congress?"

"Important people making laws that, most of the time, they have no business making." Harper grinned at him. "Like if someone wants a good friend or a girlfriend. Not Congress' jurisdiction."

"It's God's, though. Everything is God's. So what does God say?"

Noah, happy to let Harper bury herself in this nightmare, just nodded. "I'd like to know myself."

After staring at him for what felt like an hour, Harper turned to Bennie and took his hand. "Let's let your dad make that popcorn while you show me *Phineas and Ferb*. I don't know that one. And I'd say God will make everything the way He wants it to be… *in His time*."

Noah, after popping the microwave popcorn and separating it into three bowls, settled into his chair while Harper and Bennie each sat cross-legged on the couch. It was like watching two kids instead of just one. Eyeballs riveted to the screen, Harper and Bennie stuffed their faces with popcorn in near perfect synchrony while Phineas and Ferb built and advertised their epic town-wide roller coaster.

Up to that point, Harper said nothing. In fact, she looked a bit confused. However, when the mom got all sassy about Candace's paranoia and said she was off to the dairy section of the grocery store, Harper lost it. She laughed, she gasped, she howled until Bennie grabbed the remote and paused. "'If you want to yell at some cheese or anything.'" The words came out in a gasp that almost hurt to listen to.

"Yeah. I don't get that."

Harper shot Noah a look that said, *"But we do,"* and the moment cemented itself in his memory—the first time he'd ever experienced that parental understanding with someone. He hadn't even had a moment like that with his mom yet.

By the time Phineas said, "You all signed the waivers, right?" Harper was a fan. "Can we watch one every week?"

Date night. They'd just established it without actually discussing it. And Noah decided he was all right with that. But before he could agree, she leaned over and murmured to Bennie, "If I can keep from binging them all before Sunday."

"Can we watch another one, Dad? Just one more?" The kid seriously turned on the big eyes and the pleading expression. Kids shouldn't be allowed to be that cute.

Harper wasn't much better. The girl shot him a look that clearly said, "I'm good if you are" and then shot her gaze at the clock. Nearly seven-forty. By the time they got done reading…

"Not tonight. But Harper can come over and watch one any night she wants as long as she's here by six-thirty."

"Except Wednesday and Friday. Those are ballet nights. We get home late." Bennie sounded crushed.

Noah shrugged and pulled out the book, fully intending to get Harper to read it for him. "Wednesday is right. School night. But Fridays are okay if it's later. Saturdays too." And there he'd become his dad. No late nights on school nights. Even Mom had been willing to give a bit on that now and then.

But when he went to pass the book to Harper, Bennie shook his head. "No. You have to read it. She'll get the voices wrong."

She'll laugh at my voices. At least Mr. Tumnus isn't in this one. He had managed to avoid his bizarrely accented Tumnus style in any other book.

But Harper agreed with his son (the traitor—they both were) and insisted he read. His choppy style was even worse at first. Nerves, no doubt. But by the grace of God and sheer desperation, he got through it, through their short devotional, and through teeth and pajama time. Bennie insisted Harper come up for prayers and snuggled into bed. Instead, Harper kissed Bennie's cheek and told him to dream great stories before turning to Noah. "I'll be downstairs getting ready for the travesty. More popcorn?"

As President Snow turned away from the screen and walked up the steps, Harper let out a sigh. "They got a great guy to play Snow."

"But you didn't like it."

Harper looked over at Noah in his chair and shrugged. "I don't know. As a movie, it's a good one." She eyed him. "You know…" Never had just saying what she thought been nerve wracking because she cared about how the other person would receive it. Usually, it was an issue of not wanting to engage period. "If this had been a date, it would have been a good one."

"Yeah?" Noah leaned forward, arms resting on his knees. "How so?"

She shrugged and probably looked like she was faking nonchalance. She wasn't. Harper just didn't know how to explain it. "I don't really have anything to compare it to, but it's what I'd want one to be like."

This time Noah stood and moved next to her on the couch. Nerves did crazy hip-hop style dances all through her. If he tried to get all romantic…

"So what you're saying…" Noah shot her a smile that created a whole new rhythm in her heart. "Is that this *date* is incomparable?"

Maybe she shouldn't have giggled. Actually, no maybe about it. Girls who giggled were ridiculous, and there she was joining the ranks of Mr. Bennet's daughters. Great.

When he nudged her with his elbow, she nearly jumped and ran. Instead, she stared at the screen where the next suggested movie had queued up. "*Is* it a date?" Now… if she could only decide whether she'd prefer him to say yes or no.

"It wasn't." He nudged her again. "But it could be now."

"No, it can't." Her senses had returned now. She'd been so stupid. So… everything she hated women in books to be. "Dates are deliberate. Someone has to ask the other one and make it plain it *is* a date. Dates aren't accidental."

But Noah apparently didn't agree. "Unless they are. Movies are full of people meeting and turning that meet cute into a day-long date. Why can't two friends get together, watch a movie, and decide they want the rest of the evening to *be* a date?"

There she grinned and finally looked at him. "You just proved my point. You said, 'Decide.' That's the difference."

The unspoken question hung in the air until Harper decided. He wasn't chickening out or being evasive like Jake had been. He was giving *her* the out. And she'd made her decision.

Grabbing the remote, she pressed rewind until the movie should start again. The circle of death appeared. A movie trailer followed. *A Man Called Otto.*

Tears formed and fell as Tom Hanks filled the screen. "Mrs. Klair wanted to see this so much."

Noah's arm stole around her and pulled her close. He rested his cheek on her hair and said, "We'll go see it for her—together."

Epilogue

Parenting Tip #212: You don't have to love what your kid does to support his efforts.

They sat three rows from the front. Harper had gotten to the theater at the same time Noah had and had parked out front so as to save good seats. Milton sat to her right, Atticus' carrier at his feet. Noah sat to her left, gripping her hand so tight she probably would lose it from diminished circulation or something. His mom sat beside him, wriggling with excitement at every new thing and taking pictures of… nothing, really.

Somewhere backstage, his son warmed up with his class, all decked out in his "Little Lord Fauntleroy" suit, as Harper called it. At least the mouse costume looked reasonably masculine. Prelude music played—medleys of the songs to come with traditional Christmas carols mixed in. The other dance classes had already done their pre-show—a trip through Christmas music from medieval times to present, ending with a truly horrific hip-hop number that he hadn't been able to watch.

At least I have a son. A daughter would have been a nightmare if she'd wanted to do that stuff. Hard no from me. The memory of the gyrating little girls prompted a shudder. *Strong, very hard no.*

Harper extricated her hand from his and offered her

other one, despite the awkward way she had to sit to do it. "Need to get the blood back," she whispered. As serious as a judge pronouncing a sentence. Only Harper.

The music shifted and Miss Courtney, dressed in a white, flowy ballet costume stepped out onto the stage and curtsied before welcoming them all. The room swam. Black spots appeared. Somewhere, Noah heard a giggle. Then an elbow jabbed his rib, and he exhaled with a whoosh.

"Breathe!" she hissed.

Milton leaned forward and whispered, "He'll do great. You'll see."

Mom nudged him. "Told you."

But before he could find some way to tease her back, Miss Courtney slipped from the stage, the music swelled, and the curtain swung back to reveal a Victorian living room, complete with fake fireplace, settee, and an odd-looking Christmas tree. Guests arrived, children giggled and played—Bennie front and center with the little girl who had met Bennie that first day. Hilary.

Noah leaned close to whisper that to his mother. She nodded and whispered back, "He talks about her—says she's nice to him."

Please don't say he has a crush on her. Harper is better than that!

But Mom didn't. Harper freed her right hand from his and offered her left hand again. This time he remembered to hold it gently. The music became bright and sprightly as Clara danced with her doll and Bennie hopped, jumped, skipped, and did his best to take it away from her.

Harper leaned close and whispered, "He's good!"

The people around him wouldn't appreciate it, but Noah couldn't help but whisper back, "Miss Courtney said they had to change a few things. He was supposed to do a number with a few of the other girls dressed as boys, but he didn't have time to learn it, so they modified by making him sulk like that."

He couldn't say more. The music told him it was just

about time for "the battle." Hilary and Bennie began a fake tug-of-war with the nutcracker until Bennie became victor and dashed away with him. Instead of casting it to the floor, he "broke" it over his knee and pretended to laugh and jeer as he danced around Hilary with a piece in each hand.

Harper shot him a look, so he explained in yet more whispers. "The throwing it to the ground didn't work. It actually broke every time he did it hard enough to make the magnets not pull the pieces back together."

He didn't bother to tell how Miss Courtney had been relieved that the moment could then take place anywhere on stage instead of on the little carpet by the Christmas tree.

Call him awful, but Noah didn't pay much attention after Bennie left the scene. Only when the mice battled the soldiers did he drag his attention from watching Harper, his mother, and Milton.

Talking Milton into staying until the performance hadn't been easy. The guy insisted that his work was done. Harper had embraced being a book*seller* and her place in the community. Though he didn't say it, Milton also hinted that his matchmaking scheme had succeeded as well. And as if he could read Noah's thoughts, the man shot a glance Noah's way just then before turning his attention back to the stage.

Once more, Noah tried to focus on the story playing out on the stage. Through costumes, dance speeds, music, and sets, words weren't needed, but he just couldn't get into it. Maybe it was weeks of rehearsals until he was sick of it. Maybe he just didn't have the cultural intelligence to appreciate it.

Noah slid his gaze sideways and watched Harper sitting there in her glasses (that she wore as often as not these days), a close-fitting hat that had a retro air to it, and mesmerized by dancers, the lights, the music—

"Isn't he marvelous?"

He shot a glance back at the stage and saw Bennie as

a mouse sneaking off while the tree "shrank" (or rather, Clara grew to normal size). Strange... he hadn't seen that in rehearsal. But at Harper's nudge, he blurted out, "Yes."

He'd probably never learn to *like* ballet, but he had already learned to tolerate his son's love of it. Maybe he could turn that into unwavering support. And someday Bennie would realize that unwavering support of something you *don't* like means just as much as support of something you love already.

At curtain call, Harper sank back against the seat just as his mother leaned forward. She'd talked him into letting *her* give him the doll—a tiny one for their Christmas tree—instead of flowers. His mom had gone for balloons. That had left him uncertain what to do. Now, with the box out of his pocket and in hand, Noah hoped he'd made the right decision. *Should've asked Miss Courtney.*

But when the dancers raced off stage to greet family, Bennie searched the crowd until he saw Noah—not Harper, not Mom, *him*. "Dad!"

This time, Noah didn't hesitate. He wove between clusters of families greeting their dancers, doing his best not to batter bouquets in the process. His mom and Harper had been left behind, but he didn't care. He reached Bennie and scooped the boy up. "You were *so good*. I'm crazy proud of you." Hugging him tight, Noah added, "Seriously, kid. You were *good*."

"It was *so fun*! And Serenity lost her shoe, so Miss Courtney let me go get it and pretend to be the last mouse scurrying away."

So that's what it had been. Noah presented the little box to his son and said, "Didn't think you'd want flowers so..."

Bennie blinked. "Are they...?"

"Yeah. Your next shoes. Yours'll be getting too small soon."

Whatever else his son might have said was drowned out by Harper squealing and kissing the boy's cheek. She presented his ornament, kissed him again, and nearly did a jig in her excitement. Mom passed over the balloons. Milton gave him a book. A dark green book with a nutcracker on it. Noah heard him whisper, "It's for new readers. I think you're ready."

And he probably was, which was the best Christmas gift of all.

A look passed between Bennie and Harper, and Bennie grinned. "Hey, Dad! Miss Courtney says if I work really hard, someday I can be the Sugarplum Fairy!"

Noah blinked, probably turned green if the churning in his gut meant anything, and fought to keep from showing his dismay. Bennie and Harper burst out laughing before Bennie said, "Gotcha!"

Saying goodbye, Milton had discovered, was the worst part of his "side job." When he drove away from large corporations with a healthy deposit in his bank account, he rarely paused on the way out the door. He did his job, saved the company, and took off for wherever the road (or his website) took him next.

Deciding to leave after Bennie's performance had been thoughtless at best. However, if he didn't go now, it would only double the dread the boy felt, and that would be even worse. He hung back just enough that they wouldn't feel his absence or his presence. Courtney Madsen congratulated Bennie on a dance well performed and stopped only a hair shy of outright flirting with Noah.

"Many families head over to Liberty's for dessert. I hope we'll see you?"

Noah shook his head. "We have a small party planned at the store." He squeezed Bennie's shoulder. "It's a combination celebration for Bennie and farewell for Milton."

With a small smile for Noah and another "well done" for Bennie, Miss Courtney moved on to visit with the next closest family. Milton didn't think anyone but he noticed the look back at them. He couldn't blame the woman for being confused. Anyone who knew about them would assume Noah and Harper were a couple. But seeing them together rarely showed the sort of chemistry people expected. *But patience is truly its own reward, and those who embrace it will definitely be satisfied.*

While he had no doubt that when alone, Harper and Noah possessed and expressed all the feels any romance reader could hope for, his experience had shown them to be too private to display those emotions for an audience they didn't care to entertain. Only a few rare moments had proven his theory—moments when they thought no one was looking. A look, a touch…

Noah's mother probably thought Harper holding his hand was proof of their affection, but Harper would have done the same for anyone she felt safe with—possibly even Milton himself. *No… the restraint is the evidence of deep affection and possibly even passion. Time will tell. I did my job.*

Harper's, "Ready, Milton?" broke into his thoughts.

He nodded. Bennie stepped forward. "Can I carry Atticus?"

The half-block walk from the Sheldon Theater to the bookstore where cupcakes and hot chocolate waited shouldn't be too much for Atticus, even in this cold, but Milton still wrapped a scarf around most of the mesh and handed over the carrier. "There. He's all ready."

Clusters of people stood around just inside and outside the theater, most inching their way down the street as they bade friends and acquaintances goodnight. Noah led the way toward Twice Sold Tales, steering Harper around a patch of ice on the sidewalk before pausing to ensure his mother and his son were careful as well. His gaze met Milton's. Milton nodded.

This is good—very good.

Devon hadn't locked the door to the shop, so when they entered, they found a couple of customers poring over the Christmas display near the front. Harper sent a questioning look at her new right-hand man who just shrugged. As they neared, Devon said, "I couldn't tell them they couldn't spend money. That seemed dumb, but you might want to take over wrapping. I'm lousy at it."

"Me, too. If it doesn't involve brown paper and string, I'm a mess."

Mrs. Lampe stepped up to the plate. "Well, I'm actually good at wrapping, so get your backside over here and watch a pro—both of you. There's nothing easier to wrap than a book, so pay attention."

Noah moved past the stack of "must wraps" on the counter to the many stacks of books scattered from the middle to the back of the store. "What's all this?"

"They finally brought over all of Mrs. Klair's books," Milton said. "A 'few boxes' turned out to be about fifty boxes, and over half of them valuable."

He picked up a copy of *The Great Gatsby* and fanned the pages. "I suppose this one's one of the 'not so valuable' ones?"

Milton shook his head. "First edition paperback—1946 if I recall correctly. Bantam. Probably worth a hundred dollars or more."

Noah nearly dropped it. He peered inside and saw Mrs. Klair's name and the year, 1985, in pencil on the inside of the cover. He showed Milton. "Are you sure?"

"Yes. That would likely be the year she bought it." Milton stared at the inscription for a moment and then took off for the stairs. In the office, on a shelf over the desk, sat the copy of *The Mysterious Affair at Styles*. A glance inside prompted a smile.

He carried it downstairs and picked up the Gatsby. "Harper, check this out." Showing her the date and the price in the back of Styles was all it took.

"It was Mrs. Klair! But why would she put such a valuable book on a shelf where anyone could just buy it for—?"

"For five hundred? How many rare books had you sold, *in person?*"

Harper had to concede his point. "But why?"

"I think she wanted to be certain she was right about you. Remember when you told her about finding it? I think you passed a test that day."

He could see it—the grief creeping back in. People like Harper didn't let others in easily, so when they did, the pain of loss could be that much more intense. She wouldn't thank him—not at first—but Milton put his arms around her and squeezed. "She loved you. Never forget that."

The stiffening relaxed as he stepped back, but Milton could see he'd made the right decision. He also saw that his leaving would be rough. He needed to go… now.

"Harper…"

"You're leaving." Without giving him a chance to respond, she moved to the cupcakes and picked one out for him. "Take it with you." This time *she* hugged *him*. "I don't want you to go."

"That's quite the change from 'you can go' from last year."

"I was stupider last year."

Noah moved closer. "What?"

Turning away, probably to hide tears she didn't know what to do with, Harper said, "He's leaving."

It took longer than he'd have liked to say goodbye to Devon, comfort a distraught Bennie, and thank Noah for being a good friend. "Take care of them," he whispered as he picked up Atticus and his cupcake and headed for the door.

Harper, Noah, and Bennie followed him out the back door where his Land Rover sat waiting for him. Milton started the engine and blasted the heat and tucked Atticus' carrier into his coat while they waited. "You've done a great thing with this store, Harper. Keep up the good work."

She stepped forward to hug him again and immediately stepped back. "I'll crush Atticus. Drive safe. Come back." Bennie buried his head in Noah's belly, so Noah just put up a weak wave and nodded his agreement. But as Milton climbed up into his warming but nowhere near warm Rover, Devon bolted out the back door, slipping on a slick patch. "Harper! The envelope!"

When she waved him forward, Devon approached, handing Milton a business-sized envelope. "For the next store."

Milton shook his head. "Harper, you paid me. You're actually the first store to *pay* me. It's all good."

"But not everyone has been blessed like I was. And if it weren't for you, I might not have gotten any of my money back. You found it. Help someone else."

In what had become a familiar moment, Milton took the envelope, put it in his pocket, and called out, "Thanks!" as he shut the door. He unzipped his coat and put Atticus' carrier on the seat. After letting Atticus out and onto his perch, Milton put the vehicle in gear.

Letting off the brake had never been harder. He punched his playlist, and Frank Sinatra began singing about having a merry little Christmas. With a deep breath, his throat tight and heart even tighter, Milton moved his foot from brake to accelerator and rolled down 4th Street toward Plum.

A glance in his rearview mirror showed the three of them standing there, waving. It might have been his imagination, but Milton didn't think so. He chose to believe he'd seen it—Noah turning to Harper and kissing her cheek. Right there in front of God and... well, Bennie. But anyone from the Downtown Plaza building could also have seen. Even Devon *could* have seen it.

"It's a start, Atticus. Maybe next year, we'll get another wedding invitation. Christmas in Red Wing. If we do, we're staying at the St. James, and we're *going* to find those ghosts."

"Read it!" Atticus called out before he flew up to his over-the-seat perch and added, "Sucker!"

Author Notes

Ten years ago, I flew to Red Wing, Minnesota when my sister-in-law went home to be with the Lord. I fell in love with the little town and knew someday I'd write a book that took place there. I just didn't know what it would be about.

One of the things I wanted for the Bookstrings series was an immersive experience in the towns I chose to feature. Red Wing (aside from notes to follow) really is as I shared it. I kicked it off with names. Most of the surnames in the book were ones I found on the Red Wing Community Facebook page, and many first names are names of family who live or lived there. Steve Carron was named for my brother-in-law. Jamie at Hanisch's for my niece, and both Megan and Courtney are nieces, too. My mother-in-law is Lorene and about as opposite from Harper's aunt as you can get—sweetest thing ever.

For the purposes of this story, I appropriated buildings and businesses. First off, I needed the building I chose because the only building that could possibly have the windows necessary for Noah to watch his son would have to be across the street from Cornerstone Community Church. As far as I could find, no other building downtown could possibly have been able to be observed that way. So, I had a limited number of options there on 3rd Street. I felt kind of bad about appropriating the upstairs of a church, so I decided to make Miss Courtney generous enough to share her studio with the church for Sunday school classrooms.

When I told my niece Courtney about it, she laughed. It seems that the reverse is true. The church (as I assumed) does own both floors of the building, but they allow an exercise studio to operate up there during the week. Courtney says that on weekdays, you can sometimes enter the building and hear, "And one, two, three, four…"

As for the Twice Sold Tales building, it's actually a lovely hair salon, Shear Perfection. Author Cathe Swanson and I went in, told the manager what I was doing with their building, and rather than being annoyed at me appropriating it for my story, she allowed me to take pictures and videos, answered questions, and she even gave Cathe a great trim on her bangs! Thanks again, ladies! You were the BEST.

Additionally, Red Wing does have a *wonderful* bookstore, *Fair Trade Books*. I first discovered this delightful place when I returned for my niece's wedding and was eager to return on my research trip. It is, if possible, even better now, and they really do have a bookshelf at Mandy's Café where they sell hardbacks and paperbacks with coupons in them for discounts at the store. They're just a little bit further down the street and around the corner.

As for Mandy's Café, I really need to apologize to the real Mandy. From what I read in an article, her in-laws actually own the building. To give her a bit more privacy and so my character isn't *really* her, I gave her a different surname. Although I wanted to change the name of the café to protect her from misrepresentation, I just couldn't. It's a wonderful place and deserves to be recognized for what it is.

The ghost walk is real, but since I couldn't go on it, I have no idea what stories are told, aside from what is shared on the website. I doubt the Sea Wing disaster ghosts are anything like I described, although I really want to make that Pepie book a thing.

If you visit Red Wing, you'll want to visit Mandy's Café as well as Hanisch's. That bakery is amazing and wonderful, and those Fruity Pebbles donuts are a thing.

Also maple bacon. Oh, and there's a confectionery with salted caramels on Main Street that you don't want to miss. Furthermore, a trip to Red Wing isn't complete without stopping in at the Uffda Shop and to see the Red Wing Pottery museum. They have beautiful stuff there.

Memorial Park on Sorin's Bluff does have "stone tables" and disc golf. It's a wonderful view from up there, and you can actually see Cornerstone Community Church and the back of "Twice Sold Tales" from it.

Finally, the Goodhue Historical Society has a great museum and gift shop. The lovely woman there was so helpful in giving me things for Noah to do with Bennie, and I spent a small fortune on books and things to use for research. Definitely take the time to stop in and see what they have to offer. And if you need a place to stay, I heartily recommend the St. James. It's a beautiful hotel with a rich history (and it really was used as a morgue after the Sea Wing disaster!)

Oh... and for the curious, the breakup ice cream list is real. You can find it here. https://spoonuniversity.com/lifestyle/which-ben-and-jerrys-flavor-you-should-eat-based-on-your-most-recent-breakup

Thank you, Red Wing, for being such a wonderful place not only to visit but to write about. Just putting this all down is making me miss it. I wonder if I should consider a sequel...

The Bookstrings Series

Spines & Leaves (a novella in the *Song of Grace* anthology)
Hart of Noel (a novella in the *Heart of Christmas* anthology)
Twice Sold Tales
Clocktower Books (expected release, November 2023)

The Mosaic Collection

Learn more about the many Mosaic Collection authors and books at www.mosaiccollectionbooks.com/mosaic-books

Made in the USA
Columbia, SC
05 January 2023

75562376R00161